SOUTH OF

NOWHERE

Also by Minerva Koenig

Nine Days

SOUTH OF NOWHERE

MINERVA KOENIG

MINOTAUR BOOKS

A THOMAS DUNNE BOOK
NEW YORK

A THOMAS DUNNE BOOK FOR MINOTAUR BOOKS.
An imprint of St. Martin's Publishing Group.

SOUTH OF NOWHERE. Copyright © 2016 by Minerva Koenig. All rights reserved. Printed in the United States of America. For information, address St. Martin's Press, 175 Fifth Avenue, New York, N.Y. 10010.

www.thomasdunnebooks.com
www.minotaurbooks.com

The Library of Congress Cataloging-in-Publication Data is available upon request.

ISBN 978-1-250-05195-0 (hardcover)
ISBN 978-1-4668-5267-9 (e-book)

Our books may be purchased in bulk for promotional, educational, or business use. Please contact your local bookseller or the Macmillan Corporate and Premium Sales Department at 1-800-221-7945, extension 5442, or by e-mail at MacmillanSpecialMarkets@macmillan.com.

First Edition: February 2016

10 9 8 7 6 5 4 3 2 1

SOUTH OF

NOWHERE

CHAPTER 1

"He's been dead awhile," Liz Harman said, rocking back off her knees to open the field case she'd set next to her on the scarred wood floor.

The doctor, who also served as the coroner in this tiny little Texas backwater, wasn't telling me and Benny Ramirez, Azula's newly minted chief of police, anything we didn't already know. The parts of the body sticking out of the red bedsheet it was wrapped in looked like beef jerky.

Liz reached into her case, withdrew a thermometer, and leaned back down into the coffin-sized hole in the floor where the dead guy lay. I'd found it while ripping out some old linoleum in the wreck of a farmhouse I'd bought last year. I shouldn't have been working on the place, since I didn't legally own it yet, but my life had been feeling out of control lately, and the only fix I know for that is to tear up some vintage real estate and then put it back together again. I've found everything from mummified rodents to meteor fragments in the course of that therapy, but this was a first.

The hole had been covered with well-fitted, loose wood planks instead of the longleaf pine flooring that was typical in the rest of the house. The planks were easy to lift, and I'd done it, to see what was underneath: an old heating chase, full of dead guy.

Liz snapped on some latex gloves and motioned to Page, her young goateed assistant. Benny got hold of my elbow, dragging me back a few steps. "Are you for real?"

I gave him my best what-the-fuck look, but he didn't blink, so I said, "You know who I bought the place from, right?"

He didn't say, "The broad who tried to slit your throat last winter?" because we'd both been up to our ears in all of that. Instead, he just grunted and glanced toward the two medicos. "Any guesses on cause, Doc?"

"The man's a raisin," Liz snorted, with her characteristic gruffness. "He's got some holes in him, but there's no way to tell from what until I get him back to the shop and look under the hood."

Through the wavy old glass in the tall windows, I gazed down the long slope to the river at the south edge of my future property. Neffa Roberts and her father, Lavon, were out in their vegetable patch up the other side, eyes shaded in our direction. Cop cars and ambulances were rare beasts out here.

"I've got to go up to Gatesville this afternoon to finish up some real-estate paperwork with Connie," I told Benny. "Want me to ask her if she killed the guy?"

"We don't know that anybody killed him yet," he said, lowering his head to look at me from under his thick black brows, "and you oughta be hoping it stays that way."

I opened my mouth, but he didn't slow down. "This is the second dead body you've stumbled across in less than a year."

"I wasn't responsible for the first one, either, if you'll recall."

That shut him up. He looked away, adjusting his equipment-swollen gun belt with the insides of his wrists, like James Cagney. "You going up there by yourself?"

"Why shouldn't I?"

His eyes dropped to my left shoulder, where Connie had stuck the knife in. "It's just weird."

Most people don't maintain a friendship with their would-be killer, so I could see where he was coming from, but the remark irked me. "She didn't know what she was doing, Benny."

"The shrinks said she was sane."

"Sane's a relative term."

Liz got up and came over to us, stripping off her gloves. "My best guess on time of death is more than three months ago, but less than six. That's about as close as I can get right now."

Benny scratched his ear, peering at her. She gave him an annoyed look and said, "I assume you want it on the front burner, as usual."

Page had spread a body bag on the floor, and now Benny stepped over to help him haul the corpse out of the hole next to it. The back of my neck started to crawl, and then came that familiar lurch of high, cool nothingness, and my mind turned off like someone blowing out a match.

My gut has always run several lengths ahead of my conscious thought process, so I'm used to a certain level of intellectual vacancy, but this was different, and it had been happening more and more often since the events of last winter. The brain wasn't even loading into the starting gates anymore. Not all the time, but often enough that I was getting used to people looking at me funny. In addition, a recurring feeling of suffocation was waking me every morning; a sensation of pushing something wet and heavy off me so that I could float up into wakefulness. It felt like I was doing my thrice-weekly weight-training workout with my brain as well as my body.

When my gray matter came back online, everybody had changed places: Benny and Page clomping across the downstairs porch, Liz at the door on the other side of the room, watching me with a question on her face.

Not anxious to find out what it was, I stepped out into the big central hallway and shut the bedroom door. Little puffs of paint dust huffed out around the door frame, and I pulled the musty odor in, lead be damned. Nothing smells like an old house. If I could bottle it, I'd wear it as perfume.

Liz fell in behind me as I started down the stairs and said, "Have you been out to see Dr. Conroy yet?"

Liz Harman's "crusty old country doctor" act—a bit of a stretch for someone probably in her mid-fifties—hid a terminal case of motherly concern, which manifested itself in frequent bouts of unsolicited advice to her patients about stuff that was none of her business. My mental health had been at the top of that list for months now, and it was getting old.

"Do you get a kickback for referrals or something?" I cracked at her over my shoulder.

She chuckled, but when we got to the bottom of the stairs, she still hadn't taken the hint.

"Look, whatever's going on with you isn't going to get better on its own, and it might be real simple to fix. You're not going to end up in a padded cell, if that's what's worrying you."

"I'm fine," I said, letting some of my annoyance show now.

"You're not fine," she replied, with surprising alacrity, "but you're not irrational, so I don't understand why you keep resisting treatment."

Because I'd done my eight rounds with the head-shrinking profession when I'd been drafted into the U.S. Federal Witness Security Program three years ago, the prospect of a rematch was about as repulsive an idea as any I could think of. The inside of my head was no place for strangers, no matter how weird it was getting.

There wasn't any point anyway; I was pretty sure I'd have to tell the truth about my life history to get anything out of psychiatry, which meant letting someone in on who I really was. Now that I was no longer under WITSEC's wing, having been unceremoniously kicked out after my keeper had turned up dead under mysterious circumstances the previous November, that was information I couldn't afford anyone else to get. Not even a professional who promised confidentiality. That's how I'd gotten into my current situation.

A weary anger prickled across my shoulders. I was so tired of this worn little paranoid crevice between rock and hard place. The house and my burgeoning construction business helped a little—they kept my attention occupied enough that I didn't fall off a psychic cliff every fifteen minutes—so that's what I focused on. There was enough crumbling architecture in Azula to keep me off the shrink's couch indefinitely, if I could just manage to find some buildings without dead people in them.

I stepped out onto the long front porch and waited for Liz to follow suit before closing and locking the door. She headed for her county-issued Pontiac, and the ambulance started down the long caliche driveway.

"You coming?" the doctor asked, pausing at her car.

"Yeah, in a little bit."

She hesitated for only a fraction of a second before getting in, but that was enough to set off my preternaturally sensitive internal radar. I thought about it as I walked to my truck, questioning, as I always did now, whether the alarm was legitimate or if Liz had just inadvertently stepped on something sensitive but meaningless. Having to second-guess an instinct I'd been able to trust completely in the past was a pain in the ass, but I'd been scared straight by my near-death experience the previous winter. Maybe my self-doubt was an improvement. Who knows how many times I'd been wrong before and not known it?

CHAPTER 2

It felt close to a hundred degrees when I hit the town square. Benny's cruiser was parked behind the courthouse, near the basement entry to the police station, and the doctor's car was next to it. The ambulance was absent, probably on its way to Memorial Hospital, fifty miles south, where Liz did her autopsies.

I pulled in at the curb in front of Guerra's, the bar where I still held my nominal day job. I'd been living in the upstairs apartment since the previous winter. It was cooler inside, but not much. I walked down the narrow path between the old mahogany bar and the blood-red Naugahyde booths clinging to the opposite wall, breathing in that musty old-building smell that I loved, and went to the thermostat mounted on the wall by the back stairway. Remembering the "heat wave" that had been in progress when I'd arrived just after Halloween last year made me laugh now. If I'd known what summer had in store, I'd have banked my complaining. June in Central Texas was like Death Valley with humidity.

Wishing I could reverse the laws of thermodynamics, I clomped up the wood stairs, wondering how Hector Guerra, the

bar's owner and my erstwhile lover, had tolerated living up here
without air conditioning. He'd paid to have it installed downstairs, rightly grasping that a Texas bar without air conditioning had roughly the same chance of survival as an ice cube on
a hot plate, but he hadn't had enough money left over to do the
second floor. If I left the stairwell door open, some of the coolth
from the bar wafted up, but it was never enough to make the
apartment bearable during the day. At night, I opened the big
bay windows that looked onto the courthouse square and blew
the heat of the day out with a fan, but anytime before sundown
the place was a sauna.

Luigi, Hector's big black-and-white cat, was napping on the
kitchen table when I came in. He jumped down to wait by the
food bowl as I dropped my keys on the stainless-steel kitchen
counter. I'd been a little skittish around him for a while after he'd
spoken to me in Aymara last winter, but he hadn't seemed to
notice, eating what I fed him and sleeping on my feet at night
no matter how hot it was. I put down some kibble and went into
the bathroom to crank up the shower, but turned it off again
when I heard the phone.

It was Mike Hayes, the bartender who'd inherited the business after Hector disappeared. "I need the night off. Can you
cover me?"

"Why bother?" I said. "You know how slow Thursdays are,
and it's not as if we've got an on-site supervisor."

Every month, paychecks with Hector's inscrutable signature appeared in our mailboxes, and the bar bills were paid the
same way. It was the only way we knew he was still alive out
there somewhere. There'd been no word from him, to anyone,
since his hasty departure for Cuba in November with John
Maines, the former Azula county sheriff, who'd turned out to

be less of a cop but more of a human being than anyone suspected.

"Principle of the thing," Mike grumbled.

"Like you've got principles."

"Any bites on the help-wanted ad?" he asked me.

"Yeah, three or four good prospects. Hire one of them, you should be good to go next week."

He grunted his approval, then said, "You sure you don't want to stay on, just part-time? Me, I wouldn't start a lemonade stand in this economy, much less a construction business."

"Eh, it's always feast or famine with that stuff, no matter what the rest of the economy is doing," I shrugged, "and I've got my own place to work on until some of these nibbles turn into actual projects."

"You got enough to live on until then?"

"I'll be OK for a month or two." I could hear Mike's doubt crackle through the phone line, and added, "If worse comes to worst, I'll come back to work for you. Provided you're still in business."

There was a thick pause on the other end of the line, then Mike muttered, "He'll be back," like he always did.

Not for the first time, I wondered what bound him and Hector together so tightly. They seemed to share some subterranean psychic-twin connection that I knew Hector and I never would, no matter how long we swapped bodily fluids.

Which I missed. He'd been gone close to nine months, and his bed was feeling bigger and lonelier as the days passed. I sometimes wished I hadn't washed his sweet burnt-leaves smell out of the sheets.

Mike and I covered a couple of work details before hanging up, then I went back to the bathroom, still thinking about

Hector. That wasn't unusual—I thought about him a lot—but there was something in the air.

I don't kid myself I'm psychic or anything, with this radar, but I've come to understand that it picks up stuff beyond the reach of my conscious awareness, like a microexpression on someone's face, or flashing on a phone number without being overtly aware that I've seen it somewhere before. It's like magic, sometimes. I'll have a little whiff of something, and then a few days or hours later, the something will show up. Not always. That's the hell of it. It's not predictable.

So I tried not to get too attached to the thing in the air while I showered and got dressed, grabbed my real-estate folder and wallet, and headed back downstairs. Crossing to the truck, though, I glanced up the sidewalk and pulled up short. A lanky man in a tan felt hat was ambling toward me. A slow thrill prickled up my ribs.

"Doctor Livingston, I presume," I said as he approached and stopped, giving me what passed for a smile on his pale hatchet face. "How was Cuba?"

John Maines shrugged, lifting his hat to mash down the springy strawberry curls underneath with one freckled hand. "I didn't go in. Just got him there."

It had occurred to me before then that both of them might end up rotting in a secret prison somewhere, seeing as how their mission to return some artifacts to one of the island nation's most infamous families was sanctioned by neither government, and involved a historical point of some embarrassment to both. Now, seeing Maines without Hector in tow, the worry became more pronounced.

"So, did he?" I asked Maines. "Leave?"

The son of a bitch didn't answer me. Instead, he reached for an envelope sticking out of the pocket of his plaid shirt and said, "I need a favor."

He drew out the envelope's contents in his deliberate way and handed them to me. It was a typed letter, two pages, from the federal marshal's office, authorizing him to release $51,240.00 to me upon the fulfillment of "the previously stipulated requirements."

"What the fuck is this?" I said, baffled.

"It's the money WITSEC owes you."

"I know that. I thought it was forfeit when they kicked me out. How did you get involved?"

He lifted his high, narrow shoulders, looking deferential.

I wasn't buying it. "Just rip the Band-Aid off, will you?"

He went into his shirt pocket again and gave me a business card: JOHN MAINES, PRIVATE INVESTIGATOR, TEXAS LICENSE NUMBER A25843. "Got my first case this morning. Missing person. I need help with it."

"So, these 'previously stipulated requirements' are that you keep an eye on me and make sure I don't spend the money setting up a new criminal empire or something. Is that it?"

"I'm to use my professional judgment about when and how much to give you."

"Same difference."

"Hey, I don't wanna be shackled to you any more than you do to me," he said, holding up his long hands, palms toward me. "I'll give you the whole chunk if you'll just help me with this one case."

"Which is?"

"Local gal went for some medical treatment at a clinic in Ojinaga. That's in Mexico. Just across the border. Never came home. Her people are worried."

"They should be," I said. "The cartels are running wild down there right now."

"No body," Maines replied. "Those guys always make sure you find at least parts. Sort of the point, in fact."

"What kind of medical treatment?"

Maines hesitated briefly, then said, "Lap-band."

My face went hot. "Oh, I get it. You need a fat broad for a decoy. So naturally you came to me."

He kept his faded-teal eyes leveled at mine. "It's amazing how loaded that word is."

I'd used more than one, so I kept my mouth shut until he got more specific.

"'Fat,'" he said, in his terse monotone. "The way people use it now. It means all kinds of shit it never used to mean. Lazy, unattractive, stupid. None of which describes you."

He wasn't flirting with me; he lacks the gene, and we'd spent enough time together for him to know that I did, too, even if I had any interest, which I decidedly did not. The only other logical alternative was that he was giving me a legitimate compliment, which I hate.

Ignoring the possibility, I said, "So, what do you want my fat ass to do for you?"

His faint twitch of a smile flashed by. "Get you into the clinic. Yahoos who run it are way off the beam and jumpy as hell. I go in there, the place turns into a dental office soon as I clear the door."

I noticed that I was holding my breath, and realized that the tickling sensation behind my belly button wasn't indigestion. I went ahead and asked my question directly. "Where's Hector?"

Maines's expression went crafty. "It's a six-hour drive from here to the border. Plenty of time to tell you alla that."

I considered for a few minutes. It'd be nice to get the hell out of Azula, if only for a couple of days, but doing it with John Maines wasn't my idea of a vacation. Neither did I much like the prospect of letting him torment me with whatever information he had about Hector. Plus, if I stopped working, or thinking about work, even for an hour, I might have to face the black thing lurking in my subconscious. I wasn't in the mood.

"Good luck with your case," I said to Maines, and got into my truck.

CHAPTER 3

It was an hour and fifteen minutes to the prison at Gatesville, through scenery that might once have been interesting. My tenure in Texas had been completely rainless so far, and everything not bleached white by the ferocious sun was brown. Just looking out the window made me thirsty.

The women's unit was a plain white cube, with a frill of tall chain-link fence, that smelled of disinfectant all the way to the parking lot. I filled out the visitor's form and got patted down, then passed through a series of locked steel gates into a big sun-washed room with bars across the windows and a well-armed guard standing against the far wall.

Connie was sitting at one of the steel tables, flipping through a textbook. Petite to begin with, she'd grown even smaller in prison, and with her frizzy dark hair caught back in a high ponytail, she resembled a large child. It was almost enough to make me forget that she'd tried to slit my throat six months ago.

A shiver of wariness slipped up the back of my stomach, and I hesitated. I didn't feel sorry for Connie—she didn't feel sorry for herself, and seemed just as content in prison as she'd ever been outside it—so why, exactly, did I keep coming to visit her?

She looked up from her book and saw me, her sharp little face splitting into a smile. My wariness subsided, making room for something warmer. Don't ask me to explain why I still liked her, after everything we'd been through. I might have to admit that she reminded me of myself a little. The road not taken.

As I sat down, she took off her reading glasses and said, "I was afraid you might be in jail."

I made a quizzical face, and she directed her eyes at a television bolted high up on the concrete-block wall. It was tuned to a local news station. "They just ran a story about the body you found out at the Ranch. What happened?"

Her guiltless expression wasn't reading fake to my radar, so I said, "Nothing very interesting. I opened up a hole in the floor, and there he was."

"Did you dissociate when you found him?" she asked as I opened my folder.

Connie had been finishing up her graduate-school education to become a psychiatrist when everything had gone *kaboom* last year. The prospect of yet another unsolicited medical opinion coming my way irritated me. I pressed my teeth together so that I wouldn't snap at her, but then decided, what the hell: If everybody I knew was going to read me like a cheap novel, I might as well face the reviews and get it over with.

"Yeah," I admitted. "And Liz Harman's been after me to go see a shrink."

"That seems a prudent suggestion, based on my observation of your affect and behavior lately."

"Observation?" I snorted. "What observation? You've seen me an hour a week for the last six months."

"That's about as often as a licensed psychiatrist would see you," she pointed out. "And I have the benefit of a social association with you, from—before."

I got out the signature sheets for the Ranch closing. "I'm not interested in reliving my childhood, thanks."

Connie tilted her head to one side, examining me through her big black-framed glasses, lips pursed.

"What?" I said.

"You can relive your childhood experiences a couple of times in the company of a good therapist, or you can keep on reliving them over and over again, for the rest of your life, at inopportune moments."

"You're practicing without a license," I warned her.

"It just always amazes me when otherwise logical people resist treatment," she said with a small laugh, shaking her head.

"You did it," I shot back.

Our eyes met.

"That's right, I did," she said. "And you see where it got me."

We sat there measuring each other up like a couple of alley cats, then I passed the signature sheets across to her, changing the subject. "Tova says it will take a couple of days for the money to be transferred to her account. Then she'll send this in and get the title transfer done."

Connie laid down her pen and closed the book over it, sliding her fingers behind her glasses to rub her eyes. "God. Tova. She is *such* a pain in my ass."

"Too bad you can't fire her," I agreed. Tova Bradshaw, Connie and Hector's adoptive sister, was doing the paperwork for free, out of the goodness of her heart. Which was likely very little, considering the heart involved.

Connie noticed me eyeing her book, and turned the spine

in my direction: *Clinical Interventions in Post-Traumatic Stress Disorder.*

Careful, as always when his name came up between us, I asked, "Are you still treating Hector?"

"I never 'treated' him," she said, sounding defensive. "He's not a patient, he's my brother. The fact that we were adopted at different times, from different places, doesn't change that. I'm not going to let him suffer if I can do something to prevent it."

"Have you heard anything from him?" I asked, as I usually did on my visits.

She shook her head, and I didn't press. Nor did I offer that Maines was back in town. Where I was concerned, Hector was her property. She'd almost killed me to prove it, and I didn't want to get her going again, even in this relatively secure location.

Changing the subject again as deftly as I knew how, I lifted my chin at her book. "Do you think PTSD could be causing whatever's going on with me?"

The federal shrinks had suggested the diagnosis after I'd watched two skinheads blow my husband Joe's head off back in Bakersfield, which is why I'd gotten into protection. I hadn't liked that diagnosis much, so I was momentarily gratified when Connie pulled the book back to her side of the table and said, "No."

She paused, then added, "There's nothing wrong with you except that you don't know anything about yourself."

It took a second for what she'd said to register, and when it did, I found myself speechless for a minute. Then I snapped, "What the fuck is that supposed to mean?"

Connie's eyes stayed on my face. "Just what it sounds like it means."

The meat between my shoulder blades had gone cold, but I couldn't figure out why. I was talking to the woman who'd tried to kill me nine months ago; she was still working on it, that was all. I took a breath and squeezed my anger down into oblivion, pulling the closing signature sheets back to my side of the table and replacing them with the title transfer.

A few silent seconds ticked by while Connie signed it, then she murmured, without looking up, "Where did you find the body?"

Tired of playing cat and mouse, I said, "Maybe you'd better tell me what you know about it. You're the one in prison for murder, and it used to be your house."

"You of all people should know that I'm not that kind of killer," she said mildly, not looking at me.

I wasn't sure what she meant, but I was pretty sure she'd tell me if I kept my mouth shut. Sure enough, when it became clear that I wasn't going to reply, she leaned across the table and said quietly, "You and me, we're the same. We're like dogs that have been kicked too much. We're only dangerous when somebody tries to hurt us."

I dragged the title page back over to my side of the table and put it in my folder. "I'm no dog."

"If you weren't at least part dog, you'd be dead now," she said, smirking. Her manner was shifting, turning sarcastically vicious like it sometimes did near her medication time.

I got up and shot a look at the guard, who gave me a barely perceptible nod. I moved quickly toward the gate, not saying good-bye to Connie. It was too late for that. I knew too well where the conversation was heading, and how fast it could get there. I preferred to have at least one wall between us when it did.

CHAPTER 4

"It's not personal," Benny said.

"You just told me I can't leave town," I replied, annoyed. "How's that not personal?"

We were in his corner office in the courthouse basement, our voices bouncing off the stone walls. Behind his bristly black head, I could see the sky through the high transom windows that sat level with the ground outside, facing Main Street. He stacked his short brown hands on his hard belly and attempted to look patient. It didn't suit him.

I'm not much of a globetrotter by inclination, but having somebody tell me I couldn't go anywhere made me fractious. "What if I need to travel for business?"

Benny's eyebrows climbed his low forehead. "I'd be surprised if you hadda go around the block. The construction market's in the toilet all over the state."

"Maines has a case down near the border he wants me to help him on." I didn't add that I'd refused. I was simply making a point.

"A case? Like, you mean, an investigation?"

"How is this news to you? Don't all you Rollers use the same hairdresser?"

"I knew he was looking into getting his private investigator's license, but I didn't think he'd pull it this quick." Benny leaned forward in the creaky oak banker's chair, his eyes amused. "You know he thinks he's gonna make a detective out of you, right?"

"You say that like it's funny."

"It's not funny to you?"

"I'd do a better job than you clowns, in my sleep."

Benny's eyes glittered at me, but I didn't flinch. He got up, pushing his barrel chest forward. "Your gun over at the apartment?"

"No, it's in the truck," I said. "Why?"

"The holes in that dead guy were made by bullets."

"Benny, I haven't been in town long enough to know anyone so well I'd want to kill them."

"Maybe one of the Aryan Brotherhood guys that's looking for you found you," he suggested.

"So I stuck his body under the rug and then hung around waiting for his buddies to come looking for him? Come on."

"If the doc is right, and he's been dead a maximum of six months, that lets Connie off the hook."

"OK, but it doesn't automatically put me on it," I told him.

"You bought the house well before the guy died in it. So, yeah, it does."

"All of us were tied up with Connie's case until May," I reminded him. "I didn't even have time to go inside the place until the end of June, which was, like, six weeks ago."

Benny didn't reply, just wiggled his fingers at me impatiently. Ignoring them, I said, "What caliber were the bullets?"

"We didn't find any bullets. Just holes."

I frowned up at him. "What, they all went through?"

"No. Somebody shot him, then dug the bullets out," Benny said. "Some *CSI* wannabe, probably thinking that would prevent an ID."

"They couldn't have done that in the house," I said. "There would have been blood all over the place."

"Yeah. He was killed elsewhere and dumped there."

"So what good is my gun going to do you without bullets to test against?"

"Wound comparison," he said, rippling his fingers again. "Come on."

I sighed and passed him my keys. He took them and clomped out. I got up and followed him through the squad room, around the courthouse and across Main to where my truck was parked in front of the bar. He unlocked the passenger side and opened the glove compartment.

"It's under the seat," I told him. "Driver's side."

He straightened up and went around. "Loaded?"

"Yeah, but the safety's on."

He cut his eyes at me over the hood. "You know it ain't legal to carry a concealed firearm unless you got a permit, right?"

I showed him my surprised face and he made a disgusted noise. My little Kahr P40 appeared, and he handed me back my keys. "You and me, we'll be talking more tomorrow."

I watched him stride back across Main and disappear around the courthouse, then I went into the bar, locked the door behind me, and grabbed the phone.

"Tell me that piece you sold me is clean," I instructed Mauricio Torres when he answered. I'd bought the Kahr from his bunch of local bangers during the previous winter's festivities, when I wasn't sure I was going to get out of the mess I was in alive, and wasn't feeling picky about the firearm I laid my hands on.

"You didn't specify that you wanted a weapon with no history," the Inca replied in his soft, courteous voice.

"God damn it," I muttered, then said, "Can you at least tell me what that history might be?"

There was a pause, and then Torres replied, "I believe we obtained that weapon from a rival gang, whose executioner used it."

"So it's got bodies on it?"

Torres's silence was as good as a yes. I did a little swearing. He waited for me to finish, then said, "I know that you will, nevertheless, honor our agreement."

What he meant was, "I know you won't say anything to bust me, because if you do, I'll make sure the Brotherhood finds you." I was starting to wish I'd decided to just leave the damned linoleum where it was.

I stood there with my hand on the phone for a while after Torres hung up, picturing the paces Benny would put me through when the Kahr's record came back. Yes, eventually, somehow, someone would figure out who the guy in my floor was, and that I had no reason to kill him, but the stretch of time between now and then was going to be unpleasant. I was getting really tired of unpleasant.

I spent an hour or so thinking about it, at the end of which I decided there was only one solution I liked: getting the hell out of Dodge. Permanently. I wasn't on WITSEC's books anymore, and the only things keeping me in Azula were my construction-business plans and my relationship with Hector, neither of which were developing the way I'd hoped. As far as the feds were concerned, I could go anywhere I wanted, and their $51,240.00 would last a lot longer in Mexico, which, conveniently, would also put me out of reach of whatever Benny pulled out of his ass. Yes, I'd have to sell the Ranch, but I could do that remotely. Everything with Mike and the bar was sewn up. All I had to do was pack.

I picked the phone up again and called Maines. "When were you thinking of heading south?"

"As soon as I could talk you into it."

"You can pick me up first thing in the morning," I said. "One condition: I want all my money up front."

CHAPTER 5

Maines waited outside in his tan Crown Vic while I went into the bank to deposit the certified check he gave me. I was a little worried that carrying my duffel in with me might put him on my scent, but I guess he was used to women hauling big bags around.

I had the cashier convert half my money into pesos and give me the rest in American dollars. She banded up the cash into bundles, and I stowed them under my hasty packing job before heading back out to the car.

I expected Maines to loop around the block back to Main Street, which turned to highway a couple of miles outside of town, but he didn't.

"Gotta pick up our third," he said, in answer to my quizzical look.

Irritated, I replied, "When were you going to tell me this was a trio?"

We pulled up at a low stucco building with a pair of scissors painted on the glass door, a couple of blocks farther down Third. I let Maines get out and go inside, using the time to decide if an additional person would interfere with my plans. I made up my mind that it wouldn't, and Maines returned, leading a medium-sized brown-and-white short-haired mutt. He let the dog into the backseat and got behind the wheel. When we turned onto Main and started to accelerate, I realized who the third was.

"You can't be serious," I said, glancing at the dog. It was sitting up on the leather seat, looking quietly out the window.

"He's freshly bathed and groomed," Maines said, sounding offended, "and I can't just leave him at home alone for however long we're gone."

"However long we're gone? You said a couple of days, max."

Maines gave me a disgusted look. "You're gonna hafta learn to be more flexible if you want to make it as a PI."

"Look, Pygmalion, I'm a builder, not a cop, OK? And even if I were looking for career advice, I wouldn't be taking it from the likes of you."

"Bad time to start a construction business," he replied, shifting the Crown Vic into overdrive, "and you and Mike can't keep that bar going by yourselves forever."

Knowing he wouldn't support my secret relocation plans, especially if he knew what had instigated them, I didn't tell him that the bar staff had just been halved.

"Lots of places operate with out-of-town owners."

"Maybe in a big city, where nobody knows each other. People want to just drink, they do it at home. Hector was the draw for that place."

Maines was right. Despite his leftist politics, my handsome boss was well-liked, especially by the local ladies. Attendance had dropped off sharply after he and Maines had left town.

"So where is he?" I asked.

Maines shrugged in response.

Irritated, I said, "Look, you obviously made it in and out of

Cuba in one piece, which means mission accomplished. Take off the international-man-of-mystery suit already."

Maines chuckled but didn't crack. I gave up and settled back in the soft leather seat. I'd get it out of him eventually.

The rolling, rocky landscape of Azula County gave way to flatter, softer, brush country after a while, covered in long brass-colored grass and dotted with puffy chartreuse mesquite trees. It always killed me, what they call "trees" in Texas. Even the largest oaks and pecans seem stunted and misshapen in comparison to the big California pines and redwoods. Maybe that's what made the sky seem so much bigger here. It was as if you could see clear from horizon to horizon with nothing to block your view. Being under it, even inside the car, felt like a sort of mental vacuum cleaning. My head quieted down, and the vise that had become a permanent part of my digestive system started to loosen up. After a while I fell asleep.

I came up out of a dream about dancing skeletons to find the top half of a canine stretched out on the console next to me, chin on his paws. The dog lifted his head and looked at me as I opened my eyes, but, unlike my recent feline experience, didn't say anything. There was a manila folder in my lap.

"Case notes," Maines told me. "We'll stop for something to eat in a few minutes and go over them."

It was late afternoon, and my bladder was full. I glanced at the dog. "He's been holding it all this time?"

"We stopped a couple of hours ago."

I wiped a hand down over my face. "Geez."

"You didn't so much fall asleep as pass out. Been burning the midnight oil?"

"Hey, you live my life for the last six months and see how much rest you get."

The dog went on alert as I reached for my bag behind the seat, lifting his short triangular ears and sitting up.

"Steve," Maines said to him.

I laughed. "*Steve?*"

"My kids named him."

The dog scooted back off the console, and I groped for my makeup case. "I'm guessing they're not living at home anymore, or they'd be babysitting him."

Maines nodded but didn't offer any details. I tried to imagine him as a husband and father and drew a blank. I always do with him. He's one of the few people my radar won't penetrate. He's got a lead-lined soul, that guy.

My compact mirror showed no drool marks or boogers hanging out anywhere, but the sleep hadn't done my face any good. I'd turned thirty-nine on New Year's Day and looked every minute of it. Which isn't to say I was ready to start a plastic-surgery fund. My face had always looked too wholesome for my taste. I liked the edges that age was giving it.

The landscape whipping by outside was low and rocky now, pockmarked here and there with stubby eruptions of sun-browned, spiky brush. Every now and then an anemic-looking tree appeared, shading some skinny goats or cows, but there was little other vegetation. The air felt dry as a saltine cracker.

After about ten minutes, Maines started to slow down, and a gas station-slash-store came into view up ahead. We pulled into the gravel parking lot in front and got out of the car.

Maines handed me Steve's lead and angled his head at a group of picnic tables shaded by something that looked vaguely tree-like. The dog led me there and watered the stumpy foliage, then flopped down on the dry grass underneath. Maines returned with some sandwiches and drinks, a bowl of water, and

a can of dog food. He cranked the latter open with the Leather-
man dangling from his key ring while the dog slurped down
the water, then put the contents into the empty bowl.

We sat down and unwrapped our sandwiches. Maines
opened the folder, which I'd brought with me.

"Miles Darling, M.D.," he said, pointing his chin at a photo
clipped to the inside cover. "He runs the clinic."

I took the photo off the clip for a closer look. Darling was
pale and anemic-looking, with dark, thinning hair and steel-
rimmed glasses pinching the bridge of a somewhat long nose.
Clean-shaven, with an expensive tie under his white lab coat.

"He's got an American medical license?" I said.

"Yeah. Well, had. Set up shop down there after losing it.
Wrote one too many scrips for that banned diet drug. Fen-
whatever."

There was another photo underneath the doctor's, a head-
and-shoulders shot of a youngish brunette. "Is this our missing
person?"

Maines nodded, chewing and swallowing hastily to say,
"Rachael Pestozo. Divorced last year. Quit her job in November
to move back home to Arizona. Never showed up."

I was looking at Rachael's eyes, which were the same muddy-
bottom hazel as my own, but with an epicanthic fold.

"Where in Arizona?"

"Sells," he said. "It's on an Indian reservation down there."

"Oh, she's Tohono O'odham," I murmured, peering more
closely at the photo.

Maines's face went surprised.

"My mom is Chiricahua Apache," I explained. "I grew up
in Florence, about a hundred miles north of Sells. Sells is the
capital of the O'odham Nation."

Maines's sandy eyebrows rose a few more millimeters.

"I take after my dad," I told him.

"He musta been a really short Viking or something."

"He's Finnish."

Maines kept watching me, curiosity flickering in his pale eyes. Since he was so fond of keeping me in the dark, I let him swing. My family history was none of his business.

"So how'd you end up with the case, if her people are in Arizona?" I said.

"They called Benny looking for her. He doesn't have the manpower. Sent 'em to me."

"Did they know she was going down to the clinic?"

"No. Found it in her Internet history. She tracks down there, but not back out. Nobody's been able to get hold of her since."

Granted, I couldn't see Rachael's whole body in the picture, but her sharp jawline and only slightly rounded shoulders made me ask, "Why did she think she needed a lap-band?"

"The ex," Maines said. "Was always on her about her weight. Guess the divorce drove the point home."

"Oh, for Christ's sake."

A cop cruiser with a gold insignia on the door reading Texas Department of Public Safety crunched into the parking lot. Two burly guys in matching tan uniforms got out and went into the store.

The hair on the back of my neck got busy. We'd only been gone for half a day, so I doubted that Benny knew I was AWOL yet, but he'd figure it out pretty quickly, and the troopers would remember seeing me with Maines. I just had to hope that I'd be well into Mexico by then.

While I was thinking all this, Steve paused eating to give me a questioning look. Apparently I wasn't the only mammal on this mission with good radar. I lifted my eyebrows at the dog, resisting an urge to put my finger to my lips, and he went back to his food.

"Darling does a little cosmetic surgery on the side," Maines said around a mouthful of bread and cheese. "Face-lifts, nose jobs. Not actually bad at it. Seen some of his work. Majority of the clinic income is the bariatric stuff, though."

"Does he do all the work in-house?" I asked Maines, keeping a furtive eye on the store door.

"He's got admitting privileges at the hospital in Ojinaga. Mexican side, just across town from the clinic." Maines crumpled up his sandwich wrapper. "Can't get 'em to call me back. Not that it matters. The clinic gave me the 'medical confidentiality' runaround. Can't imagine the hospital is any better."

"So what makes you think I can get anything more out of them than you did?"

"I need a read on this Darling character from someone who's got better feelers than me," he said. "That'll tell me what my next move is."

I couldn't believe he was willing to haul me eight hundred miles just for that, but the troopers had come out of the store and were headed our way, so I put my interrogation on hold.

They were the multicultural set—one black, one white—both well over six feet tall, and built like large appliances.

"Good-lookin' dog you got there," the white guy said as they sat down at a nearby table. "What is that, a pointer?"

"Probably got some pointer in him," Maines replied, with that negligent drawl that men always seemed to use with each other in these parts. "Mostly mutt, though, I'm guessing."

"You seen those DNA kits they got now for dogs?" the

trooper chuckled, shaking his head. "My wife is all hot to do one for ours. Get him on the social register."

"Don't matter what DNA he got, he can tree a squirrel," his partner put in.

"Got that right," Maines agreed.

I'd closed the folder and was trying to look polite but casual while I finished my lunch.

"Y'all kinda far from home out here," the white trooper remarked, indicating the Azula County dealer insignia on Maines's Crown Vic.

My stomach tightened up a notch. Steve looked at me again, and Maines muttered to him, "Go do your business."

The dog loped out to the grass behind the picnic tables, sniffing the ground.

"Got a case down near the border," Maines told the troopers. He flipped open his wallet to show them his PI license. "Missing person."

The white trooper shook his head with a silent whistle. "It's a hornet's nest down there, brother. Lotta missing people." He glanced at me. "A lot of 'em women."

"She's my op," Maines told them, with what passed for a grin with him. "I pity the fool."

They all chuckled like they knew something about me that I didn't. I smiled gamely; the troopers weren't showing any interest in us aside from the typical roadside camaraderie, and I didn't want to give them a reason to look closer. It was bad enough they knew where we were going.

The dog came back from fertilizing the flora and looked at us expectantly. I got up to throw out my trash and didn't sit back down.

"You ready?" I asked Maines, taking care to keep a pleasant expression on for the cops.

Maines made a skeptical face. "Didn't want to come, now she's all hot to get on it."

More chuckling. I kept my mouth shut. Maines got up and nodded to the troopers, clipping Steve's lead back on, and we headed for the car.

"Seems like your opinion of cops would have improved some, considering," Maines said as we got in and buckled up.

Relieved that he hadn't read anything more into my desire for a hasty departure, I shot back, "Considering what? That you guys did such a great job keeping me out of harm's way last year?"

"Hey, that was your own fault," he said.

Before I could return fire, he went on. "There's a hot springs about forty miles from the clinic. On the American side. It's sort of an unofficial outpatient recovery room for U.S. citizens too chicken to spend the night in Mexico. We'll stay there overnight. Beat the bushes some. Unless we strike gold that way, you'll hit the clinic the next morning."

He paused to check traffic, then pulled back out onto the two-lane blacktop. "It's a walk-in deal. You show up, get examined, talk to Darling. Then he sets up an appointment for the work."

I frowned. "What, you don't have to make an appointment the first time? That's pretty relaxed for someone supposedly trying to stay off the radar."

"Probably does it so he can sniff people out ahead of time. Make sure they're not gonna turn him in."

"Did Rachael make it over that first hurdle?"

"Dunno."

Steve was listening, turning his head to look at each of us as we spoke, with his eerily intelligent brown eyes.

"Did you train him to do that?" I asked Maines, feeling a little unnerved by it.

"Came that way. He was a rescue." Maines bent his left leg and set his elbow on his knee. "Damn good watchdog, I'll tell you that. Can't get a thing by him." The corners of his dour mouth twitched. "You're a lot alike."

"No, we're not," I snapped, Connie's remark from the previous day slapping me in the face again. "I'm a human being."

"I just mean you've got an aptitude, that's all," he said, lifting the hand between us. "It could be an asset, if you used it right."

Why did the whole damned world suddenly have such an investment in my future?

"I'd say the fact that I'm still sucking air means I'm using it pretty right already."

Maines didn't answer, so I returned to the subject at hand. "What do you think happened to Rachael?"

"I can tell you what I'm hoping," Maines said. "I'm hoping she got an infection or something and is laid up in the hospital, with Darling trying to keep it quiet so he don't get sued."

"You're assuming she's still alive?"

Maines glanced my way. "I said 'hoping.' Nobody's heard from her for almost a month."

"Nobody's heard from me for almost thirty-six," I pointed out.

"She had no reason to want to disappear."

"Do you know that for a fact? Maybe she's running from that toxic ex of hers, or something else."

"She told her people she was coming home," Maines said. "Don't make any sense to worry them, if she wasn't going to show."

He had a point. I settled back to think, but with no obvious answers to keep it entertained, the brain eventually wandered to other subjects.

"OK, so tell me about Cuba," I instructed after we'd covered another twenty miles. The road had turned completely flat and straight now, stretching out ahead of us into a bare gray-and-brown eternity.

Maines cut his eyes at me. "After you've held up your end of the deal."

"You said you'd tell me on the drive."

"I didn't specify coming or going." He was watching the road with his head against the headrest, hat tipped forward. The visible corner of his mouth was twitching at me.

"Enjoying yourself?" I said.

"A little," he admitted.

"Laugh while you can," I advised him. "You're going to pay up eventually, if I have to beat it out of you."

He didn't reply or even look my way, just kept his eyes on the road and that smirk pasted on his face. I sat back and thought about the dead guy in my house. If things worked out the way I hoped, I'd never have to think about him again.

CHAPTER 6

We got to the hot springs around 10 P.M., after a bone-jarring crawl down a winding dirt track with more holes than flat places. The final hairpin ended at a small adobe cabin with several others marching up a low hill behind it. The light coming through its windows fell onto a row of metal roofs below and parallel to the cabins. Everything beyond that was darkness.

My joints cracked as I got out. It felt good to stand up. The expansive relief of driving through the flats of West Texas had shrunk the knot in my stomach to almost nothing, and I was feeling optimistic about my plans to slip into Mexico when the time was right.

A young man with a shaved head, dressed in red and yellow robes, came out of the first cabin to meet us. He was maybe twenty, with large dark eyes and a high-bridged nose that looked local.

"Welcome," he said to Maines, pressing his palms together at his chest. "Is it Mr. and Mrs. Smith?"

I shot Maines a look as he drawled, "Sorry we're so late." He'd told me to wear something that would pass as a wedding ring, but I'd assumed that was for my cover at the clinic.

"It's not necessary to apologize," the man said, gesturing toward the lighted cabin. "Please come in. Everything's ready for you."

The tiny building had a clay-tile roof and some kind of spiky gray-green plant growing in its painted window boxes. Inside, our host stepped behind a plywood counter and dragged a large ledger over, showing Maines where to sign.

"The bathhouses are always open," he said while Maines drove the pen across the indicated space. "The water is hottest at the end of the day."

Maines looked up. "That sounds good."

"I'm exhausted," I said quickly. "I think I'll just hit the sack."

The monk inclined his head with a smile, his eyes taking their time to follow. Something about my face seemed to interest him.

"Please come and go as you wish. There is always someone here in the office, but we prefer not to intrude upon our guests' time unless something is needed."

"Perfect," Maines said. He touched the brim of his tan felt hat with a finger. "Number four, is it?"

"Yes, just three doors along. You may park next to your cabin."

"Buddhist?" I asked on our way back to the car.

"I guess. They run the place."

"I thought it was part of the clinic."

"They have some kind of arrangement," Maines said, making an annoyed face. "Don't like the smell of it, but couldn't get to the bottom of it from home."

"This thing better have two beds," I growled as we pulled up next to our cabin.

Nothing in Maines's face moved, but I could feel the joke coming. "Gets pretty cold at night out here."

"The Arctic couldn't get cold enough."

Number four was just like the office, without the counter in it: one big room, with a small bathroom at the far end. The solitary double bed was covered with a colorful horse blanket, and there was a rustic chair and dresser. Steve jumped immediately onto the bed.

"Guess we're both sleeping on the floor," Maines remarked.

"You couldn't say we were relatives or something?"

"Didn't want to take a chance on our story here not matching the one we'll use at the clinic," he said, emptying his jeans pockets onto the dresser. He was maybe ten years my senior, too young to pose as my father.

"Man, I can feel that lithium doing its thing already," he said.

"Lithium?"

"It's in the water here, in the hot springs. That's why people come down here. You soak in it, makes you feel kinda loopy. In a good way."

"You haven't been in the water yet," I pointed out.

"No excuse, then," he said, getting out a pair of faded blue pajamas and a small travel case. "You coming?"

"I'm loopy enough, thanks."

He dropped his hat on the dresser. "Your loss."

I'd almost forgotten about the dog, and was surprised to feel someone watching me when I came back from inspecting the bathroom. He was still sitting in the center of the bed, wearing that attentive and slightly puzzled look that appeared to be his default expression. He lifted his long skinny tail and let it fall once, then his ears stood up. Maines's phone, on the dresser, was buzzing.

The caller ID told me that Benny Ramirez was on the other end. I waited for the voice-mail indicator to light up, then fiddled around until I found the access.

"Hey, John," Benny's crusty young voice said. "The dentals came back on that John Doe we found out at Julia Kalas's place the other day. It's Orson Greenlaw."

Benny paused, as if Maines would know who he was talking about and be surprised, then went on.

"Nobody reported him missing because he was supposed to have moved to D.C. to work with some political campaign up there. When he didn't show, they just figured he'd decided he didn't want the job and was too chicken to tell them directly. Liz is still working on it, but it looks like Greenlaw hasn't been dead long enough for Connie to have been involved."

Benny took a deep breath and continued. "I'm calling because Julia mentioned that you'd asked her to help with your missing-persons case down near the border. Her gun came back neck-deep in a couple of Zetas hits in San Antonio, but I can't find her to talk to her about it. If she's with you, just know that she may be fixing to rabbit. She cashed a big-mother check the other day and took half in pesos. Let me know, will you? I've got a bulletin out for her."

The message ended. I turned the phone off and sat there looking at myself in the dresser mirror. Erasing it might buy me a day or two, but if Maines saw Benny's name on his call log, it wouldn't matter. Purging the call log would be worse than just leaving it as is. I thought about hiding the phone somewhere, but with all that cash in my bag, I didn't want to invite a search.

After thinking a bit more, I went into the bathroom and filled the sink, then dropped the phone in. I let it soak, then took it out and turned it on. A satisfying crackle and a black screen told me I'd successfully shorted something essential. I took the back off and dried all the parts, then put everything back together and returned the phone to the dresser.

I folded the bed down and was asleep before I got horizontal.

CHAPTER 7

The awareness of a warm body next to mine startled me awake just after sunrise. It was Steve, lying with the blanket drawn up to his chin and his head on the adjoining pillow. Maines was asleep on the floor with his back to us. I was beginning to understand just how impenetrable to my radar the man really was. The comedy of tucking a dog into bed with me wasn't something I'd have thought him able to enjoy. Maybe the lithium had kicked in during his bath.

Steve felt me juking around and rolled over, giving a quiet whine. Maines slurred, "I'm coming, boy. Just a minute."

"I'll take him," I said, swinging my legs out of bed. I wanted to make sure Maines's phone hadn't leaked a pool of telltale water overnight.

Steve jumped up and bounded to the door, and I grabbed his lead off the dresser. The phone looked exactly the same as it had when I'd left it there the night before.

It was surprisingly cold outside, and the chill blue light showed a flat area about the size of a football field beyond the lower buildings, where several tents were pitched next to soot-marked rock fire rings. This camping area dropped sharply off into a dry riverbed that looked like a mini Grand Canyon, the high banks on both sides banded tan and white. An occasional spiky dark plant stood out along their top edges. Nothing you could call a tree anywhere in sight.

Steve squatted and made a dark puddle in the rust-colored dirt, then started to sniff around, pulling on the lead. Movement off to the left drew my eye: the monk who'd checked us in the previous night, walking down into the camping area. A group of people appeared over the edge of the small canyon, coming to meet him. They were too far away for me to make out anything more than general specs—a couple of men and a woman carrying a small child. The monk talked with them for a short while, then one of the men peeled off and disappeared back into the canyon. The others turned and started toward the cabins with the Buddhist.

"*Coyote*," said Maines's voice behind me. He was still in his pajamas, minus his hat and glasses. He looked about eighteen, all skinny wrists and tufts of sleep-mussed strawberry hair.

I peered back out into the barren landscape. "Where?"

"That fella who just went back down," he said, nodding toward the canyon. "They bring illegals across the border. Under the radar."

The group with the monk was heading for the office, coming closer now, and Maines motioned me back into our cabin.

"Well, that certainly doesn't smell too good," I said as he went to the dresser and put on his glasses.

"Illegals come with the territory down here," Maines replied. "It ain't unusual."

Maybe not, but it tweaked my radar. "This place is a way station for illegals in addition to being an informal recovery room for the clinic where Rachael disappeared? Maybe the two things are related."

Maines looked at me. My suspicion wasn't well-formed enough yet to put into more words than that, so I just looked back.

He held still, thinking, then said, "Might be worth looking into. Let's keep an eye on it."

It suddenly occurred to me that I'd jumped out of bed without having to crawl out from under that heavy, wet thing that camped on my chest most mornings. Getting away from Azula was turning out to be good therapy.

"I wonder if the clinic owns this place," Maines muttered to himself, then said to me, "You know how to look up property records, don't you?"

"If the county has their tax-appraisal records online, there's nothing to it. All you need is an Internet connection."

Maines grabbed his phone and mashed the "on" button. I went over to get my duffel bag off the floor, so as not to seem like I was watching him.

"What's wrong with the damned thing now?" he muttered, smacking it against his hand.

"Is there a library where we're going?" I said, putting my duffel on the bed. "I can do it on a public-access computer, if they have them."

Distracted by his phone, Maines didn't answer. I watched him fiddle with it for a while longer, then asked, "How'd the snooping go last night?"

"She stayed here the night before she disappeared. Left her suitcase with some clothes and personal items."

"She was planning on coming back here, then."

"Right. Never did."

The vague suspicion aroused by seeing the *coyote* came into sharper focus. "Maybe she somehow got sideways with whoever is killing these women along the border, the stuff those troopers were talking about."

"Those gals are all Mexican nationals," Maines said. "Whoever's doing them in knows better than to mess with Americans. Most people figure the cartels are to blame."

"Rachael probably wasn't wearing her passport on her forehead," I said, "and she could easily be mistaken for Mexican. Who's to say she didn't run afoul of some cartel business by accident?"

He pressed his lips together, then shook his head. "I ain't saying you're wrong, but that's a ways down the road. Might be worth chasing, if we don't turn up some other connections right quick." He got out his shaving kit. "You want the bathroom first?"

I grabbed my duffel. "I'm fast."

CHAPTER 8

We took a short, skull-rattling drive south to a sun-bleached general store with a rusted sign nailed to it that read RUIDOSA, TEXAS, POP. 43. There was a half-demolished adobe church next to the store, its cedar *latillas*—the horizontal roof members typical in the Southwest—caved in. Maines went into the store and bought some breakfast tacos and caffeine for the two of us, and another can of dog food and a bowl of water for Steve.

Sitting down under the front porch, which was just a piece of tin roofing balanced on top of some stripped tree trunks stuck in the dirt, I noticed a broad, sandy wash about a hundred yards from the road.

"I can't believe it ever rains here," I said, pointing my chin at it.

"That's the Rio Grande," Maines told me.

I swallowed my mouthful of iced tea. It was weak and tasted kind of like old paper, but I still preferred it to coffee. "Get out of here."

"Farms and ranches upstream are siphoning off so much it hardly runs anymore."

I gestured at the corrugated panel fence just beyond the wash. "How do these ranchers water their cattle?"

"That ain't a ranch fence," Maines said. "That's the newest thing in border security, courtesy of your U.S. government."

I'd heard about the border fence, of course, but the thing I was looking at made me wonder what the backers were smoking.

"You can't be serious," I said. "Your dog could climb that thing."

"He'd be dead in a couple of days," Maines said, tilting his tan-hatted head toward the vast expanse of bleached dirt and dry brush beyond the fence. "That's the Chihuahuan Desert. Better barrier than any damn fence."

I finished my breakfast taco, realizing that my plan to fade would have to be better planned than just wandering off when Maines wasn't looking. Even though I was dressed in boots and jeans—a sartorial tradition I'd adopted shortly after realizing that everything in Texas below about mid-thigh level was out to bite, sting, or stick something sharp into me—I wasn't ready to join the mad dogs and Englishmen.

"You think I should mention Rachael, when I get to the clinic?" I asked Maines, watching Steve scarf down his dog food. "I could say she referred me. Maybe it'll shake something loose."

Maines mashed his taco wrapper into a tight ball. "Finding her stuff out at the springs means whoever was involved in her disappearance wasn't bothering to cover his tracks."

"It could also mean that there wasn't a whoever," I pointed out, glancing back at the desert. "If you don't buy a run-in with some nefarious border types, maybe she wandered out there and got lost or something."

"She's born and raised," Maines said. "She knows better."

"I'm just trying to bring you around to seeing some logic about this thing."

Maines looked at me. "Why?"

"You're already sold on the clinic being involved when there are at least a dozen other possibilities."

"No, I mean, why do you care?" He'd taken off his clip-ons, and his ineludible eyes remained aimed at my face.

"Because I don't want to spend a week down here if we can get this thing cleared up in a day." I didn't tell him that was actually because I was anxious to get over the border and disappear before the news trickled down that Benny was looking for me.

"No possibility that solving the case holds some fascination, huh?" Maines said, mouth corner twitching.

I gave him a pitying glance. "Give it up, man. The day I turn cop is the day we all find out whether or not there really is a God."

Steve flopped down at our feet, having finished his postprandial gambol. Avoiding Maines's laser gaze, I pointed at his cup and said, "You want another one?"

"Black," he replied, still watching me.

When I came back out with our refills, he was scowling at his dead phone, which he'd hooked up to the charger on our drive here.

"You been screwing with this?" he asked me.

I gave him my surprised look as I handed him his coffee. "Why would I?"

He studied me briefly, then got up and tossed the phone into a rusted steel trash barrel next to one of the porch poles. He stood there looking out across the parched view for a few minutes, sipping his coffee, then asked over his shoulder, "Got that P40 with you?"

"No," I said, the back of my stomach going cold. "Why?"

He pointed to his left temple. "Just running the possibilities."

"You're not filling me with confidence here, man."

"Well, that's our deal, idn't it?" he said, adjusting his hat with studied carelessness. "You don't trust me, I don't trust you. Keeps us both on our toes."

There wasn't much I could say to that, so I just sat there and drank my tea until he started for the car.

We buckled in and pulled out onto the two-lane blacktop, Steve panting quietly in the backseat. I sipped silently and tried to decide if it was better to keep my mouth shut or rewind the conversation. Sometimes, if you pretend something hasn't been said, the other person starts to believe it.

A green-and-white sign flashed by, advising that we were entering Presidio, Texas. We came around a flat, wide curve with some sick-looking palm trees on either side. In the hazy distance ahead of us the blue-gray mountains were coming closer, and another sign loomed: OJINAGA MEX. PORT OF ENTRY.

We rolled by a row of battered yellow gates and guard houses under a flat tan canopy where uniformed border patrol were checking papers and searching cars coming from the opposite direction. Maines saw my puzzled expression and explained, "They don't care about people going in. Just people coming out."

We crossed a low bridge over the river and did the same song, second verse on the Mexican side: an older-looking series of gates, none of which were facing our way. The uniforms didn't even look over as we passed.

Ojinaga—a jumble of tin-roofed adobes, industrial-looking public buildings, and decaying *palacios*, all faded to pale imitations of their original colors—crowded right up to the edge of the riverbed. There were several perfectly respectable-looking hotels along the divided boulevard leading away from the crossing.

As we turned off onto a narrower street coming in at a crazy angle, I asked Maines, "People will seriously drive forty miles after having surgery when they could just stay here?"

"You underestimate the average American's fear of brown people."

I wondered, not for the first time, how he'd come to harbor thoughts like that. His good-ol'-boy Texan demeanor always made me expect something else.

We cut through another assortment of buildings that looked like they'd been dropped there from outer space by someone with no sense of direction. The air smelled of gasoline and cig-arettes. After a while we turned onto another street, this one so narrow we couldn't have gotten out of the car if we'd stopped, which didn't seem to bother the other vehicles bombing along in both directions at breakneck speed. We spent some time driving on what would have been the sidewalk, if there'd been one, then Maines spotted a parking space and made use of it.

There was a corrugated-tin shack on the corner in front of us, conjunto wafting from its open windows, which were just flaps of lumber hinged at one side, thrown open and hooked to the wall. The other side of the street was all open shops with boxes of produce, clothing, and cigarettes stacked chin high. Pedestrians boiled all around us, threading between cars, bicy-cles, and noisy scooters; browsing along the shops; standing in clusters to talk.

Maines got out of the car and clipped Steve's lead on. "The clinic's on the square. Couple blocks. I'm coming with you."

"Don't be an idiot," I said, stepping quickly out of the street to avoid being flattened by an oncoming vegetable truck. "The wedding ring might have fooled those monks, but you and I clock about as married as Margaret Thatcher and Cesar Chavez. If Darling has his ears up at all, he'll smell you coming from a mile away."

"I'm not sending you in there alone. Not after finding Rachael's stuff."

"What was the goddamned point of dragging me all the way down here, then?"

The dog took a seat. Maines watched him, pushing his jaw to one side.

"Look, I assume you wanted me on this because you know I can handle myself," I said. "So enough with the white-knight shit."

Maines started to reply, but I headed him off. "I'll take Steve. You said yourself that he's a good watchdog, and he'll be a distraction, keep their focus off me. I'll tell them he's a service animal or something."

We stood there for maybe ten minutes, Maines not looking at me and not saying anything. Then he passed me the dog's leash and pointed his eyes at the tin shack. "I'll wait for you in the cantina. If you're not back within an hour, I'm coming after you."

CHAPTER 9

The plaza was a dusty stone rectangle with a dry fountain in the center, concrete benches along the street side, and a lone palm tree guarding a whitewashed adobe church at the far end. A small sign reading DARLING CLINIC was posted on one of the pillars of a long arcade on the left.

I walked over. A smaller sign posted above the bell at the plank door inside the arcade read, PLEASE RING FOR SERVICE. I found some humor in the fact that neither it nor the main clinic sign were in Spanish. Obviously, Darling's target demographic wasn't local.

A short, hefty black woman in a nurse's uniform opened up a few seconds after I touched the bell. She didn't say anything, just stood aside and held the door. I let Steve lead the way in, expecting to get some resistance, but the nurse offered none. She merely turned and started down a narrow, high-ceilinged hall with lumpy white walls. At a corner, she led me into a large, windowless room with a desk just inside the door. There was an exam table and some painted wooden cabinets at the end of the room facing the desk, which had a single chair standing in front of it. The nurse gestured me to take this, putting on a sudden, somewhat alarming smile.

"What can I help you with today?"

Her bogus friendliness unnerved me, and I stammered, "I'm, uh—I wanted to see about getting, having a lap-band done."

Her nuclear grin brightened, and she made a note on a pad in front of her. "Wonderful!" Her face then went serious. "You do understand that you must pay cash? Because of our location we are unable to file with American insurance companies."

I bet myself that wasn't the only reason.

"Oh, no problem. I don't want my husband to know I'm doing this anyway."

"Of course," the nurse simpered, giving me a conspiratorial look. "Many of our ladies feel the same way. But you won't be able to hide it for long. The weight comes off very quickly."

I nodded, trying to look pleased. She had an accent I didn't recognize, and I started to wonder how she'd gotten roped into this gig.

"Now . . . will you be wanting the hot springs recovery package? Of course we can accommodate you at our inpatient facility if you prefer, but . . ." She trailed off, her gaze sliding down my face.

"No, I'm already staying at the springs," I said. "But is it safe, so far away? I mean, if something goes wrong, will they know what to do?"

"The procedure has very few complications," she said, "and we only release patients to off-site recovery after we're sure that they are stable following their surgeries."

"But—I mean—" I hesitated, trying to appear flustered. "Unforeseen things come up, don't they?"

"None of our patients has ever had any problem that could not be taken care of." The bright reassurance in her voice had slipped a little, and the phrasing of her answer felt odd, as if she were on the witness stand.

I kept my worried face on and said, "But, like—how? Is there a doctor out there?"

She leaned toward me across the desk, her dark eyes fixing on mine. A little flash of fear shot through me, but she just said, "Don't worry. You are in the best hands."

She gestured at the exam table on the far side of the room. "If you would, please."

Steve, who'd dropped into an almost instant sleep beside my chair, lifted his head as I got up. When he saw that we weren't going far, he put it back down.

"A handsome fellow," the nurse remarked as I climbed up onto the exam table. "I have a dog also. Not quite so well-behaved."

I nodded, still trying to place her accent. "I'm glad you guys didn't mind me bringing him. He's kind of my good-luck charm."

She glanced at him again as she pumped up the blood pressure cuff. "The doctor won't like it, but where's the harm?"

The radar found that interesting. You don't usually find a lot of insubordination, subtle or otherwise, in a crooked enterprise. It's difficult enough to stay clear of trouble when everyone plays along. Throw a wrench in there, things can get hairy fast.

"He sounds like a grinch," I said.

"Oh, not at all," the nurse replied, ripping the Velcro cuff off and making a note on her pad. "Dr. Darling is a very accomplished surgeon. A fine man."

"They say he's the best," I agreed. She stuck an electronic thermometer in my ear. "A friend of mine came down here for her lap-band. She's the one who told me about the place."

"Ah, yes?" the nurse beamed, peering at the thermometer. She didn't seem interested. I decided to save it.

After making a few more notes, she picked up her pad and said, "The doctor will see you in a few moments."

She went out, leaving the door open. Faint voices echoed in from down the hall, and Steve looked up again, then over at me, and got up.

"I wouldn't," I said.

I didn't feel like much of an authority, sitting up on the high table with my feet dangling, but he gave a noisy sigh and lay down again.

After about ten minutes, Darling came in. He looked exactly like his picture; the third dimension added nothing. Even his hair looked like an imitation of the real thing. Maybe it was.

He nodded in my direction but his eyes didn't focus on me. "Now then, Ms."—he consulted the folder he'd brought with him—"Smith."

It wasn't a question, so I kept quiet. He closed the folder and laid it on the low stool next to the examining table, taking a roll of mints out of his white lab coat pocket. He popped one into his mouth and tilted his head back to look at me. "Open, please."

I unhinged my jaw and he peered in, then felt behind my ears. His hands smelled of rubbing alcohol.

"Lie back, please."

I did it, and he lifted the hem of my shirt and began mashing my stomach around. He was watching what he was doing but I got the definite impression that he was thinking about something else.

He grabbed the folder and said, "On the scale, please."

I got down and let him weigh and measure, then we went back to the desk. He gave Steve a frown as he went by, as if noticing him for the first time.

"Have you had your blood work done?" he asked, the mint making clicking sounds against his teeth as he talked.

I gave him a confused look, and he tore a form off a pad and slid it toward me across the desk.

"You'll need to do that today, after you leave here. You appear to be a good candidate. Have you ever had surgery before?"

"On my shoulder," I said.

He looked up, drawing a bead on me for the first time. "Joint problem? That's very common with obesity."

"I was involved in an accident," I said.

"Ah." He tilted his head back and gave me a deprecatory once-over through his glasses. "Yes, excess weight often exacerbates injuries in those situations."

It's not like I hadn't heard stupid shit like that from doctors before, so I don't know how my annoyance got on top of me before I could stop myself from snapping back at him, "I was stabbed."

His expression went wary. "Stabbed?"

"Like I said, it was an accident," I said, quickly corralling my temper. "I'm a little touchy about it."

"Why's that?" he asked, his voice quiet and sharp.

I was clearly on thin ice, which is usually where I do my best skating, but with horror I realized that a predissociation chill was starting up the back of my neck. I grabbed Steve's lead and stood up. "I'm sorry, I'm not feeling well. I'll have to come back."

The doctor looked up at me, his expression turning dangerous. "Don't bother."

CHAPTER 10

God only knows what happened between Darling's office and the street in front of the clinic, where I came back into my body some time later. There wasn't a battery of guns pointed at my head, and I appeared to have all my parts, so it hadn't been life threatening, but I almost wished it had. At least then I'd know where I stood.

Crossing the plaza to head back to the cantina, Steve jerked suddenly on the lead and got away from me, turning down one of the side streets. I gave chase and saw him jumping up on a short man in a chambray shirt and faded jeans at the end of the block. It looked like the *coyote* I'd seen at the hot springs that morning.

Amazed at the dog's memory, I hurried toward them. The *coyote* was leaning over and scrubbing Steve's ears like they were old friends, and as I came up, he straightened and turned toward me. We both froze. It was Hector.

After a minute I found my voice. "What the hell?"

His hair had been shorn off close to the scalp, exposing patches of gray above his ears, and he'd lost a lot of weight, but he looked at me like I was the one who'd undergone metamorphosis.

"Julia?"

"Oh, come on. I haven't changed that much in nine months."

Steve was going nuts, dancing a circle around Hector's legs. "No, I just—Maines didn't say he was bringing you."

"God damn it," I said. "He knew you were down here all this time?"

Hector nodded but said, "I asked him not to say anything to anybody."

"Why? It would have been a lot easier to get me down here if he'd told me. I almost didn't come."

"Well, technically he didn't know my exact location. I'm on the move a lot."

"I guess you have to be, to avoid getting picked up by border patrol." His eyes jumped to my face, and I explained, "I saw you yesterday evening, bringing those people up to the hot springs."

"Gotta pay my bills somehow."

"You do know that you own a bar in Azula, right?"

"I can't go back into the States. The feds'll pick me up if I do."

"So what? You haven't done anything illegal."

The air was heating quickly in the oncoming afternoon, and the faint odors of gasoline and rotting vegetables were growing stronger. Hector stepped into the shade of the building behind him and extracted from his wallet a folded piece of newsprint, which he handed to me. It was a Spanish-language paper, but the photo of him shaking hands with Castro didn't need translation. The caption read, *"El hijo boliviano del Che regressa a Cuba."*

"Hm," I said, making a face.

"Yeah," Hector agreed grimly. "I'm sure you've had enough interaction with the feds to know how that might go down."

"Fidel's retired," I said, handing him back the clipping, "and this new guy—Obama—says he wants to normalize relations and lift the embargo."

"*Wants* to," Hector emphasized. "Even if he can make it happen, which is questionable, given how much pushback he's already getting on his agenda, that's not gonna undo fifty years of political and cultural animosity right out of the box. Not to mention that me and Maines didn't exactly get our visas in order before we left. Don't kid yourself. If I was at home and the U.S. found out how and why I went to Cuba, I'd disappear so fast it'd make your head spin."

"OK, you might get picked up and questioned," I agreed. "But you, me, and Maines are the only ones who know what you were doing there, and none of us are going to talk about it. At worst, the cops could pop you for failing to make proper travel arrangements. They don't put people in prison for stuff like that."

"That's not the point," Hector said, glancing around the dusty street. "My identity would become public. I'd never walk down an American street in peace again."

"Some people admire your father," I reminded him. I wasn't sure if I was one of them, politically speaking, but the fact that Hector shared his DNA was enough to make me approve of him as a human being.

"They're not the ones I'm worried about." Hector felt toward the breast pocket of his shirt—a gesture I recognized—but his magic herbal cigarettes weren't there. They'd been replaced by a white plastic inhaler.

"You look like hell," I said, watching him take a couple of hits off it. He didn't, really—the hawk nose and beautiful dark eyes with their long expressive brows hadn't changed. His vibe was more guarded, but that was to be expected, given the circumstances.

He coughed and returned the inhaler to his pocket with a weak grin. "You don't."

A tickle of pleasure fluttered up into my throat, but I swatted it down. The man had disappeared from the face of the earth after a pretty convincing courtship. Who knew what else he had up his sleeve?

I opened my mouth to begin the shit-giving part of the program, but Hector had spotted something over my left shoulder that was making him antsy.

"Look, I'm supposed to meet Maines up at the hot springs this evening," he said, moving away. "We'll talk more then, all right?"

I glanced behind me to see what had spooked him: a couple of uniforms getting out of a small green SUV. When I turned back around, Hector was gone.

CHAPTER 11

Maines was sitting at an upended wooden cable reel inside the cantina when I got back. He was the only person in the place, aside from the guy behind the bar, who was drinking beer and watching a soccer game on the TV set bolted to the wall.

"You'll never guess who I ran into," I said as I sat down in the metal folding chair across from him.

"Montezuma?" he cracked, watching Steve ease down onto the floor. "Hope he didn't take revenge."

I gave him the stink eye. "Why the subterfuge?"

"People see more when they face the unknown. It's a statistical fact."

I leaned toward him and enunciated precisely so that he couldn't pretend to mistake my meaning. "It's fucking annoying."

Maines adjusted his hat and asked, "How was Darling?"

"Don't try and weasel out of this."

"It ain't my fault. Hector wouldn't come over the border. So I brought the mountain to Mohammad."

"Never mind," I said. I could practically feel his boot heels digging into the dirt floor, and we had business to discuss.

He received my report on the clinic—edited to omit my last-minute fadeout—with a grim, attentive grimace, and a mut-tered, "Crap." He got up. "We'd better make tracks for the hospital."

"I imagine the good doctor knows how to dial a phone," I said, following him to the bar, where he laid down a bill and touched his hat brim at the soccer fan.

"All the more reason to shake a leg," Maines said, pushing the screen door open and stepping into the street.

We wove toward the Crown Vic, single file through the stream of bodies and cars, Steve cutting a path for us. I was be-ginning to admire the dog's ability to roll with the changes; he didn't get jumpy or overexcited by the crush, the way most of his brethren would. Just trotted along with his ears up and his eyes open.

When we stopped at the car, he spotted another dog across the street and stiffened, emitting a short, sharp bark. Maines started to shush him, then pulled up short, his eyes fixing on a group of people standing at one of the open shops.

Without saying anything to me, he came around the car and handed me the leash, then threaded across the street and ap-proached the group, touching the elbow of one of the women. As she turned toward him, I got a look at her face, which was a fairly reasonable facsimile of Rachael Pestozo's photo.

Crossing the street to join them, I observed that she'd had a lot more work done than a lap-band. To the average person, she might have passed for organic, but I'd lived in California long enough to recognize even the best plastic surgery when I see it. She didn't look "done" the way the people on those celebrity-disaster websites do, but her skin was too smooth, her expres-sion too serene. Nobody comes out of their mother like that.

"Yes, I am," she was saying when I got to where they were

standing. She gave me a wary look with eyes that seemed lighter than in her photo. This mixed-blood eye color is a weird thing, though. Some days I could swear my eyes are hazel and the next day I'll get up and they're blue or green or even yellow.

"Who are you?" she asked me.

I pointed at Maines. "I'm with him."

He handed her one of his cards. While she read it, I wondered why she'd bothered with plastic surgery. Not because the work was bad—Maines was right about Darling's skill—but because she didn't look much different from her photo. Usually, when women go under the knife, they don't want to come out of it just a slightly altered version of how they went in; they want to be eye-catching—younger looking, sexier. Rachael, while not unattractive, was none of those things, even though it was obvious to me that she'd had extensive work done on her face and body.

"You can't be serious," she said, giving Maines back his card and glancing at me. "Who hired you? If it was Orson, you're in trouble, because I have a protection order against him."

"Orson?" I said, surprised. Maines shot me a quick look, and I added quickly, "Who's Orson?"

"My ex-husband," she replied. "If he didn't send you, who did?"

My ears went offline for a few seconds while the brain assimilated. If I believed in coincidence, the fact that the dead guy in my house was the ex-husband of the woman Maines and I were looking for would have been an amazing one. Since I don't, I kept my mental teeth in the subject until the logic lined up: Rachael must have gone AWOL because she'd killed her ex, using the story of returning home to Arizona as a cover to run for the border.

"Why'd you leave your stuff out at the hot springs?" Maines was asking her when I could hear again.

His voice had that mild, friendly tone cops get when they smell bullshit, which was a relief. I didn't want to have to tell him about Benny's phone call, but neither did I want anybody getting away with murder on my ticket. I couldn't care less about Truth, Justice, and the American way, I've just never liked being on the losing team.

I could see that Rachael felt Maines's distrust, and that it was making her prickly. "I stayed out there after my surgery. I must have missed some things when I packed."

"You missed checking out, too," Maines said, those wet-pebble eyes of his shimmering behind his glasses.

"So what? The bill was paid."

"You look pretty well healed up," he observed. "How come you haven't headed to Arizona like you planned? Nobody's been able to get hold of you."

Rachael made a tsking noise and got a phone out of her fringed suede purse. "Because the cell reception down here is terrible. I texted my aunt to let her know I couldn't get there until next week. It must not have gone through."

She started poking at the phone like we weren't there. Maines let her get away with it for a few minutes, then said, "I think it'd be a good idea if you came back to Azula with us."

My stomach did a little celebration dance. I was off the hook. Hello, Mexico.

"For what?" Rachael asked, her voice cool.

Maines didn't answer. The cool blinked.

"You're not cops," she said. "You can't make me go anywhere."

Maines gave the ground a sorrowful look. "No, you're right.

I can't." His mild voice went even milder. "I can be a real pain in the ass, though."

"That's true," I told her. Anticipation was pinpricking the bottoms of my feet, turning me persuasive.

She looked like she might run for it, despite her impassive expression, but she said, "Fine. You'll be paying for my return trip afterward, though."

"There's probably a landline out at the springs," Maines said, stepping to one side and gesturing toward the car. "You can call your folks from there."

She didn't move. "I'm staying at the Waru now. Room 717."

"That's a nice hotel," Maines said. "Nice enough to have a working telephone."

Rachael put her turquoise-ringed hands on her hips. "Look, I didn't know they hadn't gotten my text until just now. What's the matter with you?"

"Overdeveloped sense of responsibility," he said.

She stared at him, hard, and he stood back, extending a gallant arm toward his Crown Vic. She turned her stare on me, then sighed and came along quietly.

CHAPTER 12

The Waru was nice enough, considering it was just a '60s-era motel with some modernist icing slathered over the top of it. Two stories with a veranda on the second, the rooms all opening to the parking lot. The lobby had a couple of big circular windows and some nice ironwork railings.

I took a seat in the cafe while Maines and Rachael went over to the front desk. I didn't want her getting away with anything, but I wasn't anxious to nail myself to the cross, either. I'd be able to tell from here whether or not my wanted status came to light during the phone call. Not that I had any plans for what to do if it did. It wasn't like I could outrun Maines, but at least I'd have a little head start if I tried.

They only made one call, and Maines didn't look in my direction while they did it. After Rachael hung up, the two of them headed back my way, Maines checking his watch.

"It's almost four," he said. "If we leave now we'll have to stop again halfway home." He watched Rachael adjust her bone-and-turquoise necklace. "Let's go get your stuff and get you checked out. You'll have to stay with us out at the springs."

"No way," she said. "I'm not spending another night at that

dive. No air conditioning, no TV. Forget it. Just pick me up in the morning."

He fixed her with a tolerant look. "I *have* been told I look stupid."

"Listen, Maines," I cut in, seeing my chance. "I'd like to hang out down here for a while, take some vacation time and catch up with Hector." His upper lip twitched, as if he were about to respond, but I kept talking. "Why don't you give me a lift back to the springs, pick up your stuff, and then you two can come back and stay here tonight. I'll hook up with Hector when he comes out for the meeting you guys had scheduled this evening."

Maines pressed his thin lips together, thinking it over, then waved us toward the car. Rachael grabbed her purse off the bed and flounced out ahead of us, along the hotel veranda.

"You're not giving her much rope," I said quietly to him as we followed a few lengths behind. "What's up?"

"Not sure," he replied, eyes narrowed in Rachael's direction. "Something, though."

That settled my stomach a little. He wouldn't be turning his back on her.

"Listen," I muttered for good measure as we descended the concrete stairs, "be careful, will you? I'm getting the same vibe off her."

"I got a throwdown piece in the car," Maines said. "Don't you worry about me."

Satisfied that his guard was sufficiently activated, I watched Rachael get into the Crown Vic. She wasn't tall, and she had an OK figure: not fat, not thin, but nothing wrong with it. If she'd had her lap-band done at the same time as her face, it had been in place for at least a couple of months. I wished that Maines had gotten a full-length picture of her so that I could see what she'd looked like before. The radar was telling me that something was off about this whole plastic-surgery story.

Nobody said much on the drive out to the springs, which was fine with me. The closer we got, the tenser I felt, worried that something would go haywire at the last minute.

It was just after sundown when we turned off the washboard dirt road and pulled up outside the office. Maines and I got out and walked a few feet from the car.

"Hope you can talk him into it," Maines said. I gave him a quizzical look, and he explained, "It's no kind of life for Hector down here. He needs to come back home."

"Leave it to me," I said. If I worked it right, Maines would never see either one of us again.

"If you can't, gimme a call and I'll wire you some bus money."

I nodded, knowing I wouldn't.

He hesitated, looking off toward the canyon. After a minute, he said, "Thanks for your help on this. Appreciate it."

He held out a hand and I shook it. A weird urge to hug him bubbled up, surprising me. The thought was mildly obscene, as if I'd caught myself thinking lewd things about a sibling.

CHAPTER 13

After Maines and Rachael left I realized that I'd been so focused on getting them on the road that I'd forgotten to eat. Wishing I'd thought of it in Ojinaga, I took a stroll around to see what might be available on-site, but beyond the six cabins climbing the hill behind me there was nothing but craggy brown rock.

While I stood there considering my options, a monk came out of the office. It wasn't the same guy who'd checked us in yesterday—this one was a wiry Caucasian—but he wore the same shaved head and red and yellow robes. He looked about my age, with dark stubble on his pale scalp and bright brown eyes that were wide and forward-looking, like an owl's. He walked with his head thrust forward, and had a curiously reluctant posture that made him seem as if he'd shrunk away from the touch of his clothes.

"I don't suppose there's a diner or anything within walking distance," I said to him.

He smiled, showing some crooked teeth, and took a bench against the adobe wall, producing a paper sack from one sleeve. He gestured for me to join him, opening the sack.

The radar tweaked. There was something slightly off-putting about him, despite the outfit. It didn't read lethal, though, so I sat down.

"Valley peaches," he said, pulling one out of the bag. It was about the size of a large walnut. He cut around its seam with a small pocketknife, then twisted it apart and offered me the half without the pit in it. "They're really good this year."

I took the tiny half peach and sat down. "I thought you guys renounced worldly stuff like enjoying your food."

"Oh, you've studied Buddhism?"

I laughed and shook my head, popping the fruit in my mouth. It had an unexpectedly rich, sweet flavor. "Wow, these *are* good."

He brought out a large puck of soft white cheese and another half-dozen peaches. "You can't learn detachment if there's nothing around that tempts you."

His gaze crawled toward me but didn't make it all the way. He offered me a slice of cheese on the end of his knife. "Now, try that."

As he reached forward, the sleeve of his robe fell away from his forearm, revealing a faded indigo tattoo. It was a watch with no hands, encircling his arm just above the wrist.

So that was it. I took a steadying breath and said, "Which prison were you in?"

His owl eyes flashed all the way up to my face this time, clear and intent. He didn't say anything.

The radar was awake, but not screaming the paint down. "It looks older than ten, so you've been out awhile," I ventured. "Must not have been too serious."

"I got this in Austin, years ago," the monk said. Then he did an odd thing: He shut up.

His pupils were still dilated, so I knew it wasn't because I was wrong, but I was clearly not working with an amateur. Most people, challenged like that, will be unable to resist their own anxiety. They'll keep talking, or get up and walk around, or do something else to try and draw you off.

I put the cheese in my mouth while I thought about what to say next. It was smooth, creamy, and slightly salty—the perfect counterpoint to the juicy peach. I chewed thoughtfully, letting the silence lengthen out.

"I drove a car," the monk said, just as I was about ready to give up on it. "A woman died. She was Mexican, in the U.S. illegally. The guys I ran with in those days didn't care for that."

My neck went tense and the radar ramped up a notch. The monk was still looking at me with that strigine intensity, so I dared not sneak another peek at his tattoo to see if it might be covering a swastika or shamrock.

He offered me another tiny half peach and I took it, weighing the odds of him being Aryan Brotherhood. I knew the Texas bunch was viewed with scorn by the original California founders, but that didn't mean that a word in their shell-like ears regarding my location would go amiss. Even if he was an ex, he might have old friends.

He gestured at the cottage behind him. "These guys have a prison-outreach program. By the time I got out, I was ready to make up for what I'd done."

A distant mechanical clatter had been drawing nearer while we ate, and now a vintage motorcycle appeared from around the corner of the office, Hector astride.

Grateful for the timely distraction, I watched him dismount and take off his helmet, observing, "Of course it's a Norton."

"Hey, Finn," he said to my dining companion, slapping the

dust off his clothes. Then, to me, "Not the same year. This one's a '65."

"Good thing. You'd go broke keeping a '39 running."

"Not the way I do it," he grinned. The wrinkles around his nose and eyes had grown deeper, but that smile was still a hit. "Where's Maines? I been trying to call him all day."

I wasn't ready to spill my long-range plan yet, so I just said, "He's in Ojinaga. His cell's on the fritz."

Hector nodded, wiping his face with a faded red bandanna and eyeing the peaches settled in their paper-bag nest on the bench. Finn saw the look and passed him a couple.

"You been for a soak yet?" Hector asked me, biting into one of the tiny fruits.

I was about as hot as I wanted to get, but I didn't want to do any more talking to the monk until I'd given my radar time to sort him out. I got up, thanked Finn for the snack, and headed for the bathhouses with Hector.

CHAPTER 14

———— ◆ ————

"What's that guy's story?" I asked Hector as we crunched along the gravel path.

"Finn? What do you mean?"

"If he's on the up and up, I'm Mata Hari."

Hector laughed, and I got a glimpse of that lazy irreverence that had been part of what originally endeared him to me. "You say that like you're not dangerously close."

"He's been in prison," I said, "and apparently used to hang out with some guys who didn't like Mexicans."

Hector's gait hitched. "Seriously?"

"He says he's a changed man now that he's hooked up with these Buddhists, but I'd sure like to see the paperwork on that."

"I bet you would," Hector muttered, searching my face, probably for signs of panic. He should have known better, but I liked the fact that he cared enough to look.

We walked a few more yards in silence, then he blew out his breath and said, "Meh, I buy it, actually. I bring my people through here all the time. If Finn was a racist, I'd have seen evidence of it by now."

"You didn't know he was an ex-con," I pointed out.

"He doesn't know I'm Bolivian," Hector returned. "That kind of stuff is easy to hide. It's not so easy to fake consistently ethical behavior over time. He's been hands-on with most of my clients at one time or another, and never done anything to make me worry even a little bit."

"Hands-on?" I said, curious.

Hector nodded. "My people will sometimes stay over, here at the springs, while I bring up a relative or wait for border patrol to clear out."

"Oh, well!" I said, finally seeing the bones beneath the skin. "Of course he wouldn't do anything to threaten the profit margin."

We'd reached the bathhouses, and Hector stopped at the first one, his long brows dropping low across his eyes. "They don't pay, Julia. I wouldn't bring 'em here if they had to."

"Well, these guys have got to be making something off your clients," I said. "People don't take that kind of risk for free, I don't care how spiritual their motives are."

"Man, capitalism's really done a number on you, hasn't it?"

I scowled at him and he knocked softly on my forehead. "Hello? Remember me? The pinko idealist?"

"Trust me," I said. "Somebody, somewhere, is making some money on your people."

"Yeah. Me," Hector replied, with a chuckle. "And the only reason I ain't in debtor's prison is because Mike sends me a check every month, and I get two pesos on the dollar."

"I'd still like to check Finn out next time I'm near a computer," I said. "What's his last name?"

"Dunno. Don't even know his first one, really. I call him Finn because he told me his family was from there, once."

Finland's not exactly a small town, so the odds of the monk

having a connection to my father were slim to none. Still, the thought did materialize.

"These guys all give up their names when they join, and get a Tibetan one," Hector was saying. "I can't remember what his is. Not that I could pronounce it anyway."

I pulled the bathhouse door open and stepped in. Except for the tin roof, it was all stone inside, carved out like a cave. A low bench ran along one side, and a tub about the size of a twin bed was sunk into the floor. This had a rough brass spigot coming out of the wall above it. I twisted the single handle, which started a steaming gush of hot water. It had a distinct odor— not unpleasant, but odd.

I turned to continue grilling Hector, but he wasn't there.

"What the hell?" I muttered, going back over to the door. He was heading toward the next bathhouse.

"Get in here," I said. "What's the matter with you?"

Hector made a U-turn and came back, his lazy grin lighting up. "Just trying not to act like an entitled asshole."

He ducked in and sat down on the bench. I got undressed and into the tub, but he stayed where he was, keeping his clothes on. I caught my breath as I hit the water. The heat was almost intolerable.

Hector passed a hand across his stomach. "Listen, some things have changed since the last time you saw me."

A shot of fear grabbed at my solar plexus. "You want me to close my eyes?" I cracked, to distract myself.

Hector continued looking at me, thinking. I could see that he didn't really want to tell me. That usually makes me want to know more, but he hadn't even kissed me yet. Just one more hour, the worst part of me begged the universe. Just let me have one more hour of the fantasy that all of this is going to work out.

Hector seemed to pick up on my reluctance to hear what he had to say, and got up to strip down. As he walked over to the tub, nude, I wondered why that particular arrangement of parts made my heart turn over the way it did. If it was just sex, why the spasm in my chest, in addition to the one lower down?

"Listen," I said after the carnal festivities were over, trying to prolong my willful ignorance, "I'm thinking of retiring to Mexico."

Hector was lying back in the tub with his eyes closed and a blissful expression on his face. The hot water did seem to have some sort of relaxing quality above and beyond a soak at home; it took him a minute to grok me. "What, you mean, right now?"

"I don't really have any reason to go back to Azula, and WITSEC finally came through with my money. I'm kind of loaded."

"What about your house? And the bar? Mike can't run the place on his own."

I sank farther into the hot water, giving the wet tin ceiling an annoyed look. The radar poked at me, but I was getting irritated with its insistence on jumping into the middle of everything I did. I slapped it away and said, "You walked away from all of it. Why can't I?"

"Maybe you don't remember my friends, the CIA," Hector said, his eyes stern under their long brows.

"If they really wanted you, why didn't they come after me when you and Maines split? The feds knew you and I were fraternizing. If you'll remember, they kind of put me up to it, without my knowledge."

"Don't ask me to explain the logic of the U.S. government," Hector sighed. "For all I know, they're watching you right now, fixing to pick me up as soon as I make a noise."

I hadn't thought of that. "Jesus."

The corners of his eyes crinkled up, and he floated over to me, slipping his wet arms under mine. "You see the risks I take for you?"

He was trying to distract me. I fought it for a few minutes, but it wasn't any good—when he got up next to me like that, skin to skin, I always went completely stupid. As his hands slid down my back and pulled my legs around his hips, I wondered if he knew that, but my blood was rushing up hot and fast again, wiping out the brain's warning about men you can't say "no" to.

CHAPTER 15

The sky outside the high window above the bed was just starting to lighten. I turned over and examined Hector's sleeping face. The weight loss had dried him up a little, but he was still beautiful. Not for the first time, I wondered if I would take the risks I had for a less attractive man. Beauty makes people do strange things.

Somewhere in his unconscious, Hector must have felt me watching him, because he stirred and opened his eyes. He looked happy to see me and slightly puzzled about where he was. Then he noticed the pale light in the room.

"What time is it?"

I shrugged, and he sat up, grabbing his jeans off the floor. "Which room is Maines in?"

"This one," I said. Hector frowned at me over his shoulder, and I explained, "He stayed in Ojinaga last night. We closed our case yesterday, and he's heading back to Azula this morning."

"Closed your case?" Hector said, turning to face me. "What do you mean?"

"We were down here looking for—"

"—Rachael Pestozo," he finished. "Maines called me last week about it, wanted me to verify that she'd shown up at a local medical clinic."

A twisting sensation under my sternum. "You're the local contact?"

"Yeah, of course. Why else am I here?"

I sat up and slid my legs out from under the sheet, heading for the bathroom. The twisting sensation persisted.

"Yeah. Why else are you here?" I repeated, half to myself.

Silence from the bedroom. I washed my face and brushed my teeth, the question reverberating in my head. The bed creaked, and Hector appeared in the bathroom doorway. He didn't say anything, just watched me rinse my toothbrush and tried to catch my eye.

"Rachael's fine," I said, refusing to consider that I wasn't part of what had drawn him to Ojinaga. "Maines and I found her walking around town yesterday. She's going back to Azula with him this morning."

I was running a comb through my hair and stole a look at Hector's face in the mirror. It froze me.

"Walking around town?" he said. "When?"

"Yesterday, right after I saw you."

Hector's expression didn't relax. He shook his head. "That's not possible. She died in December. I found out yesterday. That's what I needed to tell Maines."

My heart clattered into high gear and my toes went cold. "What?"

"She died in December," he repeated. "I assume it was something to do with her surgery, but of course the clinic wouldn't tell me anything." He paused to rub his head and mutter, "I gotta say, the lap-band thing surprised me. Orson was after her for years to get a bypass, but she was dead set against it. I can't figure why she would do it now, after the divorce."

"You knew her?"

"Yeah. Well, as much as anyone did. She was pretty private, kept to herself, but ya know—people talk to bartenders."

My toes were starting to warm back up, but there was a sour taste in my mouth. "Are you sure it was her who died? One hundred percent sure?"

"I saw the body. It was her."

"Saw the body?" I said. "It's the middle of June."

Hector shrugged. "She's still in the morgue. Ojinaga Hospital."

The radar was on full alert now, and my doubt about the plastic-surgery story solidified. I went back into the bedroom and started getting dressed, filling Hector in on our encounter with the woman Maines and I thought was Rachael.

When I finished, Hector was standing next to the bed looking flummoxed. "You're saying this woman got fixed up to look like Rachael so she could pose as her?"

"That's what I'm guessing."

Hector snorted. "Why?"

"You tell me," I said. "You seem to be the only person in town she ever talked to."

"She was just an ordinary person," he said, a shrug in his voice. "Nobody who'd make you want to look like her."

"What about the rest of her? Anything unusual in her history?"

"Yeah, sort of," Hector said, after thinking a minute. "She mentioned it one time in the bar. Her dad was from an Indian tribe in Arizona, and after she and Orson divorced, she decided to try and get official citizenship with them and move back."

That would be her cover story about returning to Sells. Maybe it hadn't all been icing. "How long since she'd been home?"

"It would have to be something like twenty years," Hector said.

That gave me some goose bumps, but I couldn't figure out why. The O'odham kids at school had always been poorer than we were, and I'd grown up in a house with holes in the walls and an outdoor kitchen. Talk of casinos and federal support was all over the reservations in those days, but as far as I knew, none of it had ever materialized for the O'odham. If our impostor wanted Rachael's specific identity—which the plastic surgery certainly suggested—it wasn't for monetary purposes.

"You could hardly make up a better scenario for someone who wanted to take over someone else's life," I said, after a couple of minutes' thought. "Ordinary woman, nothing remarkable about her, not well known around town, on her way to a new life somewhere no one has seen her in a couple of decades. Oh, and then there's the conveniently dead ex-husband."

Hector's dark eyes jumped to my face. "Orson's dead?"

I nodded. "Somebody shot him and stuffed his body into an old heating chase out at the Ranch."

Hector's face went wary, and I said, "He hasn't been dead long enough for Connie to have been involved."

He relaxed a little. "So does Maines think Rachael killed him?"

"Maines doesn't know he's dead," I said, jamming my stuff into my bag. "We've got to catch him before they leave."

CHAPTER 16

———————————◆———————————

The sun came the rest of the way up while we crossed the river at Presidio to head into Ojinaga and back to the Waru. I hoped it was early enough that we'd catch Maines and "Rachael" before they left the hotel.

All manner of motor vehicle was crammed bumper to bumper along the six-lane boulevard on the Mexican side, waiting to come into the States. As we passed through the gate, going in the opposite direction, my eye caught on a familiar-looking car, and my heart sank. It was Maines's Crown Vic.

I gave Hector a squeeze with my legs to get his attention and yelled over the traffic noise, "There they are. Turn around!"

He slowed the bike, looking for an opening in the undulating sea of metal. I craned my neck around as best I could with the bulky helmet on, and saw the Crown Vic accelerating over the bridge.

"Damn it, they just went through," I said.

Hector made a frustrated motion with his head, trying to maneuver over to the inner lane. None of the vehicles shoving along seemed to be paying the slightest attention to one another or to the lines on the pavement, pulling to the vendor-lined curb or changing lanes without warning or regard for anything in their immediate vicinity.

Hector finally found an opening, and we headed back toward the river crossing. He swerved and threaded, ignoring the shouted and gestural objections of the other drivers, until we were at the gate.

The guards were busy with a commercial truck, and one of them held up a hand, stopping us. Hector turned off the Norton's motor and removed his helmet. I followed suit, peering into the distance.

"Damn it," I breathed again.

"Highway 67 to Marfa," Hector murmured, watching a couple of German shepherds sniff the truck's tires. "It's the only route out. We'll have to step on it, though."

The truck finally moved ahead, and the guards waved us up. Hector fished out his wallet and showed them his driver's license—Mexican, I noticed, with a fake name. I really hoped they wouldn't want to look in the Norton's saddlebags, where I'd crammed my duffel full of cash.

They asked Hector in Spanish whether he'd bought anything in Mexico. He laughed and said something in a dialect I couldn't understand. The guards both grinned. They handed Hector back his license, and we were on our way.

CHAPTER 17

The cool of the morning burned off fast, and by the time we'd cleared the city limits, it felt like we were driving headfirst into a blow-dryer set on high. The road was dead flat from horizon to horizon, which would make it easy to spot Maines's car from a distance. Hector hit an easy ninety and stayed there.

We'd just passed a sign advising that it was thirty miles to Marfa when the shimmer coming off the asphalt up ahead started to form a solid blob. I squinted, trying to make it come into focus. It divided in half, and as we covered more distance, the right half gradually started getting bigger, the left half receding until I couldn't see it anymore. After a few minutes, I was sure that it wasn't a mirage.

"You see that?" I yelled to Hector, above the roar of heat blasting by.

He nodded and dropped down to the speed limit. The remaining blob was definitely a car, pulled off onto the shoulder. Something was moving between it and us. As we got closer, I saw that the moving thing was an animal.

"It's Steve," I said, my nerves jerking tight.

The dog was all alone. Hector geared down and stopped.

Steve began to run toward us. I got off the bike and caught his collar as he bounded up.

Hector pointed his eyes at a long smear on the dog's flank. "That's blood."

I straightened up and did a quick visual scan. It was maybe a hundred yards to the Crown Vic, and there were no heads sticking up above the seats. Nothing was moving anywhere out in the landscape, either.

Steve panted loudly and made whining noises, wriggling like crazy. My stomach started to hurt.

"Call 911," I said to Hector, heading for the Crown Vic.

Halfway there, Steve broke loose and ran, prancing up against the driver's-side door and barking. A wave of nausea bubbled up, but I swallowed it down and yanked the door open.

Maines was in the driver's seat, slumped to one side, covered in blood from the neck down.

"Jesus Christ," I breathed, leaning in to feel him.

He was still warm and his chest was moving. A slanted gash ran across his neck, deeper on the side facing the car door. His hand was limp at the wound, where it had apparently been holding pressure until he lost consciousness. I tore off my jacket and pushed it against his neck, climbing into his lap.

"Paramedics are coming," Hector said from the open car door. I hadn't noticed him following me.

"It can't have been long," I said, putting as much pressure on the wound as I dared. "Did you see that other car? Somebody picked Rachael—or whoever she is—up."

Steve was standing in the shade of the driver's-side door, looking worried. He didn't make any noise, but kept sitting down and getting back up, occasionally putting one paw on the edge of the blood-soaked seat. Hector watched him, looking grim.

I had just started thinking how pointless what I was doing was when the sound of a helicopter faded in from the north. Hector ran out into the road, waving his arms as it came into view over the mountains. Maines was still breathing.

The helicopter set down on the center stripe, and the paramedics moved in fast. They dragged me off Maines's inert body and began pumping blood and plasma into him like their lives depended on it. His certainly did.

A cop car bearing the legend PRESIDIO COUNTY SHERIFF materialized out of the blinding heat. Hector turned his back on it and handed me his phone. "This is yours now."

"What? Why?"

"I used it in the States," he said.

I started to argue, but the two flatfoots who had gotten out of the cop car were on us.

"Y'all OK?" the older one, a sturdy blonde woman, asked.

I nodded, slipping the phone into my front pocket.

The paramedics were trotting a stretcher over from the helicopter. The woman cop's partner, a younger Latino with a friendly-looking face, gestured to Hector, guiding him away from us.

"Really?" I said, watching them. "Why would we call you guys if we had anything to do with this?"

The woman cop peered at me from under her lacquered bangs, which stood out from her forehead in a long arc.

"What's your name?" she asked, getting her notebook out.

I gave it to her and then shut up.

She didn't care for that. "Tell me what happened," she instructed, her light eyes going hard.

"He's a private detective," I said, gesturing toward the Maines-filled gurney, which the paramedics were now pushing to the helicopter. "He was transporting a suspect who isn't who she says she is. We were trying to catch them."

Hector was looking our way. I hoped he had the sense to play stupid.

The cop squinted at me. "There's a second person in the vehicle?"

"Not anymore. Another car picked her up. We saw it from way back. Too far away to tell anything about it."

She pursed her lips, making a note.

Hector and her partner were on the other side of the motorcycle, between it and the trunk of the Crown Vic. Hector was holding on to Steve's collar.

"Stay here," the blonde cop said, and headed toward them.

She pulled her partner away and they held a short conference in the ditch, then she came back to me, flicking a look at the bike. "If I were to have a look in those saddlebags, what would I find?"

"A perfectly legal wad of cash," I said.

She gave me a short, intense look of appraisal, then glanced back at the Crown Vic, her expression turning sour. "Nope," she said, after a minute. "I don't like any of it."

I sighed and held out my wrists.

CHAPTER 18

⸻

They didn't cuff us, and even let us share the backseat of the cop car. My bag full of cash went into their trunk. There was a brief shuffle while they tried to decide where to put the dog; in the end, he rode up front.

"I paid good money for that Norton," Hector grouched at them through the security grille as we pulled away.

"Don't worry about it, bro," the younger cop told him.

Hector muttered something foul in Spanish under his breath and sat back. Across the seat we were sharing, he hooked his pinky finger under mine. I looked over at him, but he'd fixed his eyes on the scenery.

I spent the drive to Marfa trying to decide whether telling them I was wanted in Azula would buy us anything. It was hard to say if knowing about Benny's BOLO beforehand would make me look more trustworthy or not. I wondered, too, what Hector's name would bring up. All in all, it wasn't turning into a good day.

I kept feeling like I'd forgotten something; like a door was closed in the back of my mind and something behind it kept howling to be let out. In the quiet of the cop car, I realized I'd been feeling it for a while, at least since Maines and I had gotten to the hot springs. I felt around the edges of it, trying to suss out the shape, but I was too tweaked. It would have to wait until survival mode had gone offline.

Marfa was a lot like Azula: a flat, spare little town with a wedding cake of a courthouse in the middle. It was more faded, though, as if the sun were stronger here, and somebody had poured some money into the local economy, judging from the condition of the buildings. I spotted a number of pricey-looking boutiques as we passed through the square.

About a block from the courthouse we turned into an alley and parked behind a low, tan building remarkable for its complete lack of personality. The only way I knew it was the sheriff's office was the buzzer mounted to one side of the steel door. The deputies got us out and walked us up the concrete steps and into the air conditioning, which must have been set at about forty degrees. It felt good after the heat of the highway, but I knew I'd be freezing in about twenty minutes.

"This way," the female deputy said, gesturing ahead of me. Hector and her partner were behind us, with Steve.

I led the pack down the anonymous hallway into a large room with fake-wood paneling and four beat-up Steelcase desks with black linoleum tops. These were paired up facing each other, with each pair dead center in its half of the room, side-on to the door so nobody could sneak up on whoever was sitting at them.

Hector and his factotum went to the pair of desks on the right, and the female deputy guided me to the left pair, indicating a side chair. Steve flopped onto the floor next to me. The cop waggled the mouse in front of the enormous CRT monitor on her desk as she sat down, waking the computer.

"Wow, that thing must be twenty years old," I said.

Right away I wished I'd kept my mouth shut. She gave me a derisive look that was half smirk, plainly convinced I was trying to suck up.

They'd patted us down before putting us in the car, and now another uniform came in, carrying my duffel and a clear plastic ziplock bag stuffed with my cash. He brought these over to the female cop, giving Steve a wide berth. The dog seemed annoyed by this, but kept his mouth shut.

"Is he housebroken?" the female cop asked me, setting the cash on the far side of her desk.

I shrugged, watching her unzip the duffel and get out my wallet. There wasn't much in it; she found my driver's license pretty quickly and wedged it upright on her keyboard. I watched her tap my information in and then sit back to wait. It took some doing not to fidget, but I managed it with an old trick: giving myself permission to fidget if I wanted to. It's the prohibition that makes it hard to resist.

The cop's eyebrows rose after five silent minutes of staring at her computer screen. I couldn't see it from where I was sitting, but she'd plainly discovered my skeletons.

"You're"—she squinted at the screen—"you *were* in federal witness protection?"

Genuinely surprised, I paused a second before replying, "That's in your database?"

"Hey, Hol," her partner called over. "You come here a minute?"

She got up and crossed the room. I had my back to it, so I couldn't see what was going on, but I could feel eyes on me, so I kept my hands to myself. "Hol" came back shortly, looking stressed.

I kept quiet, but it wasn't easy. She did a little more typing on her keyboard, letting me cook. Finally, she said, "You coulda saved yourself a lot of grief if you'd told me who John Maines was."

Careful not to let anything show on my face, I replied, "Aren't you guys supposed to ID everybody on a scene?"

"Oh, don't be thinking you're in any position to get smart with me, girl," she shot back.

I reeled it in a little. "I'm just saying, I thought you already knew who he was. Not that I have any idea why it matters." For all I knew, they'd dialed up his trip to Cuba with Hector and were freaking out at having an international fugitive in their crosshairs.

"Texas is a small state, where county sheriffs are concerned," the cop said. "When news goes out on the wires about one of our own, we tend to remember it."

Still not sure which news she was referring to, I switched to more neutral ground. "Any word on how he's doing?"

"He survived the ride to the ER," she said, picking up her phone. "Ask me, that right there is a goddamn miracle."

I waited to see if she had anything else for me, but she was focused on her computer screen, dialing a number from it. A few rings, then she said, "Yeah, this is Deputy Sheriff Hollis Zulke, out in Marfa? We just picked up your BOLO."

CHAPTER 19

I spent the afternoon and most of the night listening to the meth cook across the hall perfect her impression of Janis Joplin. At the literal crack of dawn, a deputy appeared with Benny and Steve.

"Jesus, you must have left right after she called you," I said to Benny as the deputy let me out.

"And I got so much time to spare right now," he growled.

The deputy led us to the squad room where Hector and I had been booked the night before, him in front and Benny behind me with the dog. When we got there, Zulke was at her desk. Hector was nowhere in sight. They sat me in a chair out of earshot and did some paperwork, then Benny put Steve on the lead, handed it to me, and herded us down the hall and out into the alley.

Maines's Crown Vic was parked there, next to Benny's cop car. Steve eyed a nearby telephone pole with a wistful whine, and I stepped over to let him water it. When he was done, Benny unlocked the passenger side of his cruiser and gestured us in.

"How's Maines going to get home?" I said, nodding toward the Crown Vic.

"The hospital'll fly him in when he's stabilized," Benny said. "He won't be driving for a while."

My guts were trying to do all the knots in the Boy Scout handbook. "How bad is he?"

"We'll stop by the hospital on our way out," Benny said, sliding behind the wheel.

"What about—Juan?" I asked, needing the pause to remember the name from Hector's fake ID.

Benny gave me a quizzical frown, and I felt a blip of relief. If the cops had busted Hector's identity, Benny would know about it.

"There was a local helping us with the case," I explained. "They locked him up last night, too."

"Oh, the Mexican dude? His wife came and sprang him last night."

Benny was focused on getting his cruiser out of the parking space and into the street, which was a good thing. I couldn't see my face, but I felt the blood drain out of it like someone had pulled a plug at the bottom of my neck. Steve seemed to sense that I wasn't feeling like I'd just won the lottery and watched me with what I could swear was sympathy as he settled down on the console next to me.

The concept of Hector having a wife, even a fake one, gave me some unpleasant moments, especially in light of the feeling I'd had earlier about him not telling me something. He had to be portable, considering his *coyote* work and his concerns about the feds, so where the hell had he picked up a female accomplice? I won't try to pretend I wasn't jealous, because that was at least fifty percent of it, and the rest was resentment. I'd tied myself in knots more than once for a man who didn't deserve it, and it hadn't been enjoyable. I wasn't looking for a repeat performance.

CHAPTER 20

———————◆———————

It was about forty minutes to the medical center in Alpine, which gave me plenty of time to stew. I ran through my recent interactions with Hector in my head, trying to find cracks, but I knew it was pointless. Once my hormones are engaged, my radar is no better than anyone else's. I'd just have to wait until the other shoe dropped.

Benny pulled into a vast parking lot in front of a low, sprawling building almost indistinguishable from the flat brown landscape around it. I put thoughts of Hector away and got out of the car.

"You can't bring pets in here," the guy at the reception desk said when he saw us.

Benny expanded his considerable chest. "Service dog."

"He don't got no vest on."

"He's undercover," Benny said, keeping a straight face.

Receptionman didn't look convinced, but he gave us directions to ICU without any more argument. When we got there, Benny showed his ID to a passing nurse, who took us to Maines's private room. A young blond doctor was inside, making notes on a clipboard.

Maines's eyes were open, but he looked pretty out of it. He lay completely flat, his neck swathed in bandages and gauze. A couple of IVs ran into one bare, bony arm, which was pale and freckled, like a kid's.

The doctor came around the bed and shook hands, introducing himself as the surgeon. "If he can survive the next twenty-four hours, he'll probably be OK."

"What's the hurdle?" Benny asked him.

"Stroke," the doctor said. "We repaired the vascular injuries—the veins—and everything seems to be flowing fine right now, but as healing sets in things can change fast. We have to run the gauntlet—with his medications, I mean—between him bleeding too easily or clotting up."

"Makes sense," Benny muttered, looking over at the bed. Maines's eyes had moved in the direction of our voices. "Can we talk to him?"

The doctor looked down at Steve, who was gazing anxiously toward the lumpy, disinfected form on the bed. "Go easy, OK? No Frisbee or anything."

Maines's fingers lifted toward us as the doctor left, and Steve pulled me over to lick at them. A faint smile crossed Maines's face, which was so pale it looked almost blue. His eyes moved slowly up to my face.

"Nice work," he croaked.

"Same to you, smart-ass," I murmured in reply.

His gaze shifted to Benny. "Get her?"

"Sorry, John," Benny said, coming closer. "Julia gave us a description, and I put a bulletin out on that, but we been waiting on you for full specs on the car."

Maines swallowed carefully and looked at the ceiling. "Bronze four-door. Arizona plates. Sells dealer."

"Get a look at the driver?" Benny asked, taking out his note-book.

Maines started to shake his head, then thought better of it. "No."

Steve had hopped up onto the side chair and laid his head gingerly on the edge of the mattress. His nose was almost touch-ing Maines's left ear.

Benny fiddled with his tiny pencil, looking away. Finally he asked, "How'd she get you, man? You ain't that easy to blindside."

"My fault," Maines croaked, closing his eyes. "Took my eye off the ball."

I've seen a lot of horrifying stuff in my day, so I couldn't fig-ure out why watching an ex-cop that I didn't particularly like struggle to form simple sentences was ripping me up so much. Then Benny said, "The ex-husband full of bullet holes didn't make you kinda wary?" and my head split open.

"He didn't know," I said, the words almost choking me as they spilled out. "He never got your message."

Maines's eyes closed, his lips compressing into a faint smile. Benny glared at me.

After what seemed like a decade, he asked Maines, "You want me to call Grace?"

"Better," Maines said. His sluggish eyes moved to me. "You gonna fill us in?"

Afraid Benny might hit me, I stepped around to the end of the bed. "That's not Rachael Pestozo. It's somebody pre-tending to be her. The real Rachael Pestozo died six months ago." I looked into Maines's half-closed eyes. "Juan identified the body."

I saw him understand who I was talking about. A kind of weary merriment passed across his face.

"Why would anyone want to impersonate Rachael Pestozo?" Benny said.

"She had cut her ties in Azula and was moving to a new job in Arizona," I said. "If she mentioned that to someone around here before she died, maybe they took advantage of the opportunity to get a U.S. passport."

Benny snorted. "And then fucked it all up by trying to kill a man on American soil? Kinda stupid."

"Rachael was also a member of the Tohono O'odham Nation," I said. "Sells is the capital. They have their own justice system."

Benny frowned at me, and I explained, "My mother is Apache. I grew up in Florence, just south of Phoenix."

"Well, whatever deal they've got, I doubt it covers attempted murder off their lands," Benny said. "That's a capital crime."

"It depends on the deal they've made with the state," I said, trying to remember what had happened to the guy who lived next door to my cousin Norma on the Gila River reservation when I was in my teens. He'd shotgunned his wife while drunk one night in August. The smell of hot, dry dirt and cigarettes came back to me, his murky ramblings and her sister screaming.

My brain slammed shut before the memory could come all the way up; something ugly had been trying to come with it. I couldn't imagine a memory more disturbing than the sight of that woman's brain matter all over the front wall of the house, with her almost-headless body sprawled on the porch below, but the filter in my head makes these decisions without my input.

"I'd better call the feds," Benny muttered, feeling for his

phone. He headed for the door and stepped out into the hall.

"Pointless," Maines croaked as the door swung shut, leaving us alone together in the quiet white room. I could barely hear him, and stepped closer to the bed.

"Pissed them off going to Cuba," he said. "They won't do jack, they hear I'm involved."

"Listen," I said, as much to keep him still as anything else, "Benny didn't say that Orson was Rachael's husband, in that message. By the time—"

The look in his eye stopped me. "Don't matter now. Forget it."

It was worded like a forgiveness, but both his tone and his face told me it was something else. I couldn't tell what.

The ache in my chest was too much. I pushed it away and turned on the brain. "Hector says Rachael died in December. When did she leave Azula?" I asked Maines.

"Fifth," Maines croaked.

I narrowed my eyes, thinking. "Liz Harman's still working on Orson's time of death, but her first guess was between three and six months ago. It's June 15 now, so that would make the earliest he could have died December 15."

Maines blinked at me. "Close."

"Maybe close enough for Rachael to have killed him before she left." I nodded. "Estimating time of death isn't an exact science."

I remembered Hector's report that Orson had been pressuring Rachael to have surgery, and the impostor's comments when we'd found her in Ojinaga.

"Did you find anything about a restraining order when you were looking into Rachael's history?" I asked Maines.

"No . . ." He paused to take a slow breath. "Wish I had. Would have slowed us down."

My chest convulsed again. What the hell *was* that? I swallowed it away and said, "Well, Rachael and her ex both dying under mysterious circumstances, within six months of each other—there has to be a connection."

"Beware the obvious," Maines replied.

"Sometimes the obvious is the answer," I told him. "Although I'm not seeing the obvious on why this woman wanted to pose as Rachael." I paused, then asked, "Are you sure there's nothing about her that would make her identity worth trying to kill you to keep it?"

"Did a pretty good check on her," Maines said. He swallowed, and I could tell that talking was costing him. "Nothing unusual in her background. Except the O'odham thing."

I sighed, frustrated. "Two-and-a-half dead people to play Indian Princess just for the fun of it seems excessive. There must be a reason for it that we're not seeing."

Benny came back in, looking wounded.

"I see you mentioned my name," Maines rasped.

Benny's caterpillar eyebrows jumped up his low forehead. "Something you want to tell me?"

Maines produced that near-death smile again, and I started thinking about brain damage. He's not usually much of a smiler.

"They'll look into jurisdiction and get back to me," Benny said, when it was apparent Maines wasn't going to answer him. "That's fedspeak for 'fuck off.'"

Maines moved his fingers at me and opened his mouth to say something, but the monitor above his bed started to beep. Steve leapt to the floor, barking, and a couple of nurses rushed in. Benny and I hustled out of the way as the doctor appeared.

"Y'all need to wait outside," he said.

CHAPTER 21

It was a long two hours in the waiting room, a mint-green ice-box with a view of the parking lot and a television blaring in one corner. When the young blond doctor finally reappeared, he looked completely different.

"Stroke," he informed us, affability gone. "We've got him stabilized, but the bleeding was pretty extensive."

Benny was sitting with his elbows on his knees, hands clasped, looking at the floor. I'd been standing up, but now I needed a chair. The doctor watched me sit down, then went on.

"We won't know the extent of the damage for a while, but he's almost certainly going to need rehab, and maybe long-term care." The doctor paused. "Does he have any family?"

Benny's head dropped so that all I could see was the top of it, sprigged with his stiff black hair. "I called his ex-wife. She's on her way."

A cold horror was seeping up through the soles of my shoes, climbing toward my head. I've killed people, and been responsible for their deaths in other ways, but they mostly deserved it. Never anything like this.

The television faded into silence, and the glint off the silver

sports car I'd been watching while the doctor talked burst into
supernova, obliterating everything else. I sat there blind and
deaf until I felt a hand on my shoulder. It was one of the nurses.

"Miss?"

I blinked the blinding light out of my eyes and looked up.
Benny was standing behind her, his face alarmed.

"I'm fine," I said quickly, getting up. "Let's get out of here."

CHAPTER 22

———— • ————

Benny's face was even grimmer than usual as we walked to his cruiser and got in. My mind was going in circles, spiraling out into space and then back into the present moment again, over and over. I couldn't stand being in either place. I put my hands up over my ears. I don't know why. It was quiet in the car.

Benny glanced over at the movement.

"You've got to let me make this right," I said, dropping my hands.

"I don't see how that's possible," he replied, turning his stony gaze back to the windshield. He didn't start the motor.

"Let me go get her."

Benny made a noise that was somewhere between a snort and a laugh. He didn't answer.

"I can do it," I said, looking at him. "You know I can."

"So can the cops," he said. "And they won't make a bigger mess in the process."

"She'll be gone by the time they finish drawing straws for the job. She had no qualms whatsoever about trying to kill Maines. Whatever she's up to, she knows she's got to get it done fast and then disappear."

"I put a BOLO out on you and found you in twenty-four hours," Benny reminded me.

"Once she gets to the reservation, no BOLO of yours is going to bring her back," I said. "Half of the Tohono O'odham lands are in Mexico, and the tribe doesn't let anybody patrol that border. There's absolutely nothing to keep her from crossing over and disappearing forever, whenever she wants to."

As the words came out of my mouth I was struck by the absurdity of what I was saying. Why would "Rachael" go all the way to Arizona to disappear into Mexico when she could do it way easier from here? All she had to do was get across the bridge.

"I don't care," Benny said, sounding tired. "Tribal cops, Arizona state troopers, FBI—it don't matter to me who gets her, as long as someone does. And someone will."

"Look at me," I said.

He did it.

My voice felt like a slush of ice pouring out of my throat. "You can lock me up, but as soon as I get out—even if I'm a hundred—I'm going to find this broad, wherever she is. I can do it now, while it's easy, or I can do it later, when it's hard. But I'm going to do it."

Benny and I sat there staring at each other for a long time.

"Be a human being," I pleaded. "Just this once, be a human being instead of a cop."

He didn't say anything, just leaned forward and started the car.

"Where's Rachael's body?" he said.

CHAPTER 23

The Ojinaga hospital was a surprisingly modern-looking teal-and-white building just off one of the big main boulevards. The building directory was in both Spanish and English, and we quickly found our way to the morgue. Nobody gave us any grief about Steve, who trotted along next to me like we were related. I was just starting to think our task was going to be easy when the white-coated young woman at the front desk shook her head.

"You have to be a relative," she told Benny, in Spanish.

He pointed to the badge pinned to his shirt pocket, as he had at the hospital in Marfa. "It's a criminal matter."

"Do you have a warrant?" she asked him.

He sighed and looked at me, taking a step back from the window with one hand braced against the counter edge. After a minute, he stepped back up and took another shot at it.

"I need to confirm the identity of a U.S. citizen whose body has been here since December," he said. "If I have to get a warrant, it might turn into an investigation."

She glanced at me, uncertain, then said, "One moment," and shut the reception window.

We watched her roll to the telephone and make a call, talk for several minutes, then come back and slide the window open.

"Dr. Darling will be with you shortly."

"This is going to be tricky," I murmured to Benny as she shut the window again. "Darling and I have already crossed paths, and it didn't go well."

"Meh," Benny said, lifting one shoulder. "Maybe it'll worry him enough to play us straight."

I doubted it, but I didn't say so.

Darling appeared after a short interval, and hesitated, frowning, when he saw me. Benny assumed his professional stance—chest out, legs apart, thumbs hooked in his equipment belt—and told the man what we wanted.

Whatever Darling was hiding wasn't worth fighting an American cop for. He motioned us to follow him out of the waiting room and down the hall, where he opened the door to a large, cold room lined with stainless steel. Without saying anything, he led us to a drawer and gave it a pull. A white-draped body on a slab rolled out. Darling folded down the sheet and stood back.

Despite the intervening months, the body was still in pretty good shape. I wondered if she'd been embalmed, and then realized that Darling must have been keeping her around as insurance against her doppelgänger trying to roll over on him. The resemblance was remarkable. He really did do good work.

Benny sighed and wiped one hand across his mouth. "You got a cause of death on her?"

"Blood clot," Darling said, his eyes still lurking in my direction. "It's not a common risk with lap-band surgery, but it does happen."

"Notified her next of kin?" Benny asked Darling.

"She didn't list any. That's why we haven't put her in the ground yet."

I gave him a skeptical look, but he ignored it.

Benny thought it over, then said, "I'll need a DNA sample."

Darling stepped forward and rolled Rachael back into the cooler. The drawer closed with a soft click. "I'm sorry, for that you really will need a warrant."

Benny said, "Pretty damned interesting, a patient dying and then you fixing up a second woman to look just like her."

Darling gave him a surprised look. "Excuse me?"

"If you tell me why, I won't shut you down," Benny said.

The doctor continued to look at him with mute shock, not answering. It was pretty convincing, but my radar wasn't buying. Darling was in this up to his neck, but felt confident enough about it to shine Benny on. It didn't give me a good feeling.

The two men gazed at each other for a long couple of minutes, then Benny sighed and headed for the door.

Out in the hall, once we'd gotten out of eavesdropping range, I told him, "Rachael left some personal items out at the hot springs where Maines and I were staying. You might be able to get something off that."

Benny made a dissatisfied noise as we got on the elevator. "Yeah, but I won't know if it's the real Rachael's DNA or the stand-in's."

"It might still be useful," I pointed out. "If you could find something of hers in Azula you could run a comparison."

He thought about that as we walked down the white hallway and out to the parking lot.

"We gotta go out there to pick up your stuff before we head home anyway," he said.

So, it was going to be the hard way. I didn't like it, but there wasn't much I could do about it.

CHAPTER 24

Benny's cruiser was a much stiffer ride over the rough, narrow track leading down to the hot springs than Maines's cushy Crown Vic was. I felt pretty shaky getting out. The young monk who'd signed me and Maines in on our first night came out of the office to greet us.

"I understand some belongings were left here last December by a woman name of Rachael Pestozo," Benny said, showing the monk his badge.

The monk nodded and stood to one side, gesturing Benny to precede him into the office. Benny turned to me.

"Why don't you pack up and wait for me in the car?" he said.

I looked at him. Our eyes met.

"Here's the keys, in case you need to get into the trunk," he said, holding them out.

I stepped over and took them. He continued looking into my face for a long minute, then turned and went into the office.

I didn't hesitate. I walked straight to the cruiser, opened the trunk, and got out my ziplock bag of cash. There was a small pistol in a Velcro ankle holster lying there, and a half-full box of cartridges. I grabbed those, too. Then I closed the trunk, dropped the keys into the driver's seat, and scurried up to the cabin where Maines and I had stayed. Shoved my stuff into my duffel bag, along with the gun and the money, then back out and quickly down the path to the campground.

I stopped at the edge of the canyon, wondering if I were walking into oblivion. It was at least five miles to the store where Maines and I had stopped for breakfast the previous morning, and the temperature already felt well over a hundred degrees, even though it was still early in the afternoon.

I looked back up the rise to the cabins. Benny was nowhere to be seen. He was taking his time, giving me a head start. I scrabbled down the canyon side, into the gravel wash below, and started walking south.

The canyon ran for what I guessed to be less than a mile before it flattened out into rolling desert again. The sun was merciless, but the scariest thing was the silence. It made the noise in my head seem deafening by comparison. After a while I wasn't sure whether the voices I was hearing were inside my skull or outside it. I started to understand why people went nuts out here.

Just in case the voices were external, I stopped to get out the Glock I'd taken from Benny's trunk, and loaded it. It was a sub-compact .45 automatic, barely bigger than my hand. The sound of cartridges clinking quietly against each other in their stiff cardboard box was an almost physical relief. I stuck the gun in the back of my waistband and started walking again, carrying the cartridges in one hand. When I started thinking I was hearing voices again, I shook the box, to remind my ears what was inside and what was out.

That kept me sane until I came out onto the road again about an hour later and saw the Ruidosa store up ahead. My throat felt like baked sandpaper, but I wasn't lying dead under the sun, feeding the buzzards. That was nice.

I stopped and dug through my stuff until I found the phone Hector had given me. It was a pretty nice one, a smartphone type with a decent-size screen. Scrolling though the contacts, I saw something called LANDLINE and touched it. It rang five times, then Hector answered.

"Thank God," I said.

"Hey," he said, sounding surprised. "Where are you?"

"I'm in Ruidosa. Can you come pick me up?"

"What, right now?" He sounded slightly breathless. "What happened?"

"I'll tell you when I see you."

There was a muffled noise, as if he'd covered the mouthpiece, then he came back. "Be there in about an hour."

I'd come up with an idea during my walk down the canyon, and now I found the Internet browser on the phone and looked up an e-mail address. It was risky, but I was already flapping in the breeze. If I was going to do this thing, I might as well go all in. I set up a free e-mail account and typed in a message that I knew the recipient, and no one else, would understand.

CHAPTER 25

"So you're on the lam again," Hector said, walking up to the picnic table where I was drinking iced tea. The dust was still settling around his Norton, which he'd parked in front of the store.

"Not technically," I said, watching him swing one leg over the opposite-side seat of the picnic bench. "Do you know where I can buy a car around here?"

"Depends. You want a local clunker or something more road-worthy?"

"It needs to get me to Arizona."

Hector paused halfway to sitting down. "Arizona?"

"Maines had a stroke in the hospital," I said. My eyes blurred, and I had to take a couple of breaths before I could add the rest. "He's going to be permanently disabled."

Hector dropped onto the bench seat, looking like someone had just punched him in the stomach. I had the feeling that seeing me produce tears affected him more than what I'd just said.

"I'm going after her," I told him.

Hector had put one hand to his mouth, and now he dropped

it, releasing an incredulous sigh. "Jesus, Julia. Let the cops handle it."

"By the time they sort out whose job it is, she'll be in South America. Plus, I don't know, I just—" I stopped, looking across the scrubby landscape behind him to the steel-gray fence in the distance. "I've been living on credit for a long time."

We sat there, not talking and not looking at each other, for several long minutes. Then Hector said, "You'll never get her by yourself. Especially if you drive in there guns blazing."

I opened my mouth, but he held up one hand. "Don't bother telling me that isn't the plan. No matter how you slice it, that's where it will end up. You can't help it. It's in your DNA."

"That's pretty rich, coming from you," I shot back.

Hector was thinking, only half listening to me. "I can probably help, if you'll let me go with you."

"How's your wife going to feel about that?"

His eyes jumped up to my face. "My wife?"

"Yeah. The one who bailed you out of the Marfa jail."

He looked away, smiling. "That's Juan's wife. Not mine."

I'd hoped that springing it unexpectedly would make him give me something the radar could work on, but his reply felt genuine. For some reason that annoyed me even more. "I hope she knows that."

His smile turned surprised, wrinkling his forehead. "You're pretty possessive for someone I ain't seen in almost a year."

"That wasn't my choice, if you'll recall."

He studied my face for a second, and I could feel his pride arm-wrestling his judgment. His judgment won. "I know. I'm sorry about that."

The heat went out of my neck. "So who is this broad? You're

so jumpy about everything, I can't believe you let someone else in on your situation."

"I have friends here," Hector said. "We don't know everybody's details, but we're all on the same side. We cover for each other."

"She's a *coyote*?"

"Maybe you'll understand why I wouldn't want to tell you something like that," Hector said, his eyes sharpening.

Any other day I might have kept at it, but John Maines's bleak future was taking up a lot of space in my head. I took a breath and closed my eyes. When I opened them again, Hector was on his phone, pacing back and forth a few yards from the picnic table and carrying on an animated conversation, but he was too far away for me to follow it. I cursed my hormones as I watched him move, the curve of his forearm bringing up a lump in my throat. The truth of the matter was that, beguiled as I was by his physical beauty, I knew very little about Hector Guerra, even though I was privy to his biggest secret. Our fling the previous winter had gone from zero to sixty in record time, and he'd disappeared before it could slow down and let me take a good look at it. I should be doing that now, instead of putting more gas in the tank.

He rang off and came back to the table. "OK, I got us transportation to Sells."

I didn't argue with the "us." A second pair of hands wasn't going to hurt a thing.

I grabbed my duffel and we got on Hector's Norton, pulled out onto the road, and turned toward Presidio. Just before we hit town, Hector took an exit to the north, and about ten minutes later a pair of isolated steel buildings appeared up ahead, on the left. A sign at the entrance told us it was Lely International Airport.

I'd really like to know who names airports, because the only thing "international" about Lely was that the steel on the buildings had probably been manufactured in China. The hangar stretching out toward the south, behind the main terminal, looked the same as most of the agricultural buildings in the area, except that a row of overhead doors ran down the side facing the asphalt landing strip.

The door at the end was open, and Hector drove down and maneuvered the Norton inside, where a small, white plane stood at a jaunty angle. A figure in a floor-length dress appeared from the office at the rear as we dismounted. My eyes were still adjusting to the change in light, so it took me a minute to realize that it was Finn, the monk from the hot springs.

"You're lucky you caught me here," he said, shaking hands with Hector and aiming his bright brown eyes at me. "It's about an hour and a half to Sells. If the wind is against us it could be more."

"You own a plane?" I asked him, surprised.

"No, I just fly it. It belongs to the Sangha."

"The sang-what?"

"The bunch who runs the hot springs," Hector interjected. "That's what they call their group."

"I don't see how this is any better than my plan," I said to him.

"That's because you don't know all of it yet."

I waited, but he just stood there looking at me.

"What about ground transportation when we get there?" I asked.

"Taken care of," he replied.

Flying would certainly shave some time off my task, but

Hector's secrecy annoyed me. I gestured him over toward the open door of the hangar, out of Finn's hearing range.

"Listen, does he know it's aiding and abetting if we get caught? I doubt his buddies would appreciate being dragged into this."

"They aid and abet me every day," Hector pointed out. "They don't care about that stuff. They do what they think is right, regardless of legalities."

I looked over at Finn, who was doing his preflight check, carrying a small clipboard around the plane. The radar had apparently decided that he was OK, because it still wasn't giving me any major warning signals. There was something not quite straight about the monk, but it felt harmlessly familiar, almost comfortingly so. I'd spent my life feeling that way about the people I lived and worked with.

That didn't mean I'd turned stupid. I went over to the Norton and got my duffel bag, retrieving the little Glock. I walked back to the plane and handed it to Hector.

"Turn around and put your hands on your head," I said to Finn.

His eyes widened, and he glanced over at Hector, who said, "Just go with it, man. It's easier than trying to change her mind."

Finn laughed and raised his arms, turning slowly. I gave him a good patdown and stepped back, satisfied at least that he wouldn't be shooting at us in the air. That didn't mean there wasn't a plethora of other things that could go bad. I looked at Hector, who was standing with his arms folded, the Glock's short muzzle protruding from his left armpit.

"What were you going to do if he jumped me?" I said. "Take pictures?"

"If I thought he would jump you, I wouldn't have brought you out here in the first place," Hector replied.

I looked at him a little longer, and he sighed and added, "Look, I know it ain't easy for you, but at some point in your life you're going to have to trust someone else's instincts."

"Why would I do that?" I snorted.

"Because yours aren't always right."

I raised my eyebrows at him.

"You're sensitized to certain things," he said. "You see trouble where there isn't any, and miss trouble you should pay attention to, because you got bent a particular way by your life experience. No shame in it, that's just how things go. But you don't have to take that road every time."

Finn was listening to this exchange with his hands folded across his midsection, leaning slightly forward and looking to one side.

Hector kept talking. "You know my story. I got the same shit. Seems to me our respective instincts could work kind of like a system of checks and balances, make both of them more accurate."

"Thank you, Dr. Jung," I said, holding my hand out for the gun.

Hector passed it over, making a noise that was half laugh, half sigh. I returned to the Norton and put the Glock back in my duffel bag, then hoisted the bag onto my shoulder. Finn and Hector were both watching me expectantly when I turned around.

"All right, let's get this circus in the air," I said.

The plane was quite roomy on the inside, and felt heavily smooth as we taxied out and accelerated down the runway, but once we were airborne, it jumped and slid around in the air like a paper kite. Finn seemed not at all bothered by this, maintaining a placid expression while we achieved altitude.

"I notice you didn't put on your seat belt," he said after we'd leveled off.

I'd flipped down a small jump bench directly behind him, and was now leaning into the cockpit doorway. "What, does it void your insurance or something?"

"It's just an observation."

I snorted derisively. "There's no such thing as just an observation. Just say whatever's on your mind, will you?"

The monk smiled. "You don't waste much time on social niceties, do you?"

Hector had taken the copilot's spot, looking out the window. Now he came around to the conversation. "Man, you don't know the half of it."

"Both of you can kiss my ass," I said. Hector opened his mouth, but I pointed at him before he could speak. "Don't."

"Have you read Freud?" Finn asked me.

I looked at his ear. It was delicate for a man's, with a small lobe.

"Only on the Internet," I said.

"His 'death drive' theory has always interested me," Finn said. "That unconscious thing that makes people do things like walk too close to the edges of cliffs, smoke, and not put on their seat belts."

"I just consider that evolution at work."

Hector laughed, exchanging a glance with the monk.

"The death drive is considered the opposite of the 'pleasure principle,'" Finn went on. "Freud's theory is that, without the death drive, the human race would just sit around eating cake and fucking all day."

He'd turned his head another fifteen degrees so he could watch my face. I felt the blood rush up into it. He returned to watching his instrument board.

"Interesting," he murmured. "Still some modesty in there somewhere."

I enjoy being someone's psychological guinea pig about as much as the next person, which is to say that it annoys the shit out of me.

"Modesty is overrated," I said.

"Maybe," the monk answered, adjusting something on the instrument pad, "but it's natural to some people."

A burning sensation crawled across the back of my neck; it felt like humiliation. I remembered a couple of the *cholas* who had hung around with Joachin back in the day, advising me to toughen up, when they'd caught me crying over a boy. I'd done it. It hadn't been easy.

"You don't know anything about me," I snapped at Finn.

"Neither do you," he said.

The similarity to Connie's recent remark made this sting more than it might have otherwise. Hector must have smelled my fuse lighting, because he intervened quickly, saying to Finn, "Hey, man, I got a bone to pick with you."

Finn made another instrument adjustment, then looked over at Hector. "Pile on, brother."

"Julia says you got a record. That you helped some eight balls kill a Mexican woman."

"I didn't 'help,'" Finn said, his voice as placid as ever. "I was outside, in the car. Didn't know what was going down, or why."

"When was this?"

"Got out in '07. I did five of ten, which should tell you how deeply I was actually involved. The other guys are still in the joint, on death row."

Hector digested this in silence for a while, then asked, "How'd you get mixed up with these Tibetan guys?"

Finn glanced in his direction. "I never want to go back to what I was."

"So don't," Hector advised drily.

Finn turned back to the instrument panel. "You've obviously never been in prison. Even after you get out, they want to keep you in the system. Counseling, parole, all of that. Yeah, OK, it's supposed to help you 'reform' or whatever, but how can it, if it's coming out of the same system that made you? I wanted to be out of it. All the way. Like, on another planet."

I watched them, fascinated, as always, by the way men talked to each other. Guarded and succinct, yet somehow attuned to each other, linked by unspoken understandings beyond my ken.

"I'm hip," Hector said to Finn, "but I ain't wearing robes."

"Life just felt thin," Finn shrugged. "Everything felt meaningless. People kept telling me I needed to behave myself but they couldn't give me a convincing reason why."

"Staying out of jail seems like it'd be high on the list," Hector said.

"I was hardcore for a long time," Finn replied. "I spent a lot of nights in the can. If wanting to stay out of it was going to straighten me out, it would have done that years before any of this happened. I needed something actively constructive, something other than the carrot-and-stick routine."

"It might have been smarter to pick something legal," I put in. "If you get popped helping those border-crossers, I doubt you'll get in the cushy quarters, given your record."

Hector frowned, but before he could say anything, Finn replied, "I'm not going to let human beings die in the desert when I have the ability to prevent it from happening. If I have to go back to prison for that, so be it."

"Why not put your efforts toward getting them in legally?" I said.

"There are plenty of resources going to that already."

"OK, but by helping them do it illegally, you're just encouraging more people to take the risk," I pointed out.

He and Hector exchanged a look. The monk took a deep, resigned breath. "I can't explain samsara to you. It's a concept that takes years to grasp, and you have to want to grasp it."

"Well, at least provide a 'for dummies' version, if you're going to keep talking about it," I told him.

He gave it some thought, then said, "Everything's temporary. Clinging to stuff like happiness and success and rules is pointless. And, yes"—this before I could open my mouth—"that means exactly what you think it means. Most effort in life is absolutely meaningless. At the end, you're gonna croak, and it will all have been for nothing. Because nothing here is real."

"Oh," I said, sitting back. "You're a nihilist."

"No, because there's a way out: letting go. Letting go of wanting anything, including your own life."

"That's a way out, all right," I agreed.

Finn turned to give me a quick look in the eye. "No. See . . . What makes people miserable?" He paused, watching my face, then went on, "Wanting things. It's not the lack of the things, it's the wanting of the things to begin with. Eliminate that and you eliminate all human suffering."

I glanced at Hector, who'd been listening with an air of having heard it all before. "Are you buying this?"

He shrugged, smiling. "Makes about as much sense as any other philosophy I've listened to."

"If you're going to give up wanting everything, then why not just jump off a bridge?" I asked Finn. "For that matter, why bother to go straight?"

"That's an excellent question," he replied.

I waited for him to answer it, but after five minutes passed without him saying anything else, I realized he wasn't going to. I was growing tired of talking on the subject anyway, so I sat back, out of the cockpit, and settled in to think about more interesting things, like the details of my plan to find "Rachael," and what to do with her once we found her. I was horrified enough about what had happened to Maines to just take her out on sight, but I was doing this via Benny's good graces, and doubted he'd want something like that on his tab. He'd known Maines longer than I had, so by rights "Rachael's" head was his to do with as he pleased. If she gave us any trouble, though, I wouldn't balk at making her regret it.

CHAPTER 26

"I'll have to insist that you fasten your seat belt while we land," Finn said to me. "It's not going to be as smooth as taking off."

"You can put it down right there," Hector said, craning to see over the nose of the plane.

We were coming in low over a lumpy brown landscape. I didn't see an airstrip anywhere, but I buckled into the jump seat and braced myself. A hard bump, then the plane burst into a deafening rattle that lasted about a minute and died down as we came to a stop.

"Shit," Hector breathed. "Sorry about that. It looked a lot smoother from up there."

"I've had rougher," Finn said, popping his seat belt loose.

The two men got out and I pushed the side door open. The plane was perched in the middle of a badly potholed asphalt road. There were dark-green crops growing on either side, and low hills hazy in the distance. No buildings anywhere.

Hector scanned the horizon, then got out a flip phone. He must have picked up a new one after he'd been sprung from jail, because I still had the one he'd given me after we found Maines.

"¿*Dónde estás?*" Hector said. "*Somos aquí.*"

A tail of dust kicked up toward the west, where the sun was starting to drop. Hector closed his phone.

As we watched, a vehicle gradually materialized out of the dust. It was an old Chevy Suburban, blue and white, making a beeline for us. When it stopped, a kid of eleven or twelve got out. There was a thick stack of newspaper leaning against the back of the driver's seat, to push him forward far enough to reach the pedals.

He gave me a saucy, curious look and said, "*Aho, mami.*"

I advised him, in Spanish, that I was way too old for him, lifting an eyebrow. It didn't wipe the smirk off his oddly mature young face.

Hector stepped forward and gestured at me and the monk. "Julia *y* Finn."

"*Me puedes llamar Aguilito,*" the kid said, looking us up and down like we were zoo animals.

"Little Eagle," Hector chuckled. "That figures."

Finn extended a hand, and the boy shook it, peering at his robes. "*Qué* are you?"

"*Hermano de dios,* like the guys you see in church," Finn replied, spreading his robes as if he were showing off an evening gown. "You like 'em?"

Aguilito gave an adult-sounding chuckle, then turned back to Hector, who had produced his wallet and extracted a hundred-dollar bill. He held it toward Finn, who waved it away.

"There are some brothers up near Sonoyta I haven't seen in a while," he said. "Give me a call when you're ready to head back. I'll be around."

I was surveying the Suburban, which didn't look like it would get us over the next hill, much less however far it was to Sells.

Finn shook hands with me and Hector and headed back to his plane. Hector, Aguilito, and I piled into the vehicle, the kid in back.

The phone in my duffel bag made a tinkling noise, and I dug it out with a satisfied grin. There was a text from my contact, telling me she could meet us on the reservation within a couple of hours. I typed in a quick reply, telling her to go ahead and start down, and to message me again when she got there. Hector watched me do this with an expression of worried curiosity, but I let him dangle. If he could be mysterious, well then, so could I.

The air was cooling off fast, now that the sun was going down, and the sandy ground between the saguaros and agaves was turning purple in the fading light. We drove west for about half an hour, and stopped at a collection of board-and-batten shacks that looked like they had grown right out of the rocky ground. Hector parked and turned off the motor. We all got out.

Aguilito came around to the driver's side and extracted a shotgun from behind the seat, lifting his chin toward the shacks and telling Hector in Spanish that "they" were by the fire. I wanted to ask who "they" were, but figured I'd find out in person soon enough.

The plane buzzed low overhead, toward where the sun was setting, tipping one wing at us. Hector and I walked through a tumbledown cedar gate to an open clearing enclosed by the rickety buildings. The kid and his equalizer stayed behind.

Four adults were sitting around a pyramid of burning cedar wood. One, a chubby man in a black dress shirt and slacks, with a Vandyke beard and a shaved head, was smoking a short cigar. He extended a hand toward Hector without getting up, and asked if he'd brought the fee.

Hector shook hands and nodded. The man rose from his

plastic folding chair, grabbing the dark blob at his feet. It was a chopper—an AK-47—with a night sight mounted on the side rail. His homies rousted themselves, producing similar weapons, and one, a skinny youngster of less than twenty, shouldered a grenade launcher along with his rifle.

Aguilito was leaning on the Suburban smoking a joint, his shotgun resting against the quarter panel, when we returned. Cigar Guy gave him an affectionate rub on the head and stopped to say a few words. A dark SUV with blacked-out windows had appeared and sat with its motor idling.

I took the opportunity to whisper to Hector, "Seriously?"

"This is Sinaloa country," he murmured back. "Nobody crosses through here alive without an escort."

"So why are we trying?" I hissed back.

"Two reasons," he said, holding up a pair of fingers. "One, element of surprise. No one will be expecting us to come onto the reservation from Mexico. Two, I won't have to go into the States."

"That last thing? It's really getting old," I told him.

Cigar Guy and Grenade Launcher were coming our way. They climbed into the back of the Suburban, and Hector took the wheel. The other two of the crew disappeared into the SUV. Aguilito headed back to the circle of shacks.

If you've never been to the Mexican desert, save your money. It has a beauty, but once you've seen one square mile of it, you don't need to see the rest. The uniformity of the landscape, especially in the rapidly darkening evening, made me wonder how our navigators knew where the hell we were going. There were no roads; we simply drove along the unmarked dirt, dodging cacti and the occasional chunk of colorless rock.

The two guys in the back didn't say much, and Grenade

Launcher fired up a joint about fifteen minutes into the drive. He politely offered it to me across the seat after taking a hit. I declined. The last thing I wanted to do right now was relax.

As I turned forward again, Hector slammed the brakes. The SUV in front had stopped short, and their two riders jumped out and assumed defensive positions with their backs to the vehicle. For a few tense minutes everything froze like that. Then one of the people from the SUV—a stout, sun-browned woman somewhere in the neighborhood of forty, with her hair in two long braids—skittered around the vehicle to examine a pale lump about the size of a small ice chest lying in their headlight beam.

"*Chaca!*" she called back to us.

Cigar leaned over the seat and said something to Hector in Spanish too rapid for me to follow. Then he shouldered his AK, got out, and trotted up to join the woman bent over the lump.

"What's going on?" I said.

"Might be an ambush," Hector replied, reaching across me and getting a pistol out of the glove compartment. He nodded ahead. "That's a dead body up there. The cartels will do that. Leave them along a route to make you stop, so they can jump you."

"Pft," I said. "That's too small to be a body."

Hector looked at me. "We'll probably find the rest as we go along." He flipped the pistol's safety off. "Assuming we survive."

Grenade Launcher had gotten out at the same time as Cigar, and was leaning against my side of the Suburban, his T-shirt wrinkled flat where it pressed up against the window glass. I felt a sudden, intense affection for him.

We idled there for about five minutes without any warheads coming in, while Cigar and Braids talked over the body. He came back to the Suburban and got in. The SUV's brake lights went off, and we started to move forward again.

"Not one of ours," Cigar said to Hector, in Spanish. He got out a lighter. "A woman."

"Somebody's hit?" Hector asked.

Cigar shrugged. "Too long to tell. She might have died crossing."

"She didn't cut herself into pieces," I said.

I don't know why it surprises people when I speak Spanish to them. It's not a dead language.

Cigar applied the lighter flame to the cold end of his smoke, to cover his pause. "Lots of animals out here." His eyes met mine briefly. "Some of them human."

Grenade Launcher spat noisily out his window, making a face. "Fucking *chavas*." Hector gave him a look in the rearview, and he elaborated. "Men who kill women have no balls. They take it up the ass, all of them."

I couldn't see his face from where I was sitting, but the intensity of his disgust radiated over me from behind.

We passed the victim's head and arms a few miles farther. They'd been worked on by insects, but it was clear from the clean cuts that their removal had been effected by something with opposable thumbs. We never did find her legs.

After about an hour of driving, the meandering course we were taking across the landscape changed to a dirt road, and we stopped at a steel cattle guard in a weather-beaten barbed-wire fence. The sky had turned an intense dark blue and stars were starting to show.

Cigar leaned forward and thrust a hand over the seat toward Hector, who got his wallet off the dash and counted out a thousand dollars. Cigar took it, and the two men got out and piled into the SUV. It did a messy 180 and sped off into the desert, leaving us alone.

"Jesus Christ," I said, into the silence. "Remind me never to go anywhere with you again."

Hector looked at his watch. "It's seven thirty and we're probably an hour away from Sells. If we'd done it your way, we'd still be in Texas."

I didn't argue, but I silently promised myself to get all the details out of him beforehand, next time.

I reached over the seat for my duffel and brought out a roll of cash. Hector glanced my way and waved it off.

"Seriously?" I said. "Weren't you just telling me you're practically homeless?"

"We get this bitch, I'll submit a reimbursement to Benny," Hector said, putting on his seat belt. "Otherwise, it's on me. I mean, this *was* my idea."

He paused with his hand on the ignition key, looking down the low wire fence that radiated into the distance from the cattle guard in front of us. There was no sentry house, no lights, no gate, no indication of life anywhere. Not even a sign telling us we were entering the reservation, in Spanish or otherwise.

"Man," he said. "I know the O'odham refuse to observe externally imposed borders, but this is ridiculous."

"This is the one between them and Mexico," I told him. "They have good relations with the Mexicans. The U.S. border is the touchy one. It's farther in."

We rolled across the cattle guard and drove about a mile before the dirt road turned to asphalt. It wasn't long after that when another car materialized behind us, seemingly out of nowhere.

I couldn't see it in the dark, with the headlights blinding me, but Hector gradually slowed down until we were doing well under the speed limit, and the car went around us. It was a beat-up old Mopar of indeterminate hue, the rear end riding low on bad shocks. The passenger-side window was open, which tweaked my radar, but the only thing sticking out was someone's elbow. I got a glimpse of a circular tattoo on the forearm as they went by.

Hector let his breath out. "Just some girls."

"Just?" I scoffed.

Hector looked over at me.

I said, "In the old days, when the tribes went to war, the men brought captives back for the women to torture, instead of killing them on the battlefield. It was way worse. My grandmother was barely five feet tall, and she scared the shit out of me. She could tell you stories that'd curl your hair."

Hector's eyebrows went up, and I remembered, too late, who I was talking to.

"I'm sorry," I said.

"Don't be. I certainly don't hold the patent on family horror."

The remark reminded me I still hadn't gotten the full story on his trip with Maines. I let things settle a bit, then said, "So. Cuba."

"You saw the clipping."

"OK, you met Castro. I'm sure he wasn't waiting at the gate when you arrived."

"Of course not," Hector said. "Nobody knew I was coming."

"So what'd you do? Look up your relatives in the phone book?"

He flashed his eyes at me across the front seat, smiling. "Crazy, huh?"

"Are you serious?"

"My dad is a hero there," he said. "His picture is everywhere. His other kids don't try to hide who they are."

"So, what? You just drove over to their house and knocked on the door?"

Hector rolled his eyes. "They *do* have telephones."

I made a "go on" gesture, impatient.

"I called 'em up, told 'em who I was and what I had, and they invited me over. Fidel was there when I arrived."

"Jesus."

"Apparently people show up claiming to be related to Guevara on a pretty regular basis. Castro asked me some questions, gave me a good going-over, and pronounced me legit." Hector fidgeted, looking out his window at the cool blue darkness. "I think he's been a little bored since his retirement."

Sensing that he might be getting ready to launch into a political tirade, I made haste to keep him on track. "Then what?"

"Well, after I gave them my father's remains, they wanted to do a whole thing—throw me a parade, state dinner, stuff like that. I asked them not to, but the news still got out."

"I bet Castro was pissed you were coming back to the States."

Hector looked over at me again. "I wasn't. I didn't."

We were approaching a better-lighted section of road, and I could see some buildings up ahead in the distance, beyond another wire fence, so I got my question out fast. "When did you decide that?"

"After I saw that newspaper article," Hector replied, keeping his eyes on the road. "The U.S. monitors all the Cuban media. Someone who could make trouble for me has seen it. You can bet money on it."

"I was watching the news like a hawk," I said.

Hector snorted. "You think they'd let that just go out on the airwaves uncensored?"

I wasn't in the mood for conspiracy-theory talk, so I nudged things back to the personal. "You know, they have phones here, too."

"I couldn't risk it."

"So send me a postcard," I said. "Something."

Hector sighed. "It's not like I was on vacation, Julia. If I'd known I was gonna attract enough attention that I'd have to stay out of the States, I'd have made arrangements ahead of time, but I had to play the whole thing by ear."

"You kept in touch with Maines."

"I couldn't not," Hector protested. "He was with me the whole time."

"That lying sack of shit said he didn't go in with you."

Hector shrugged. My chest did that funny flexing thing again as I thought about Maines. His kids would know by now; the family would be at the hospital, having those heartbreaking talks with the doctors, watching everything they'd planned for the future go up in smoke. Because of me.

The guilt was almost more baffling than it was painful. I've done plenty of devious, destructive things in my life and lost no sleep; in fact, where I come from, that skill is a point of pride. Maines had done me some favors, but he'd also gotten me kicked out of WITSEC and nearly driven me insane trying to manage my life ever since. By the standards I habitually apply, what happened to him was just one of those things—an accident of circumstance, collateral damage caused by his own stupidity. So why wouldn't my conscience shut up?

The border fence at the United States entry looked slightly

more official—three strands of barbed wire stretched between steel bollards that alternated in height from about five feet to about three feet—but the only other difference was a sign telling us we were entering the country. It was just as deserted as the Mexican border had been.

Hector shook his head as we crossed, and something kicked up in my brain.

"Is the official border fence up everywhere else? I mean that big one, the panels?"

"Not yet, but that's the plan."

"If the O'odham don't do something before then, illegal traffic through their lands is going to ramp up significantly."

Hector nodded. "As I recall, that was kind of the point. Funnel people toward certain areas, and then concentrate border patrol in those areas."

"OK, but that's not going to happen here," I said, waving at the fence. "The O'odham have never let border patrol on their land. Why would they start now?"

"I dunno," Hector said thoughtfully. "They already have problems—theft, trash, dead bodies found in people's yards—maybe the U.S. figures that if those problems were to increase significantly, the O'odham would be more open to letting border patrol in here."

I laughed. "Is it just me, or do you see the irony in intentionally increasing the likelihood of illegal immigration in order to force the O'odham to accept something meant to curb it?"

"No, I feel you," Hector said. "Even more ironic, the O'odham have actually discussed sealing up their Mexican border, which they are legally entitled to do, but they can't get the resources because the U.S. won't authorize it."

I laughed again.

"Well," Hector qualified, "that's not really the whole story. Some tribal members object to the idea of borders on principle."

That made sense to me. As far as the eye could see in all directions had once been open range, home to hundreds of tribes who'd managed to thrive on it without any concept of land ownership. In fact, the people Hector and I were referring to as "illegal" had ancestors who'd been members of those tribes. The O'odham were more "American," culturally and genealogically speaking, than most people who claimed the nationality.

"It's almost like the U.S. *wants* to split the reservation in half," I remarked.

"Can't blame 'em," Hector said, putting on a mocking white-man voice. "Let these injuns congregate, next thing you know they'll be bitching about all those broken treaties." He returned to his normal voice. "Divide and conquer, baby."

A cluster of faded-orange stucco buildings appeared up ahead on the left. Hector flipped the turn signal, and we pulled into the parking lot of a neat little shopping center. There was a corner store open at the end closest to the street.

"You want anything?" he asked me, unbuckling his seat belt.

"Lots of things," I grumbled.

"I'm currently limited to foodstuffs."

I ordered some iced tea and watched him amble into the store. My phone jingled again, and I reached back and grabbed it. My contact had arrived and was asking where to meet. It had been a long time since I'd been on the O'odham, and I'd only visited once or twice, so I texted her back to pick a spot and we'd see her there shortly.

CHAPTER 27

———◆———

Like most of the architecture I'd seen on the reservation so far, the cafe where my contact had said to meet her was relatively new, and the cedarwood table the hostess led us to looked like it had been handmade. Subdued lighting and sisal carpet gave the place an expensive and sophisticated air. The menu was a surprise, featuring things like cholla-bud salad, nopalito sandwiches, and drinks made with saguaro syrup. I'd grown up on traditional suburban poor-kid fare and wasn't sure how this stuff would go down, but I was starving. I ordered the tepary bean-and-short rib stew. Hector went out on a limb for the ha:l enchiladas, made with a local squash.

"Nice," I remarked, after the waitress had gathered our menus and disappeared. I'd asked for a table well away from other diners, so that we wouldn't be overheard, and she'd seated us next to a big window that looked toward the west. The contrast between the quiet, neutral interior of the cafe and the brilliant dark-blue sky with its scattering of early stars was exhilarating.

Hector nodded, glancing around nervously. "You gonna tell me what the hell we're doing here?"

"I'm hungry," I said.

"So let's hit the drive-through," he growled. "We've got shit to do."

"Shit that'll be harder on an empty stomach."

He gave me a withering glance. "Seriously. This is stupid. Someone might remember seeing us here."

A slim young Native woman had just come in. She wore big tortoiseshell glasses with gold accents, and her stick-straight black hair was cut in an '80s shag. It had been fifteen years since I'd seen my cousin Norma, so I wasn't completely sure it was her, but I took a chance and lifted my hand. The woman came over, a smile growing as she neared the table.

"Well, I'll be damned," she chuckled softly, pulling out a chair. "It really *is* you."

Her black eyes, magnified behind her enormous lenses, ran quickly over Hector and lit with pleasure.

"Yeah, he's pretty," I told her, "but he's a pain in the ass."

"Aren't they all?" she laughed.

Hector looked like he was about to blow his top. I took pity on him. "Hector Guerra, this is my cousin, Norma Tafoya. She lives up in Salt River."

They shook hands, Norma giggling a little, then she said, "So what are you doing here? I heard this crazy rumor you went into witness protection after Joe was killed."

I held my hand toward her. "Julia Kalas."

She stared at me for a short minute, then breathed, "Oh, my God! It's true?"

I glanced around the cafe, motioning her to keep her voice down even though we were well away from the handful of other diners. "Yeah, but they kicked me out last year. I've got nowhere to go if those Aryan Brotherhood guys find me. So, please, OK?"

She started to laugh, saying again, "Oh, my God. Oh, my *God*."

I waited for her to get a grip, which took a good five minutes and involved some snorting. She'd always had trouble with her adenoids.

By the time she'd gotten herself under control, I'd relaxed a little. When the widow of a known mafioso's son disappears from the face of the earth after her husband is gunned down in the street, she's either gone into protection with the feds or with the family, so if you take a guess you've got a fifty percent chance of being right. It's not a given that your cover has been blown. The rumor she'd heard about me could easily be just idle speculation. Still, I didn't waste time with the customary family niceties.

"Listen, the reason I contacted you is because I seem to re-member some O'odham in-laws on your side of the family," I said. "You think you could put me in touch with them?"

"Maybe," Norma allowed. "Why?"

"I'm trying to find an O'odham woman by the name of Rachael Pestozo. She's been living in Texas for a while, but had recently re-established ties here and was moving back."

"Why do you want to find her? Does she owe you money or something?"

I glanced at Hector. "Could we just leave it at 'or some-thing'?"

Norma pushed her glasses up the bridge of her nose with her pinky, a gesture I recognized, and my old affection for her creaked awake. She'd been the nerd of the family, an A-making, socially awkward, straight-arrow solace to my aunt for her brother, who'd been destined for prison and the streets from day one. I don't know why Norma and I gravitated toward each other, given that I always identified more with Joachin, but we did.

We all shut up as the waitress approached and set down our food, then Norma said, "There's a Bronson Pestozo who lives down by the river. He and my ex used to go fishing together. Could be the same family, but you know how that is."

I did. There were only a handful of surnames on the reservation, and even those who shared one didn't necessarily associate with or know anything about the outer limbs of their family tree.

"Would you be willing to ask him about Rachael?"

Norma made a reluctant gesture with her head. "I'd rather not. It wasn't the prettiest divorce in the world."

"I can pay you."

She made an offended noise. "Don't be ridiculous."

"OK, then," I said. "How about just as a favor to a cousin?"

Norma had always been romantic about family. She was the kid who shacked Barbie and Ken up and birthed them a litter of kids. She kept up with all the cousins and uncles and in-laws and sent out Christmas cards every year. There were high-minded claims about wanting to preserve the culture, but it always felt distinctly personal with her. Which baffled the shit out of me. I consider my relatives cosmic accidents and treat them accordingly.

She looked at me in silence for a couple of breaths, then said, "You should go see your mom. She talks about you all the time. You're on her amends list."

"Her what?"

"She's been going to A.A. You know, the steps and everything. They have to make amends to people, and you're on her list."

"I'm on some other people's lists, too," I said. "The ones who are probably camped out in her front yard, waiting for me to stick my head up."

"I'll bring her down here. No way those Aryan guys try to follow us onto the rez."

"Hector and I got in without anybody clocking us," I pointed out.

Norma's eyes went sly. "You think so, huh?"

I remembered the carload of women going by us.

"Don't you remember how things were on the Gila?" Norma said. "It's the same here. I pity the white supremacist trying to go unnoticed around these 'skins."

The idea made me laugh, recalling the shameless curiosity and quiet observation of the locals whenever I went over to hang out with Norma and Joachin. Nobody was rude about it, but I had never had to stop and remind myself that I was in a foreign country.

"I'll go talk to Bronson right now if you'll promise to hang around until tomorrow," Norma said. "I can bring your mom down in the morning."

I looked at Hector. "We weren't really planning on staying overnight."

Norma pushed her thin lips forward, not saying anything. I looked at Hector again.

"It's a bad idea," he said, picking up his fork.

"OK, we can just hang out on the curb and wait for Rachael to walk by," I said. "Or we could start going door-to-door. That shouldn't raise any eyebrows."

Hector took a bite of enchilada, shrugging angrily. "I'm just the wheel man. What the fuck do I know?"

Norma got up. "I'll call you in a bit."

I nodded, and she hurried out.

Hector and I ate in silence for a few minutes. I could feel his temper looking for a release valve, and didn't feel like taking the job. I focused on my stew and the scenery.

My wandering eye, running over the other people in the restaurant, stopped on a couple of women near the front. They were both fortyish; one was quite rotund, with short salt-and-pepper hair, and the other was taller but slimmer, with long dark hair trailing down her back. They both wore Huichol blouses over tiered cotton skirts, and a flat-brimmed hat lay on the chair next to the long-haired woman. They were looking directly at me and Hector.

When they saw me catch them at it, they went back to their dinner. The other diners had given us the usual politely curious look all strangers in these parts typically receive, and then turned away; these two seemed a lot more interested. I withdrew my gaze, but kept my attention focused in their direction.

"Those two women are watching us," I told Hector, shifting my eyes to the right to indicate who I was talking about. I kept my voice down so it wouldn't travel.

He glanced over, then returned a grim gaze to my face. "I hate to say I told you so."

"No, you don't," I said, "but you're entitled. I won't hold it against you."

"You think they heard us?" Hector murmured, making it look like he was commenting on the meal.

I shook my head. "No way. I mean, I can't hear them, and neither of them is wearing an ear trumpet."

There was a quiet pause while Hector bisected an enchilada and got it on his fork. He raised it to his mouth and said, "So, do I get to meet your mom?"

I gave him a look. "You want to meet my mother?"

Hector paused to chew, smiling, then swallowed and said, "I'm curious about her, knowing you."

"Save yourself the agony," I said, picking up my spoon. "Garden-variety alcoholic. They're not that interesting."

"Don't you want to see what she's like sober?"

"Not particularly," I replied.

"Not even for her benefit?"

I put the spoon down. "Listen, I spent eighteen years cleaning up puke and used condoms and getting the emotional and physical shit beat out of me for my trouble, so don't try and tell me what I owe my mother, all right?"

Hector pursed his lips and kept quiet. I went back to keeping a surreptitious eye on the two women at the other table. After a while they got up to pay their tab at the register. The one with the long hair had put on her hat, which shaded her eyes, but I could tell that she was still looking at me. Her companion started for the door, but she turned and came over to our table.

"Where you from, girl?" she said, putting her hand flat on it, near the edge. It wasn't threatening, but it had a proprietary air.

"Texas," I said, looking up at her. I wanted to add, *if it's any of your business*, but didn't want to make myself any more memorable than I already was.

She met my gaze, her eyes steady. After a few seconds, she looked over at Hector. "And what are you? The chauffeur?"

He was busy eating, but spared her a negligent glance and a mild chuckle. "I wish. I might get paid, that way."

Her upper lip lifted. "It's always about money with you guys, innit? Money or pussy."

Hector kept looking at her, chewing. He didn't say anything. I kept my teeth together, too. It wasn't easy.

A couple of the other restaurant patrons were watching us. The silence started to stretch out, then the tall woman's companion came over and muttered something unintelligible in her ear, and they moved off. I watched them mosey out into the parking lot, get into a nondescript panel van, and drive off.

"Dang," Hector breathed.

"Yeah," I said. "So much for blending in with the locals."

He wiped his mouth and put down the napkin. "What do you think? Anything to worry about?"

"Hard to say. I've never had anybody rez up on me like that before, but it's been a long time since I was down here." Hector gave me a quizzical look, and I explained, "Most of the full-bloods I knew back in the day were fine with outsiders, but some still hold a grudge against white people."

Hector's eyebrows went up. "They consider you white?"

"I *am* white," I said. "I wasn't raised on the reservation or in any tribal traditions. Blood's not what makes you Indian."

My phone rang. It was Norma.

"Got some info for you," she said, sounding a little breathless. "Bronson says that Rachael was supposed to be starting a job with the O'odham women's shelter this week. They're having a committee meeting tonight."

"It's almost ten," I said, looking at the clock on the buff-colored wall.

"They meet late," Norma said, "and they almost always run past midnight."

"Did he say for sure that she was here?"

"Not in so many words, but that's the impression I got."

"Score," I said to Hector, then, to Norma, "Where?"

CHAPTER 28

———— ◆ ————

The women's shelter was a stand-alone building on the opposite side of town from where we'd come in. It looked a little bit like a school gymnasium from the outside: a big concrete-block rectangle with a strip of tile running all the way around it, halfway up. Like most of the buildings in Sells, it didn't seem to have much age on it.

There were lights on and maybe a dozen cars in the parking lot. Hector pulled the Suburban to the curb on the opposite side of the wide street and turned off the motor. His open window framed the building, painted a glowing orange in the blue-black darkness by a single pole light.

"So how are we gonna work this?" he said.

"Let's just wait until they come out. If we see her, we can follow her home."

"And then what? We knock and ask politely if she'd like to come with us?"

"No," I said, keeping my eyes on the building. "We'll have to wait until she's somewhere out in the open and alone."

"Even then, I don't like our odds," Hector said. "Not after what she did to Maines."

I lifted the hem of my jeans to remind him I was armed. "Plus yours, in the glove compartment. We're strapped."

"So was he," Hector reminded me.

"He didn't know who he was dealing with. We do."

"I am not liking any of this," Hector complained. "We've already attracted unwanted attention, now we're gonna try and grab this woman off the street? It's asking for trouble."

I knew he was right, but I wasn't ready to give up. "Let's just wait and see what happens. We might get lucky somehow."

Hector pressed his lips together and sat back, not saying anything else.

It was almost eleven when people finally started leaving. Hector turned toward me so that it would look like we were talking while I watched them walk to their cars and pull away. I didn't see "Rachael."

The cell phone in my shirt pocket rang, nearly sending me through the roof of the Suburban. I'd forgotten all about it.

I grabbed it, my heart hammering. "Jesus. What?"

"Thanks for not locking the keys in the trunk," Benny said. He sounded like he was smiling.

Not sure what I was in for, I played it safe. "Uh, you're welcome?"

"You'll never guess what I found."

"I hope it's a gross of tranquilizer darts," I said, keeping my eyes on the people leaving the women's center, "and that you can overnight it to me."

"Just for laughs I ran all the fingerprints I got off Rachael's stuff from the hot springs, while I'm waiting for the DNA, and an ID came back." I heard him tapping a computer keyboard. "Mikela Floyd, thirty-two. She was a receptionist at Darling's clinic, so it's not weird her fingerprints would be on Rachael's stuff. But get this: Mikela disappeared on December 12, the day after Rachael's surgery."

I shifted my eyes to Hector's face, my eyebrows up. Benny kept talking. "Here's the part you'll love. She and her older sister are wanted by the FBI for domestic terrorism."

"Holy shit," I said, unable to suppress a wry laugh. "Well, I guess the feds'll be interested now."

"Fuck 'em," Benny said. I could practically see him squaring his shoulders. "I'm gonna love calling them up and rubbing their face in the fact that this 'wetback loser' got one of theirs."

"What'd the sisters do?"

"Shot and killed a cop during a May Day protest against the border fence last year, near Juarez. Mikela lay low for a month, then took the job with Darling in June. They're not top ten, but they're both on the list. Sister's name is Jennifer Floyd, she's thirty-six."

"I wonder if she bought herself a new face, too."

"Actually, there's a rumor Jennifer's dead, but nobody's been able to confirm. The Mexican cops found a body that matches her description among the *feminicidios*, but they—"

"The what?"

"You've seen it in the papers. This rash of female workers from the *maquiladoras*—factories in the free-trade zone—being murdered around Juarez and El Paso. It broke into the news for a while and then faded away, although the killings haven't stopped."

"So why haven't they been able to identify Jennifer?"

"'Able' isn't the word," Benny said. "Nobody's trying. The Mexican government's position on the *feminicidios* is that the cartels are doing it, but they've got much bigger problems than identifying all these women, so the ones that aren't claimed immediately by the families—they just write them off as anonymous collateral damage in the drug wars. Since Mikela was on the lam when they found the body we think might be Jennifer, she wasn't anxious to step up and make an identification."

"What happened to it?"

"No idea," Benny said. "They found her on June 10, so it's been almost exactly a year. My guess is that they just went ahead and buried her when nobody stepped up to claim her."

"So we don't know for sure that she's dead," I said.

"Right," Benny replied. "But nobody's seen her since. So . . . ya know."

He cleared his throat and went on. "Anyway, even if the feds did figure out that Mikela stole Rachael Pestozo's identity— which would be really tricky, between Rachael dying in Mexico and Darling's shady clinic operation—trying to extradite anybody off an Indian reservation is incredibly difficult."

"So, really, we're doing them a favor," I said, grinning.

"It's not funny," Benny said, his voice solemn. "Mikela Floyd is no sweet young thing. She killed a cop, and domestic terrorism charges aren't something the feds just throw around. So if she's gotta come home in a bag, I won't cry, and neither, probably, will our government friends."

You won't catch me defending the law on my worst day, but that startled even me. "Jesus, Benny."

"Christ, I'm not telling you to *kill* her," he said. "Just know that you're dealing with someone who won't hesitate to take you out if she feels like she has to. Don't let her get around behind you."

Hector nudged me. "Rachael" had appeared in the parking lot.

"Speak of the devil," I muttered.

Benny made a puzzled noise, and I said, "Just clocked her. I'll call you back."

Our quarry went to one of the two cars remaining in the parking lot—a late-model Mustang with a homemade paint job—and opened the trunk. She retrieved a rucksack and went back into the building. I looked at Hector's watch. It was 12:45.

"You gonna give me the 411?" he said.

I told him what Benny had learned.

His eyes widened. "Holy shit."

"Yeah. But kind of nice to know that we're on the right side of the law, if anything goes haywire."

"What do you mean?" Hector said warily.

I gave him a knowing look, and he shook his head emphatically. "I've seen enough killing. I'm not going to be party to any more of it, legal or not."

"Even after what she did to Maines?" I asked him, my face turning hot. "I almost wish she'd killed him. The life he's got ahead of him is worse than being dead."

"One more body isn't going to change any of that," Hector muttered.

I was angry now, but I didn't know why. "If you could get your hands on the guys who hacked up your mother and sisters, you wouldn't be tempted to pay them back in kind?"

"Yeah, I'd be tempted to, but I wouldn't do it."

I made a skeptical face at him.

"Not because of them," he said. "Because of *me*. Because *I* couldn't live with it."

There wasn't much I could say to that, so I shut up and went back to silently watching the women's center. Nothing was moving over there. It was getting on my nerves, along with Hector's moralism.

"All right," I said finally, leaning down to get the little Glock off my ankle.

Hector watched me, looking alarmed. "What the hell do you think you're doing?"

I got out of the Suburban and took the safety off my gun. "I'm a woman. It's a women's center."

He started to laugh, but it wasn't all humor. "You're fucking insane."

"OK, we can sit here all night debating situational ethics." I stuck the gun in the back of my waistband. "I, for one, do not have that much patience."

"I knew you'd find some way to drive this thing off a cliff."

"Relax," I told him. "I'm just going to take a look, that's all."

Hector started to answer, but I'd already gone around the front of the Suburban.

"I'd tell you not to do anything stupid, but I know better," he whisper-called at me as I crossed the street.

The building had a recess in the front where a pair of glass doors looked into a large room, with several doors in each wall. There was an intercom to one side of the entrance with a notice above it: PLEASE RING FOR HELP, 24 HOURS.

I watched through the glass doors, from a distance, for a little while, but didn't see or hear anything. Then I circled around the back side of the building to have a look in the windows.

At the third one down from the front corner of the building, I hit pay dirt. There were shadows moving across the window-sill. I crept up and stood flat against the building wall, inching toward the window opening. When I was close enough, I craned my head carefully forward, inching it ahead until a person's back came into view.

The person wore a long denim coat and had a thick black ponytail. Considering where we were, the ponytail could signify either gender, and I couldn't tell from this angle whether it was a man or a woman. I held still, waiting, and heard voices, but the person didn't move. I risked leaning farther forward, and caught the edge of a naked leg, sitting in a chair. It looked male. Another inch forward, and I saw that "Rachael" was standing between the chair and the window with her back to me; I recognized what she was wearing. The rucksack she'd just retrieved lay on a folding table to her right, surrounded by a collection of tools: hammer, ice pick, vise grips, utility knife. It only took me a second to understand what she was using them for.

Feeling slightly nauseous, I backed quickly away, around to the parking lot, and ran across the street, getting the cell phone out of my pocket.

"What's up?" Hector asked as I came within range.

"They're in there torturing somebody," I said, dialing the phone. When the 911 operator answered, I told her what I'd seen without giving her my name.

"That was the most sensible thing I think I've ever seen you do," Hector said as I got into the Suburban.

He started the motor, and I said, "Where do you think you're going?"

"I'm not anxious to make the acquaintance of any of the local cops, even if they *do* approve of our mission," he said. "I know this is a sovereign nation and all, but it's still the U.S. as far as I'm concerned."

I put my hand on the door handle. "I'm not leaving until I see that broad facedown on the pavement, in handcuffs."

Hector tilted his head toward the road behind us. "Let's go

watch from the rise back there. Then we don't have to blow our cover unless we want to."

I nodded, and we pulled away from the center, drove a few hundred yards, and nosed the Suburban across the shoulder and into the brush. Hector turned off the lights, and we got out and walked up onto a low hill where we could see down into the women's center parking lot. There was a clear view of the front door.

Fifteen minutes went by with nothing happening. No sirens, nothing.

I looked at Hector's watch again. "What the hell is taking them so long?"

"Heads up," he said.

The denim-clad person I'd seen through the window had come out of the center. It was the tall woman who'd questioned us on her way out of the cafe a few hours earlier. She'd put on the long coat over her Huichol blouse and skirt, but wasn't wearing her hat now.

She was talking into a cell phone, pacing back and forth in front of the door and looking around. Another ten minutes went by, and then headlights appeared from the direction of town. A tribal cop car turned into the parking lot, and the tall woman went over to it. She held a short conference with whoever was inside, and then it slowly pulled away and went back in the direction it had come.

"What the hell?" I said, under my breath.

I got my phone out and punched in 911 again. When the dispatcher answered, I said, "You guys need to be way more suspicious."

"Your name, please?"

"That woman your guys just talked to is helping the other one put the screws to their victim," I said.

"I'll need your name, ma'am," the dispatcher insisted.

The needle on my radar jumped. I turned off the phone and threw it out into the brush.

"We need to get out of here," I told Hector. "Fast."

CHAPTER 29

We took a different route out of the reservation than we had taken in, so that when we crossed into the desert again, I had no idea where we were. Fortunately, that seemed not to matter. Hector made a call, and our armed escort appeared as if by magic.

We hadn't said much on the way, both of us tensely scanning for police cars or any other sign of the law, and probably praying silently to our respective gods. When we passed through the fence into Mexico and saw the black SUV, I let my breath out and put my head back, eyes closed, wondering how we'd escaped the unofficial border patrol. Coming in, I hadn't seen any sign of them until they'd magically appeared behind us. I couldn't imagine that they'd suddenly decided to take the night off. Maybe they were like the crossing guards between Presidio and Ojinaga—they only cared who came in, not who went out.

The driver's-side window of the SUV rolled down to reveal our friend with the cigar. He saluted Hector and turned south into the darkness. Hector geared down and followed.

"So what are we looking at here?" he said to me, after a few minutes.

"I have no idea," I said, "but I don't like any of it."

"Maybe that woman is a cop and they were doing something official in there," he suggested.

"If that's how the cops around here conduct business, we've got bigger problems than Mikela Floyd," I said, then shook my head. "If she were a cop, I'd know. I can smell them coming for miles."

Hector nodded grimly. We were quiet again while he focused on staying glued to our lead, winding over the rocky ground ahead of us.

There was still a fire going at the encampment, and Cigar gestured us to join the circle around it, after leading us in.

"Let me use your phone," I said to Hector, before I sat down.

He gave me a guarded look. "Why?"

"I need to let Benny know the local law is rotten before he sends them anything about Mikela Floyd. I don't want her going to ground before we can get a crack at her."

Hector said something to Cigar in Spanish, and the gangster gestured across the fire at the stout woman with braids who'd stopped our caravan earlier to examine the dead body. She stood up and passed him a flip phone, which he gave to me.

I stepped away from the fire and dialed Benny's number. When he answered, I told him what had happened, and he muttered, "The plot thickens."

"Something is certainly rotten in Denmark," I agreed.

"Good thing I sent you. If I'd tried to go the official route, I'd have gotten completely stonewalled."

"If Mikela's got the local law on her side, I don't see her walking quietly out of here," I said.

There was a pause on the line, then Benny said, "I know you hate the idea, but I'm going to deputize you, right now, and backdate the paperwork to Friday. That way, if anything bad goes down, you'll be protected from prosecution, since you'll be acting as an official arm of the law."

"And by bad, you mean . . . ?"

"Do what you gotta do," Benny growled. "Just get her."

I gave a few seconds' thought to how I'd navigate that with Hector, then said, "Listen, you may not hear from me again before I get back. I had to ditch my phone."

"Pick up a burner. I'll reimburse you."

"I'll try. But if not, I'll see you when I see you."

"Yep," Benny said, and the line went dead.

I went back over to the fire and took a lawn chair, handing Cigar back the phone. He turned it off, slid out the battery, and threw the phone into the fire. A surprised look appeared on his face as he reached inside his jacket to pocket the battery.

"*Santa Maria,*" he chuckled, bringing out a dark oblong. "I thought I'd smoked all these up."

Hector, perched on a tree stump next to him, reached over and took the cigar. "Goddamn. That's a real Cuban." He glanced at me, humor in his face.

Cigar gestured at him. "It's yours, my friend. My last one."

Hector bowed his head in thanks, then took the band off and held the end of the cigar into the fire for a minute, puffing it every now and then to get it going. As he sat back with it clenched in his teeth, grinning, my blood went cold. He looked just like his father. His long hair and trained musculature had obscured the resemblance before. I wondered if Cigar's bunch knew who Hector was. Looking at him now, it seemed hard to miss.

I've never cared much for the odor of smoking, but the contraband cigar scented the air with a rich, woody perfume that was in a completely different category than cigarettes or our host's local stogie. I took a deep breath. It was like eating a piece of cake. Hector held the cigar toward me, but I shook my head.

"Too bad," he said. "There's nothing like these."

"So," I said to Cigar, "are the cartels really behind this *feminicidio* thing?"

Hector coughed, shaking his head. Cigar gave me a hard look and said, "Perhaps you should ask them."

"I'm asking you."

He made a negligent motion with one shoulder, looking off between the shacks into the chill darkness. "I can only speak for my own group. We do not kill innocents."

"Then who's doing it?"

"It's possible the cartels are responsible," he admitted. "But I doubt it."

I gave him a quizzical look, and he explained, "Those guys kill people other than their enemies for only two reasons—as a warning, or as revenge. None of these women had any connection to them. It would be foolhardy and a waste of resources on their part to do such a thing. The *federales* blame them only to cover their own incompetence."

"It *is* somewhat incredible that over three hundred women have been killed with no more plausible suspects on the radar than some nebulous group of bad guys," I agreed.

Cigar tilted his head back and blew a slim stream of smoke into the air. "Were I investigating the matter, I would consider who might want these *particular* women dead. They are young, single, attractive. If not for their jobs, they would be considered very marriageable."

He said this last word with a peculiar emphasis. I frowned at him. "What do you mean?"

Cigar took a silent draw from his smoke, not replying.

Hector said to me, "Mexico is still a very traditional, *macho* culture. Women go up against it at their peril."

"So, what, some sexist psycho—or psychos—are offing these women because they have the temerity to get jobs instead of stay at home and take care of the menfolk?" I said. "You're getting into tinfoil-hat territory there."

Cigar and Hector exchanged a look.

"Perhaps you should visit the less-traveled portions of Mexico some time," Cigar said.

The woman with the braids had been listening to this conversation impassively, and now I lifted my chin at her. "What do you think?"

She adjusted the AK between her knees and pursed her lips, looking away from the fire. "I dunno who's killing those girls, but they better be careful. People all over the country are really disgusted by the government's lack of protection from organized crime." She ran her eyes around the fire circle. "We're not the only group taking matters into our own hands."

"My bad," I said, surprised. "I thought you guys were mules."

Hector gave me an incredulous look. "You think I'd associate with those fuckers?"

"Why do you speak in such a disrespectful manner?" Cigar asked me. "It is not wise."

He sounded scary, but nothing in my alarm system went off, and a thought shot across my consciousness: Out here, sitting under the stars with a bunch of outlaws, I felt in my element in a way I never did elsewhere. I'd always assumed that I gravitated toward these kinds of people because I was somehow naturally criminal, but it didn't follow. Real thugs—lifers—are like Cigar: hard, slow, and methodical. People like me, who pop off at the drop of a hat, usually end up underground by the time we're thirty. It's natural selection. I knew this; I'd known it since I was fourteen. So why did I persist in behaving the way I did?

"*Aho*," someone shouted from outside the circle of shacks, to the north.

Faster than I would have believed possible, the group around the fire shouldered their weapons and dissolved between the buildings. Hector and I were alone in seconds flat.

I got my little Glock out and crept to the edge of the firelight, squinting to see where our hosts had stationed themselves. I heard a hiss and spit and looked back to see Hector crouched next to the fire, pouring the contents of the coffee pot onto it.

"You got that white girl from Texas in there with you?" the voice from the north said. It was throaty and androgynous and seemed to expand in all directions.

My eyes had adjusted and I could see Cigar, lying on his stomach in a narrow valley between buildings, his eye to the sight on his AK. He didn't reply to the voice, just held still, waiting. I crouched and scurried up behind him, keeping the Glock in front of me. He glanced over his shoulder at my approach, making a sign to keep quiet.

We held like that for a long while, the dark desert silence ringing in our ears. The smell of wet wood smoke washed over us. There was a moon, so I could make out the broad strokes of the landscape in front of us. There was nobody on it.

Hector crept up next to me, a shotgun in one hand. I gave him a surprised look and he gestured behind us.

"Leftover," he whispered.

As I turned back to watching the perimeter, there was a muffled scuffling noise, and two figures appeared over a small sandy rise about thirty yards away. They drew closer, and it became apparent that the one in the front was a man, covered with some kind of light-colored sack down to his shoulders. He was naked below it, pale and skinny, covered with blood and wounds that did nothing for his modesty. The figure behind him kept shoving him forward, and he stumbled and jerked along until they were within speaking range.

The figure behind gave him a final hard shove, sending him to his knees in the sand, and said, "You may watch me kill this piece of shit, or I will trade him."

It was the tall Native woman. She was still wearing the long denim coat over her skirt and Huichol, and had added her flat-brimmed hat, despite the darkness. She held a large automatic rifle in her left hand; I couldn't tell, in the dark, what kind.

I nudged Cigar, but he waved me off. The tall woman reached forward and yanked the hood from her victim. It was Finn.

She prodded him with the rifle and he lifted his head. His bright owl eyes flashed in the darkness. To my surprise, there wasn't much fear in them. His mind seemed to be elsewhere.

I poked Cigar again and made a circling sign, indicating that I was going to try and creep around behind them. He shook his head with a frown, but I ignored it.

Hector followed me through the dark compound and out between the shacks on the other side. I stopped before I stepped out from the cover of the buildings and said to him in a low voice, "Listen, I'm the loose cannon here. You don't have to be."

He indicated that I should proceed, looking annoyed. I crouched down and took a quick peek around the corner to make sure the coast was clear, then stepped quickly out and skittered silently to the nearest clump of brush.

I could hear the low rumble of a man talking, and realized that Cigar was engaging with the tall woman, to cover us. I heard her reply, which gave me a location. I headed around behind it, keeping my eyes wide to take in as much as possible in the dark.

Hector was holding position at the edge of the circle of shacks, with the shotgun aimed in the direction of the tall woman's voice. I doubted he could see much from where he was, but the gun was a Benelli—a military-class toaster that would level anything within fifty yards. Including me, if I wasn't careful.

I moved in a wide circle so that I would come in directly behind the tall woman, and then started closing, very slowly. Ten paces; stop, crouch, listen. Lather, rinse, repeat.

Four rounds of this brought me up at the foot of the low rise. There was a rim of rock there, over which I could just see the top of the tall woman's head. I raised up a bit, and my heart jumped like a startled horse; a row of women squatted about twenty yards away, with their backs to me. I counted eleven of them, most with long guns propped at their side.

The third from the end was wearing the same jacket I'd last seen Mikela Floyd in, a brown leather blazer. I held still, keeping my eyes on her until she turned her head to glance at the woman next to her. It was indeed our girl.

I lowered back down, thinking. My count around the fire had been six, including me and Hector. All were armed to the teeth, but so were the eleven women I'd just spotted, from what I could see.

I slunk back the way I'd come and between the shacks into the clearing. Hector turned in behind me.

"We're outnumbered," I told him, keeping my voice low and putting the Glock back in my ankle holster. "Mikela's out there, about twenty feet behind, with ten others. All armed."

Hector's mouth compressed, his eyes lighting.

"Let me see your phone," I said. He gave me the usual suspicious look, and I assured him, "I'm not gonna call anybody with it."

He reached out the tiny flip phone and handed it over. I set the ringer on silent and slid it down the front of my shirt, under the center of my bra where the cups met.

"Call Benny," I said. "He can track it."

Realizing what my next move was, Hector dropped the shotgun and tried to grab me, but I was already around him. I sprinted between shacks and out in front of Finn and his captor.

"Ready when you are," I said.

The tall woman raised her gun, and an odd thrill ran up from the soles of my feet. Finn looked over at me, and I could swear he smiled. Shock, probably.

The woman grabbed the back of his left arm and pulled him up to his feet, then gave him another shove. He stumbled forward a few steps, looking at me again. I took a step toward the woman, whose eyes were lifeless caverns under the brim of her hat. Her gun barrel shifted down, and she beckoned me to keep coming.

I walked toward her, watching Finn. He wasn't navigating well because of his injuries, but managed to ambulate in the general direction of the shacks, and within a few seconds had disappeared from my peripheral vision. I quickly covered the last couple of feet between me and the tall woman, who turned and indicated that I should walk past her over the rise. I wanted to look back and make sure Finn had made it, but I didn't want to see Hector's face.

As we came over the rise, the tall woman muttered a command for me to pick up the pace, and the waiting eleven arose and began moving quickly north, away from the encampment. Mikela made sure that I saw her raise her rifle. I wasn't sure why she hadn't shot me on sight, but realized that I'd gambled on it. The radar had told me she wouldn't. I put the brain to work on why.

A few minutes' trek through the desert and we came upon two old Chevy vans parked on the sand. Mikela handed her weapon to one of the other women and approached me. She gestured for me to turn around and put my hands up on the side of the van, which I did without complaining. She felt up both sides of my legs, along my pockets and the waistband of my jeans, patted and squeezed my sides and stomach, then up under my breasts. I tensed my abdominals, praying to whatever gods might be listening that Hector's phone would pass for part of them, or of my industrial-strength bra. The higher powers were on duty; she missed it.

The tall woman opened the back doors of one of the vans, and three of the women, including Mikela, climbed in. Boss Lady indicated I should join them and slammed the doors behind us.

Mikela took the bench seat directly across from me, her AK between her legs. I wanted to sass her, feeling cocky about the phone, but I knew it was a bad idea. I kept my mouth shut.

The van jerked forward.

CHAPTER 30

When we stopped and got out about half an hour later, the land-scape looked exactly the same. Big sky frosted with stars, shoulders of dark hills in the distance, pale rocky sand stretching out in all directions. If not for the derelict house the women were walking me toward, we might as well have driven in a big circle.

I tried to figure out what had possessed the builder to put the house where it was. There were no signs of anything else nearby—no ruins of a town, a road, or even fences. It looked like it had just grown up out of the sand by accident, a farmhouse seed dropped by some stray bird. It looked like it had been recently lived in, and was in fairly good shape for its age; I guessed that it had been built in the late 1800s, from the proportions and simple floor plan—it was just one big room with a porch across the front. A small laugh leaked from my mouth as we clomped up onto the wood porch. I'd probably be cataloging the architectural style of my gallows while they put the noose around my neck.

This wasn't the first time I'd faced death, but it was the first time I'd noticed what I was thinking while I did. I was acutely aware of every physical sensation: the dusty dry smell of the house, the chill of the desert night prickling up my arms, my light, fast breathing. It was almost as if I were anticipating, with some sort of pleasure, what might come next. That's what was strange—the sense of anticipation. I wasn't afraid, or even nervous. I was hungry for something that I couldn't name.

Some dilapidated furniture loitered inside the house: an old sofa, a painted wooden table with three mismatched chairs, a sagging mattress on an old iron frame. There was a TV, unplugged, on the floor next to the bed, which had a stained blue sheet draped over it.

The two women who weren't Mikela came inside with me. She and the tall woman remained on the porch, speaking to each other in low tones. It sounded like Mikela was trying to talk her boss into something and failing.

After a few minutes, Mikela came in, and one of the two women with me went out onto the porch with the boss. The remaining one, a petite young bottle blonde whose eyes and skin tone put the lie to her hair, pulled one of the chairs over to a rear window, where she sat side-on, looking out. Mikela took the sofa and indicated the bed was mine.

After a minute, the lookout on the porch, the short woman with salt-and-pepper hair, came back in with an open bottle of soda in her hand. She looked over at Mikela, who nodded to her, then propped her rifle in the corner and came over to give me the bottle.

"Drink it," she said.

I don't argue with firearms. I did what she said, then lay down and closed my eyes. Almost immediately, I became aware of the furious pace at which the wheels behind my eyes were working. I turned my attention off and let them do their thing until the drugs took hold.

CHAPTER 31

The cold end of an AK nudged me. I opened my eyes to sunrise, my head a swamp. However, the eight hundred-pound gorilla on my chest had gone on a crash diet, which surprised me. Given the circumstances, I'd expected my morning suffocation to feel more oppressive than ever. Maybe the drugs they'd given me had something to do with it.

Dye Job was absent. It was just Mikela and me in the dry heat of the big room. Only now my right wrist was handcuffed to the bed frame. A quick glance out the window showed Salt-and-Pepper still sitting in the folding chair on the front porch.

I was pretty foggy, but gradually the brain came back online, along with the work it had done before I'd passed out the night before. Somehow the tall woman had gotten wind that the white girl she'd taken a dislike to in the cafe was looking for Rachael Pestozo, and that presented a threat worth kidnapping me for. What I couldn't figure out was why it had gone down the way it did.

First of all, if I was the target, why had she grabbed Finn and then gone to all the trouble and risk of making a swap? I was right here in Sells, and Finn had been up the border some one hundred miles. Granted, I'm not that easy to grab, but there were other, better targets closer by, if the idea was to get someone I'd be willing to trade myself for—Norma or Hector, for instance.

Secondly, why did the mere fact that I was looking for Rachael rate an operation of this magnitude? I hadn't said that I was looking for Mikela Floyd. I *had* told the tall woman that I was from Texas, though, which might have been enough, if she and her minions were somehow involved in the whole identity-theft thing.

That was about as far as I had gotten before the dope hit me. Sometimes I'll go to bed with a problem and wake up with an answer, but I hadn't gotten that bonus this time.

"So what's the plan?" I asked Mikela, stretching and sitting up as best I could with my new restraints.

"Nalin will be here shortly," she replied, lighting a cigarette from a pack on the side table next to her.

"Who?"

"The boss," she said.

"And then what?"

She didn't answer me, just took a long drag off the cigarette and sat back into the sofa.

Annoyed, I turned to needling her. "Why'd you do it?"

She looked at me, and I watched her expression shift around while she decided what I meant. She finally settled on, "He's a man, isn't he?"

"That's a hell of a reason to try and kill somebody."

"It's the only reason I need." She observed the dubious look on my face and said, "Still drinking the Kool-Aid, huh?"

Not entirely sure what metaphorical beverage she was referring to, I threw her a frown.

"You're a fucking sheep," she said. "Men run every single aspect of your life. They always have, and unless you fight back, they always will."

Well, that was interesting. It was also borderline insane, but I didn't argue. If I let her rant maybe she'd tell me something useful in the process.

"Look at what you're wearing," Mikela ordered. "The neckline of that shirt was designed by a man to show off your tits. The fabric it's made from came out of a deal made by men with other men, and it was made in a third-world sweatshop owned by a man, by a teenage girl selling herself to the highest bidder. Those jeans emphasize your ass—"

"Maybe in your size," I interrupted. "I can't find the ones that do that for asses my size. Everything above a ten is basically a denim girdle."

"My point," Mikela cut in, "is that some old, white CEO with a trophy wife somewhere has decided how you should look, for the sensibilities of his brethren. How you wear your hair, what soap you use, the way you speak, how you see yourself in the mirror—all of it."

"Men look at women," I shrugged. "Women look at men. Welcome to the human race."

Mikela shook her head, sighing. "Fish don't understand water until you take them out of it."

I thought about asking if her sister's death had anything to do with her enlistment in the gender wars, but it occurred to me that the reason she hadn't shot me yet was probably because she didn't know that I'd figured out who she was. I hadn't clocked her until after she and Maines had started back to Azula, so he wouldn't have told her. And my coming after her didn't necessarily mean I knew anything more than that she'd tried to kill the guy she'd met me with.

"Listen, Rachael," I said, using the name to test my theory, "I get annoyed with the male of the species as much as the next chick, but that doesn't make me want to wipe out the entire brotherhood."

Mikela's lips curled into a disagreeable smile. She seemed to relax slightly, making me hope I'd been right about her feeling safe with her anonymity.

"We don't want to wipe them *all* out," she said. "Just the ones who are trying to wipe *us* out. I think that's fair, don't you?"

Before I could figure out how to reply, heavy steps clomped up onto the porch. Mikela looked out the window behind me and got off the sofa. I turned and saw that Nalin had arrived, and was talking to the woman on the front porch. Mikela went over to the door and opened it, remaining inside so that she could listen through the screen door and still keep an eye on me.

I leaned my head back against the windowsill, grateful for the interruption, and put the brain to work on how I could use the angle I'd just realized existed. Did Nalin know that Rachael was a fake? If she didn't, outing her might give me some kind of edge. If Nalin did know, the effort would be pointless, and letting them know that *I* knew might get me killed. Just once, it'd be nice for that not to be one of the choices.

It was colder today; someone had started a fire somewhere, and the faint sweet smell of wood smoke hovered in the room, drowning out Mikela's cigarette. I reached for the blanket folded at the end of the bed, glancing toward the far end of the room, and something tickled my brain. I let my eyes slide casually across the other windows, which gave a full 360-degree view around the house. A fire going within fifty miles would have shown smoke out there in the landscape, but there was nothing.

Then I realized: the smell. It wasn't wood smoke. It was that Cuban cigar.

A quick look out the front window showed me that neither of the women on the porch was smoking. It was possible another member of the crew had lit up nearby, but something made me doubt that any of these women were cigar aficionados. I supposed it was possible, it just didn't seem that bloody likely. What was more likely was that Hector and his *compañeros* were somewhere nearby.

My hand wandered toward my chest. The phone was still there, pressed up against my breastbone. I could feel the warmth of the battery, so it would still be sending out a GPS signal. Hector must have had Benny track me here during the night. Hector would have Cigar and his crew along, easily outnumbering the three women holding me, but maybe the rest of Nalin's force was fanned out around the house.

Nalin stepped inside, and she and Mikela stood near the front door speaking to each other in low voices. Nalin said something through the screen to Salt-and-Pepper, who propped her rifle against the siding and stepped down off the porch to head for the van parked some ten yards away. After a few minutes, Nalin and Mikela came back over to my end of the room.

I had closed my eyes, forcing myself not to turn away from the memory of my mother's face, scrunched into that eviscerating sneer. The old words coming from her mouth—those were what I wanted. I selected the ones I needed, then opened my eyes.

"She's not one of you," I said to the tall woman, in Apache. At least, I hoped that's what I'd said. I'd never learned to speak it fluently, just picked up words and phrases here and there from my mother.

The two women glanced at each other, then Nalin looked at me. She took a breath, measuring me with her eyes, then replied in the same language, "Neither are you."

A flash of adrenaline shot through me. As I'd hoped—and maybe remembered—the two tribes still shared enough in common after all these centuries as neighbors to understand and speak each other's languages. Also, the puzzled look on Mikela's face told me that she didn't know that. If she was trying to hide her identity from Nalin, which was the bet I was rolling the dice on, making that apparent would sink her.

I took another shot at speaking Apache to Nalin: "Her face is not her face."

"What's she saying?" Mikela demanded.

Nalin turned her head, gazing carefully at Mikela, and I saw her realize that if Mikela was who she said she was, she should understand what I was saying. Mikela's already wary expression intensified, and she took a quick step back, leveling her AK at Nalin and me.

"Turn around," she said to her boss.

Nalin did it, without haste, her expressionless eyes sliding across me.

Through the window above the bed, I saw Salt-and-Pepper coming back from the van. Mikela saw her, too. She sidled up and grabbed the collar of Nalin's coat, planting the muzzle of her AK at the base of the tall woman's neck.

"One word, one sound . . ." she muttered.

Nalin's dark eyes glittered, and a smile touched her wide mouth. "You might take me down, but that won't get you out of here. You've been among us long enough to know that."

Mikela froze for a second, wheels turning, then unwound her

hand from Nalin's collar to reach quickly into her coat pocket. She brought out a set of keys, which she tossed onto the bed.

"You'll go out first," she said to me.

"No, thanks," I said.

She took two quick steps back, away from Nalin, so that her gun covered both of us again. "It's not a request."

I unlocked the cuffs and scrambled to my feet, glad to be at liberty again, but trying to figure out how not to get shot when I opened the front door.

Mikela gestured me over with her AK. Salt-and-Pepper was on the porch now, stretching and yawning next to her chair. Her rifle was still leaning against the house.

I put my hand on the screen door and pushed.

Then I was on the far side of the porch, looking at a widening pool of blood underneath Salt-and-Pepper's prone body, the echo of the shot that had killed her dying away.

I hadn't had any warning this time, as I did when I'd watched Benny and Page move Orson Greenlaw's body—no cooling of my limbs, no high, drifting feeling. I'd just disappeared like a light switch going off.

Mikela was standing to my right, her hand wrenched up in Nalin's collar again, her AK still pointed at Salt-and-Pepper. Both of them were staring at the body with wide eyes.

The fragrance of the cigar seemed stronger now. I don't know why Mikela and Nalin didn't smell it. Maybe they did. It's not like they were keeping me in the loop.

Mikela brought her AK back up to Nalin's neck and gestured at me to head for the van. I stepped down off the porch and began to walk toward the afternoon sun like a daytime ghost. It struck me that Nalin had to be fronting about us not being able to get out. That shot on the porch would have brought the rest of her gang running, if they'd been within earshot.

It also should have brought Hector out. What the hell was he waiting for? Once we started driving, we would be very difficult to follow. Plus, I had no idea where Mikela might take us. It might be somewhere with an even scarier crew than Nalin's bunch.

By the time we reached the van, the cigar odor had become so strong that it almost made me cough. Finally realizing that Hector must be waiting for me to create a diversion, I paused.

Mikela, a few steps behind me, snarled, "Don't even think about it."

I turned my head to look at her over my shoulder. She still had the end of the AK pressed against the base of Nalin's skull. If she pulled the trigger, it wouldn't be my brains painting the desert.

I turned the rest of my body, facing them. Mikela moved back, away from Nalin, who stayed where she was, holding completely still. The muzzle of the AK swung toward me.

I took a step toward Mikela. Her hand flinched at the trigger of her rifle, drawing my eye. I kept it there as I took another step.

It wasn't that I somehow knew she wouldn't shoot me; it was that I didn't care if she did. As my right hand moved out away from my body, toward the barrel of her AK, that truth hit me full force: I was ready to die. I wasn't afraid of it. That's what the weird thrill I kept feeling was. It was hope. My provocative talk to dangerous people, my rash behaviors, the suffocation that crushed me upon waking, maybe even this weird checking-out thing I kept doing. I didn't want to be here anymore.

Mikela did fire, but I had already started to pull the AK toward me, and the rattle of shots went past my right side. She lurched forward, following the gun, and I brought my left arm up, pointing the elbow at her face. She fell into it and separated from the rifle, her head snapping back. The rest of her did likewise. She tilted backwards and sat down hard on the sand, the wind grunting out of her.

I lifted the AK and stepped sideways so that I could get Nalin in my sights without taking my eye off Mikela. The tall woman wasn't there.

It was flat all around, but she was nowhere to be seen. Unless there was a hole in the ground nearby or someone had invented the transporter without my knowledge, disarming Mikela had taken longer than I thought.

"Hector!" I shouted out into the heat.

There was no answer. The smell of the Cuban cigar was overpowering.

"Hector!" I called again.

Nothing. No movement, no sound. The odor of the cigar suddenly disappeared. My heart was pounding.

I gestured at Mikela to get up and into the van. I climbed into the back so that I could keep her covered while she drove.

The going was slow, dodging rocks and plants, but at the end of an hour, the compound of shacks where Nalin had traded me for Finn appeared in the distance. It was sundown, starting to get dark, and smoke rose from between the buildings. I made Mikela park some distance away so that we wouldn't have to dodge gunfire. Then we got out and walked, me behind her with the AK.

As we neared the compound, Aguilito appeared. He'd been on lookout, concealed behind a section of wood fencing. He shaded his eyes in our direction, then called behind him. Hector and Cigar appeared, and when Hector realized it was me, he trotted out toward us.

"What the hell, man?" I said to him as he came within earshot. "Did you go deaf or something out there?"

He was on me, hugging me, muffling me with kisses, and these last words were smothered in his shoulder. He pulled back and said, "What?"

"I knew you were out there, I could smell that cigar," I said. "Why didn't you come in after that first shot?"

Hector glanced at Cigar, his face baffled. The gangster had taken the AK, to cover Mikela. He returned Hector's look in kind, with a shrug.

"Not sure what you mean," Hector said. "We've been here since daybreak. Fanned out and searched through the night but we couldn't find a trace. Aguelito drove Finn back to Sonoyta to get his plane early this morning, so we could search from the air. We've been doing it in shifts since then."

Annoyed, I fished the phone out of my bra and waved it at him.

"Yeah," he said. "I tried. Benny couldn't get a signal."

"Stop gaslighting me," I told him, a hot anger rising up into my throat. "It's not funny, and I don't like it."

Hector appealed to Cigar with a gesture.

"He's speaking the truth," Cigar said. "You can ask any of my people."

I remembered the scent of the Cuban suddenly disappearing, the lost minutes between being inside the house and seeing Salt-and-Pepper dead on the porch, Nalin vanishing into nowhere. I was apparently losing whatever grip on reality I had left.

"I need some rest," I murmured. My limbs felt hot and weak and my stomach was doing bad things.

"No problem," Hector said. "We need to lay low until dark, and it's gonna be too hot to do much of anything until then. We can take a siesta in the bunkhouse."

Cigar prodded Mikela with the AK, and we started toward the compound with the two of them in front. Hector kept hold of my hand, and I made myself focus on the warmth of his rough palm, the sensation of being pulled forward. If I thought about anything else, I'd be gone again.

At the compound, Cigar called out, and Grenade Launcher and Braids appeared from one of the shacks. Hector pulled me toward another.

It was cool inside, the windows, walls, and doorway hung with blankets to keep out the heat and light. There was a twin-size mattress on the plank floor, with a crate next to it serving as a side table. I dropped onto the mattress and stretched out, sighing at the sweet pleasure of finally being able to relax.

"I'll get everything set up and wake you when we're ready to head out," Hector said.

There was a soft scuffle at the door, and Cigar came in. Hector turned, and I rolled up onto one elbow.

"She won't be any trouble," he said, looking amused. "She's scared shitless."

"Of what?" I said.

"These women, the group she joined, they call themselves *Kokoi'uvï*—ghost women. They consider themselves dead already. They are greatly feared in these parts, for good reason."

My head started to feel cool and light as I remembered Nalin's sudden disappearance. I pulled Hector's hand over to my wrist and wrapped his fingers around it.

"They don't normally kill their own kind," Cigar went on, "but they are ruthless with traitors."

"What do you mean by 'their own kind'?" I said. "Women?"

"*Las mujeres Indias*—Native women. The *Kokoi* know all the old tribal torture shit, and they use it generously on traitors. Being captured is considered treason." Cigar lifted his chin toward the shack containing Mikela. "If they ever see her again, I would not like to be present."

Hector glanced at me, no doubt remembering what I'd told him about my grandmother's war stories.

Despite my exhaustion, Cigar's remarks were exercising the brain. "How long have they been around?"

"It's hard to say exactly, but they formed in response to these women being killed along the border in recent years," he said. "They extract the vengeance denied the families."

"The *feminicidios*," I sighed, falling back onto the bed. "Why does everything go in fucking circles?"

"I'd say 'wheel of life,' but I don't wanna get slapped," Hector cracked.

I laughed and lay there looking at the rough-hewn rafters, just breathing and trying not to think. It didn't work.

"The *Kokoi*, they only accept Native women?" I said to Cigar. He nodded.

"Well, that explains why Mikela stole Rachael's identity, but it doesn't explain why she wanted to join up with them in the first place."

"Didn't you tell me that her sister was killed by whoever's doing this *feminicidio* shit?" Hector said.

"That's right," I said, remembering. "That's the party line, anyway."

Hector made a "there you go" gesture.

Voices rose outside the shack. Cigar excused himself and left.

"You want me to tuck you in?" Hector said, sitting down near my feet.

"God damn it," I said, the maternal phrase reminding me. "I was supposed to meet Norma and my mother yesterday."

"Call her," Hector said. "That phone I gave you has already been spoiled."

I got it out of my pocket. "You're going to go broke replacing these things."

"They're cheap," he said.

I punched in Norma's number, then clicked "call." She answered right away.

"Sorry," I said.

"Where are you?"

"I could tell you, but then I'd have to kill you," I joked. "You guys didn't drive all the way down from Florence, did you?"

"Of course we did," Norma complained. "What happened?"

"Are you still on the O'odham?"

"Yeah, we stayed over. Your mom was too tired to drive all the way back."

Hector had gotten up and was doing something at the table on the other side of the shack.

"Just put her on the phone," I said.

Norma made a scoffing noise. "You know she won't."

I'd inherited my loathing of telephone communication from my mother, but thought maybe she'd gotten over it after all these years.

"Well, I dunno what to tell you," I said. "She'll just have to write me a letter or something."

Norma muffled the phone, and I could hear her talking to someone in the room with her.

"Where are you?" Norma said when she came back.

"Not that far away, actually, but I can't come back onto the rez."

"We'll come there."

I laughed at the idea of Norma and my mother trying to make polite conversation with our hosts. "Uh, no."

"Well, somewhere in between, then," Norma replied, sounding irritated.

I sighed, watching Hector raise a cracked blue mug to his lips on the other side of the room. "It's just not a good time, Norma."

"You promised," she said. "I did what you asked me, and it wasn't easy."

The chances of me being anywhere within driving distance of my mother again—ever—were slim, especially after I pulled the trigger on my Mexican retirement. I'd probably never get another chance to see her in person, and if I knew Norma, she'd find a way to make my life a living hell until I held up my end of the deal.

"Let me call you back in a minute," I said. I hung up and asked Hector, "What's halfway between here and the reservation that's not on it? That I can get to?"

He thought a minute, then put his cup down and said, "Let's go ask."

I got up and followed him through the blanket covering the door. Finn was sitting at the fire with Cigar and the rest. They'd found him some clothes, but he looked like hell. Hector took the stump next to Cigar and asked him my question.

"Sasabe," Cigar said. "It's on the border, right outside the wildlife refuge. They got a nice little church."

"How long does it take to get there?" I asked him.

"It's about three hours, if you drive," he said. "The country gets rougher up that way."

I groaned. "Man, am I ever going to sleep again?"

Finn, who was sitting in one of the folding chairs, said, "I'll fly you."

I let out a dry chuckle. "You can't even walk."

"I got the plane back here," he reminded me. "I don't need to walk to fly."

"You should write inspirational posters," I told him.

"Sasabe straddles the border," Hector said. "Which side is the church on?"

"Mexican," Cigar said.

Hector turned to me. "I'll slap Finn if he passes out. Let's go."

CHAPTER 32

———— ◆ ————

The church in Sasabe did have some nice qualities, namely that it was a clean, simple adobe building with three plain arched windows on each side. A bell tower clung to the north corner, but didn't look like it had rung since Coronado came through.

The surrounding town—population fifty-four, according to the sign—was dead quiet and appeared to be completely deserted except for a couple of dogs and a horse penned in the field next to the church. Finn had stayed with the plane, so it was just me and Hector in the battered truck that had been waiting for us after we landed on the road a couple of miles away. The only sound I could hear was the quiet shrilling of grass crickets. It was just past noon and hotter than East Jesus.

Hector stretched, looking around. "Bet the real estate is cheap here."

"Hm," I said.

He looked at me. "This is one of the quieter spots on the border. Pretty safe, and easily accessible to the States. I think they got one guy at the crossing, and he probably won't even look twice at Norma and your mom."

"Down, boy," I said.

He grinned, his high cheeks crinkling up under his eyes. "Yeah, because you moving to Mexico was my idea."

"I gotta live somewhere."

"Mike's gonna be pissed."

"Not my problem," I said.

"Seriously, Julia," he said, coming over to lean on the truck. "Living in Mexico isn't like being on vacation in Mexico. You should give it some serious thought before you start packing. Don't come down here just because I'm here."

"It's almost like you don't want me in the neighborhood."

"It's just not going to be some kind of domestic bliss situation, that's all I'm saying. I'm on the move all the time, gone for days, sometimes weeks. I get shot at, hounded by *los perreros verdes* like it's their hobby. And I don't always shower on a regular basis."

"Do I look like a soccer mom to you?" I said.

A car was coming; we could see the dust. Hector opened the truck and got out the denim jacket he'd been wearing over his T-shirt when we left the encampment.

He saw my look and said, "Gotta make a good first impression."

His concern about my mother's opinion was endearing. I almost forgave him for trying to talk me out of moving.

Norma's car was a classic rez pony, a nameless Mopar of some sort, covered with rust spots and dents but purring like a race car under the hood and showing plenty of tread on the tires. Down here, where everything was hundreds of miles apart, you didn't care what your ride looked like. It just had to get you there.

A weird excitement grabbed me as I watched the tiny woman on the passenger side get out. I hadn't seen her since my wedding;

fifteen years ago, but she hadn't changed much. She approached us with her characteristically slow, measured pace, her eyes half averted, as if she were simply taking a walk and hadn't yet noticed the people in her path. She maintained this nonchalance until she was standing directly in front of me, at which point she finally raised her eyes to my face.

I'd forgotten how small she was, and she'd shrunk a little with age, so that the top of her head now only reached about earlobe height on me. At five-two on a good day, I could count on the fingers of one hand the number of people I knew who had to look up to me. There was some gray in her dark hair that wasn't there the last time I'd seen her, but her eyes were still like live coals in her expressionless face, full of appetite and uncertainty.

"Thank you for seeing me," she said.

Her voice was quieter than I remembered; certainly the manner in which she used it was unusual.

Norma had gone to see if the church was unlocked, which it was, and called over to us, "Let's go inside. It's hot out here."

My mother had shifted her gaze to Hector, so I said, "Hector Guerra, Nascha Tafoya."

Hector put his hand out, and my mother examined it for a brief second before extending her own. Hector shook it, doing a poor job of hiding his curiosity. I watched my mother read him like a book and produce a small, closed-mouth smile. From her, that was equivalent to a bear hug, and it stung. She liked him better than she liked me.

It was much cooler inside the church, which was just as clean and plain on the inside as on the outside. Simple cedar pews, a tan clay-tile floor, and a table at the far end with a plain wooden cross perched on it. Everybody but me genuflected automatically, then my mother and I sat down side by side in the rear pew. Norma tugged on Hector's sleeve, and the two of them went up front and sat down with their backs to us.

My mother pressed her hands together. I was surprised to remember how small they were. She'd always seemed larger than life to me.

"I don't really know how to start," she said, laughing quietly. She seemed slightly nervous, which surprised me. I'd seen my mother do a lot of things, but show her nerves was not one of them.

"It's been a long time," I allowed, keeping my voice low. Hector and Norma were chatting quietly and far enough away that unless things went seriously wrong, they probably wouldn't hear us.

"You look so much like your father," she told me, gazing toward the makeshift altar.

My neck muscles tightened. "That's probably not your best opening salvo."

"I can start there," she said, suddenly sure. "Your father."

Of course she could. She'd start where the blood showed, where the weakness was, where I didn't want her to. She always had. I was suddenly glad we weren't sitting face-to-face.

"Those Finns," she said, chuckling. "They can drink. I can't. Couldn't, really, even back then." She tapped the side of her head. "The genes, you know. We don't process alcohol like the white people."

She was looking at the altar, her black eyes narrow. "He was so blond. I'd never seen anything like him."

"You never told me how he ended up in Florence."

"I never knew," she said, lifting her shoulders. "I was just out at a bar with some people and there he was."

"And so you got pregnant," I prompted, hoping to cut her off at the pass. The last thing I wanted to hear from her was some tale of youthful romance.

My mother turned her head and looked at me with those black eyes of hers, thoughtful.

"And so I got pregnant." Her eyes went back to the altar. "He never knew."

"Why's that?"

"He was gone before I was sure," she said. "And it wasn't like we were dating or anything. We didn't exchange phone numbers and addresses."

Anger began to creep up my neck. "A wild weekend."

"Yes, something like that."

Her expression was still thoughtful, which surprised me. Remarks like the one I'd just made usually sent her into a fury. I don't know why I hadn't learned to stop making them. "Do you have problems with addictions?" she asked me suddenly.

"Me? No."

"Ah. Thank God."

This calm, rational woman next to me was bearing less and less resemblance to the person I'd grown up with. I was becoming disoriented.

"Is that what you wanted to say you were sorry for?" I asked her. "That you got pregnant with me by accident?"

"I'm not sorry I got pregnant with you," she said. "I regret some of the things I did after you were born."

"You mean the drinking and whoring around?"

My mother took a deep breath, but she kept her eyes on the altar and didn't react. "Yes. The drinking and whoring around. And some other things, things you may not remember."

"If I don't remember them, what's the point of apologizing?"

"It's for my own sanity," she explained. "We make amends so that we can stay sober."

"Oh, so this is all about you," I said. "How unusual."

Anger finally flashed up into her face, but she didn't say anything, just closed her eyes and took a deep breath.

"I was very self-centered," she said. "Alcoholism does that. I was diseased, and you suffered for it. I regret that every minute of the day."

I started to reply, but she kept talking. "The things you don't remember, the things that I worry about the most—"

Her voice caught, and she stopped. I've never seen my mother scared, and for a minute I didn't realize that's what was wrong.

She closed her eyes again for a few seconds, then shifted on the pew, turning so that she could look directly at me, and said, "I tried to kill you."

"You—" I started, then stopped. My brain wouldn't take it in. My hands and feet started to tingle and feel cool.

"We were up at the lake," she said. "Me and my brothers—your uncles Nitis and Taza. It was a bad day for me, too much drinking. You were just a baby. You kept crying. I didn't know what to do with you. I was on the dock with Taza and my head was hurting. He said you were scaring the fish. So I threw you in."

I wanted to get up and leave but I couldn't make my body do it. I just sat there staring at her, only half hearing her now.

"Taza jumped in after you and got you out," my mother said. Her voice was its usual calm, measured weapon, telling the story plainly, without any drama. "He took you home and they kept you for a little while, until I sobered up."

I'd found my voice again, although my limbs were still threatening to check out. "How old was I?"

"I don't remember," she said. "Young. Less than a year old. You weren't walking."

That smothering morning sensation, like coming up out of water that was trying to drown me. Could it be this simple? Just an old memory?

"Why did Uncle Taza and Aunt Retta give me back?" I asked.

"They didn't, really," she said. "Maybe you don't remember."

"No, I do. I was always at their place. But I never thought it was home. Are you saying that they adopted me or something?"

"No," she said, looking away again now. "Not formally. You just stayed there when I was drinking bad—which was often— after."

"After you threw me in the lake, you mean?"

She nodded slowly.

"I don't know how to make amends for something like that," she said. "I don't even know if it's possible."

I didn't know, either, and it was taking all my energy not to disappear, so I kept quiet. Focusing on the back of Hector's head seemed to help.

We sat there for a while in the cool, dark church, listening to the silence, then my mother said, "Joachin and Norma ask about you all the time."

I nodded, glad to be moving on. "Norma says she's got a couple of kids now."

"Yes, two. Well, two left. They lost a little girl a few years ago. Lucia."

I looked up toward Norma and Hector again, surprised. "She didn't tell me. What happened?"

"She went missing down here while she was visiting her

father." My mother made a contemptuous noise. "Not surprising. He's no good. I'm sure he just let her run wild while he drank."

The words dropped between us like hot rocks. Realizing what she'd just said, my mother bowed her head, taking another deep breath.

I changed the subject. "What's Joachin up to these days?"

"The same," she said. Which meant he was still running around with criminal elements, probably blowing shit up. Or in jail. One of the two.

I didn't have any more questions, and my mother seemed to be finished talking, so I stood up. Hector and Norma, hearing me, came over and rejoined us. Norma helped my mother out of her seat, and we all proceeded silently back out into the heat.

"I'm sorry to hear about your daughter," I said to Norma after she'd gotten my mother into her car and it was just the two of us and Hector.

She shot a look at him and said, "Nothing to be sorry about. We know who took her. We just can't prove it."

"Took her?" I repeated, surprised.

Norma's eyes shifted toward the car where my mother sat looking out the window, away from us. "Some people would rather believe she's dead. I can understand that. It's easier." Norma touched her chest. "I know better. I can feel her still breathing out there somewhere."

"How old was—is—she?"

"Seven when she left," Norma said. "That would make her almost ten now."

I didn't tell Norma that if Lucia really were still alive, there had to be a reason she hadn't returned home. Norma probably knew that, under her hope. She didn't need me saying it out loud.

"So I know you can't really call me or anything," she said, veering away from the doubtlessly painful subject of her daughter, "but ya know, if there's some way to keep in touch, I wish you would."

That was as close to "I miss you" as any Indian would ever get, and I was glad. I'm no good at that stuff.

She gave me a quick hug before I could stop her, jumped into her car, and drove off.

CHAPTER 33

It was late afternoon when we got back to the encampment. Aguilito came out to greet us from his watch spot again and told us that most of the group had gone on "an errand," but that Ruben—the one I'd been calling Grenade Launcher in my head—was keeping Mikela on ice. Finn gave Aguilito's head a friendly rub as we passed through the gate.

The fire was still going, and Ruben was sitting next to the open doorway of one of the shacks, playing with his phone. He raised his chin at us, and Hector said, "Anything in the kitchen?"

"Yeah," Ruben replied, not looking up. "Help yourself."

I hadn't even thought about food since our dinner at the reservation cafe the night before. It seemed like a year ago.

Hector went into one of the shacks and came back after a couple of minutes with some bread, dried meat, water, and various hot-weather condiments. It wasn't cordon bleu fare, but it would get the job done.

Hector put a pan of water on the fire and handed me a mug. There was a tea bag in it.

"Score!" I breathed.

"I'm gonna go lie down for a bit," Finn said.

Hector nodded. "Good test run. You handled her OK. Didn't have to slap you once."

"I told you," Finn replied, looking at me. "Next time try and remember that I used to be a badass."

"If there's a next time, my opinion of you will be the least of your worries," I assured him.

Finn snorted a short laugh and gave Hector's shoulder a soft slap on his way to the bunkhouse.

The two of us noshed in companionable silence while the sky took on the juicy blue of sundown and the temperature dropped. After I finished eating, I put my jacket back on and stretched out on a folding chaise longue to drink my tea and watch the night come in.

When I woke up, the fire had burned down to coals and there was a thick, wool blanket over me. Hector was on watch, slouched in one of the lawn chairs with the Benelli resting across his knees.

"What time is it?" I asked him, sitting up.

"Just now five," he said.

"How's the prisoner?"

"Asleep," he said. "I just checked."

I pushed the blanket off and swung my feet to the ground. "Let's get a move on. I'm ready to be done with this mess."

He nodded and got out of the chair, stretching and yawning, and went to roust the troops. Cigar, Braids, and Ruben appeared about fifteen minutes later, and, shortly afterward, Finn. The sleep had done him good. He was standing up straight now, and except for the bruises and cuts on his face he looked almost normal.

"Ready when you are," he said to me and Hector.

"We're going to need at least one additional gun," I told

Hector. "She tried to kill an armed man last time, and Finn's going to be busy keeping us in the air."

He shook his head. "You know I can't risk it."

Ruben leaned forward. "I'll go."

Hector and Cigar looked at me.

"OK," I nodded. "Thanks."

Ruben went to fetch Mikela from the shack, and Hector and I took a short walk away from the fire to say our good-byes.

He pulled my arms around his waist and set his chin on top of my head. "Give me some warning next time, will you?"

"How am I supposed to do that?" I said, disengaging so I could look at him. "Send up a flare?"

"You can leave a message with the hot springs," he said. "They always know how to get hold of me."

We stood there listening to each other breathe for a while, then Hector said, "I wonder why the *Kokoi* were so hard on Finn."

"Their whole thing is avenging crimes against women. I'm guessing they've probably got their own 'most wanted' database."

"But he was just an accessory, and it was a long time ago," Hector reminded me. "If they're gonna go after every man who's ever been downwind of a crime where a woman's involved, they'd have to take out half the population."

I remembered Mikela's remarks at the desert house. "I don't think that would be an ideological problem for them."

"It's a waste of manpower," Hector insisted. "Or woman-power, in their case. I mean, with all the shit that goes down around here, if they didn't prioritize what they put their people at risk for, their whole organization would go extinct right quick."

"Maybe it was just luck of the draw," I suggested. "One of

them saw Finn somewhere and recognized him, so they nabbed him because they could."

"He was a hundred miles away. These broads are local."

"Maybe he didn't go straight there," I suggested. "He stopped somewhere for a snack or something."

"There ain't a 7-Eleven on every corner, around here. He'd have had to go all—"

"Jesus," I cut in, growing impatient. "You're worse than me."

That made him grin. "Nobody's worse than you."

I gave him a playful slap, which started an ersatz wrestling match that ended the way it usually does. We got it out of our systems and then headed back to the encampment.

Mikela was in one of the folding chairs, cuffed at the wrists and ankles with a hood over her head, but I still didn't trust her. I got my Glock out and took the safety off, and Ruben picked up his AK. He shook hands with Cigar and Hector, then pulled Mikela up, and we headed out between the shacks. I kept everybody in front of me.

The Suburban was waiting, with Aguilito at the wheel. Ruben got Mikela in, then Finn followed. I got into the seat in back, and we pulled away.

CHAPTER 34

It took about half an hour to get to the road where Finn's plane was parked, and the takeoff was as rough as our landing had been. Once we were airborne and stabilized, I took Mikela's hood off. Ruben was sitting several feet away from us, toward the rear of the plane, well out of range if she tried anything.

"So. Let's hear it," I said.

She glanced at Ruben. "Hear what?"

"Oh, right, sorry," I said, miming contrition. "Let me just fill you in on what I know, so we don't have to do this answering questions with questions shit." I set my Glock on the bench seat next to me and got comfortable. "You're Mikela Floyd. You and your sister Jennifer are wanted by the FBI for killing a cop in El Paso last year, and some other stuff. Classified. Federal."

Ruben stopped playing with his phone and raised his eyes. Finn's head turned. I hadn't realized that he could hear us over the plane noise, but it didn't matter. Having him listen in might induce Mikela to tell more of the truth.

"I'm guessing that's what sent you to Darling," I continued. "You wanted a new face. I'm not sure why you waited so long, but it worked out in your favor. If you'd done it earlier, you'd have missed the opportunity to become Rachael Pestozo."

Mikela's hard stare dropped and she let herself fall back against the fuselage behind her. She sat with her eyes closed for a while, then raised her head and asked for a cigarette.

Ruben reached into his jacket, and I went back to take his place while he got her lit up. It was tricky, with her wrists cuffed, and she hung one hand from her opposite shoulder so that she wouldn't have to keep lifting both while she smoked.

Ruben and I returned to our original places. She hadn't answered my question, so I didn't bother asking her anything factual this time. I just said, "Why didn't you pull the trigger?"

She'd returned to gazing into nothingness with her first drag off the cigarette, but now she focused back on me. "What?"

"Out there," I said.

Her eyes went away again. "I remembered who I was."

That wasn't the answer I'd been expecting; in fact, I hadn't been expecting an answer at all, and its correspondence to the things I'd been hearing and thinking about myself lately gave me a little chill.

"What made you forget it in the first place?"

Mikela gave a short, wry laugh. "Well, I *was* pretending to be someone else."

The little chill dropped a few degrees. Could all my recent psychic weirdness be due to my change in identity? The WIT-SEC shrinks had given me some lectures about people who went nuts after leaving their homes and families, but I'd never felt that connected to California, and Joe and I hadn't had any kids. He was the only person I really missed, and he was dead, so I was going to miss him wherever I lived. I did think about Pete, Joe's dad, from time to time, but the rest of the family had been involved in their own ventures and never came around enough for me to really get to know them.

In fact, in a lot of ways, leaving California had been kind of a relief. I wasn't reminded of Joe every time I went to the grocery store or paid the phone bill. Being married to the mob also meant I'd learned not to talk about things to other people, so I didn't have chats with my girlfriends to miss, because I'd never had them to begin with. The girlfriends or the chats.

"No, I forgot way before that," Mikela said. She paused to think, then added, "It was after Jenny found out about this fence thing."

I didn't want to push her so I didn't say anything, just looked at her with mild curiosity. Oddly enough, she seemed to want to talk about it.

"My sister was something," she said, in a slow, thoughtful voice. "Not like me. Really something. Genius IQ, special classes in high school, but she never wanted to do the whole child prodigy thing." Mikela chuckled. "Too boring, she said. So she ran off and joined the circus—the actual circus—at sixteen, then the pipe-fitter's union up north to learn how to weld." Mikela paused to take a drag off the cigarette. "That's what got her into the service, that certification."

"The service?" I said.

"The army," Mikela replied. "She went in as a warrant officer, repairing Humvees that didn't get blown completely to pieces in Kandahar."

"Ouch."

"Yeah," Mikela said, twisting her mouth. "Talk about a waste of talent. She liked it, though. It was exciting. When she came back, the NSA offered her a job translating radio transmissions. She spoke, like, five languages. That's where she found out that there are people who say they want the border fence who don't really want it, and vice versa."

"Surely that's not a state secret."

"I don't mean people like you and me," she said. "I mean in the government."

"Dishonest politicans," I marveled. "Who'd have believed that such a thing existed?"

She cut her eyes at me, exasperated. "No, moron. I'm talking about the people who are buying those politicians. The real power behind the throne. The lobbyists, the people with the money."

Now the radar was kicking in. "Are you saying that your sister got crossways with some of these people?"

"You had to know her," Mikela said. "It wasn't just crossways. She was organizing, and it was working."

"I'm guessing that's where the demonstration that resulted in this dead cop comes in."

Mikela nodded, looking pensive. I thought she might try to justify frying the bacon, but she just took another drag off her cigarette and went on with her story.

"Jenny and I split up after that, figuring it would make us more difficult to track down. Then I saw an article in the paper about a white girl being killed near Juarez." Mikela cleared her throat, tapping ash onto the steel-plate floor. "Mexican papers aren't as ticklish about publishing gory pictures as papers in the States."

"So it's not just a rumor that she's dead?"

Mikela started to shake her head, then said, "Well, to the rest of the world it probably is. I couldn't go and identify her without risking my own neck, but they didn't even *try* to find out who she was or what had happened to her. She was just, like, roadkill or something."

I felt the unholiness of it, imagining what it would have been like for Joe to have been treated that way. There's something horrible about anonymous death, even to me.

Mikela looked like she was ruminating over something. I didn't want to interrupt that process, so I kept quiet, and after a minute she started to talk again.

"Not knowing what had happened to Jenny, I started worrying I was next. I'd already been talking to Darling about a job, but he wanted to pay me shit—not enough to take the risk of working for him. After I saw Jenny in the paper, I went back to him with a deal: if he'd give me a new face, I'd work for him for free for as long as I could evade the cops. I'd volunteered at the low-income clinic back home, so I had experience and stuff. I guess that—plus the fact I was wanted, and unlikely to turn him in for anything—made me worth it to him."

"But Rachael didn't show up until six months later," I said. "Why'd you wait, to get your new face?"

"Hang on," she said, lifting the hand she'd hung from her opposite shoulder. "If you're going to make me tell it, at least let me tell it my way."

I sighed and sat back, pressing my lips together.

"So Darling hires me," Mikela said, "but then he keeps stalling. First he says he can't afford for me to be laid up for a couple of weeks, and then he says what if he does the surgery and I run off before he's gotten his money's worth out of me. Then it's something else . . ." Mikela blew an annoyed breath out through her nose.

"What changed his mind?"

"Rachael did."

I raised my eyebrows, and she shifted on the bench, leaning forward. "During her intake interview, she talked about going back to Arizona and joining up with this Native women's militia group. They hunt down people who've committed crimes against women but escaped prosecution."

"And they don't take white women," I said.

"Right," Mikela replied, looking surprised for a minute. "You have to be Native, which Rachael told me isn't just a matter of showing up with a DNA certificate. You have to be known by someone who knows someone."

Just like I'd told Hector. You had to have been raised in it. It didn't matter how much blood you could prove. It mattered who you knew and who you grew up with, which ceremonies and prayers you could recite from memory, the traditions you observed and believed in.

"I was totally down to join up with these women, considering what happened to Jenny," Mikela continued. "So I tell Darling, just turn me into Rachael. I'll take her ID and stuff and go to Arizona, and neither you nor the El Paso cops need ever see me again."

"He went for that?" I said, surprised.

Mikela pressed her lips together, looking away. "She'd brought a bunch of cash with her."

"Ah," I said. "Which he adopted off the books after she died I'm guessing."

"I took what was left over." Mikela said. "It wasn't like she was going to use it."

"Well, that'll sure work for motive," I said, half to myself.

Mikela's eyes jumped to my face. "I didn't kill her! Jesus, what kind of sense would that make, killing one woman to avenge another?"

"I guess the chick you shot out in the desert doesn't count."

She flinched, closing her eyes, and took a couple of breaths before replying, "Rachael died after surgery, on her own. Darling said it was a blood clot."

"There are drugs you can give people that will cause blood clots," I said, remembering the discussions with Maines's doctor. "I'm sure Darling is aware of that, and crooked as he is, I doubt he'd hesitate to use them, for a price."

"Well, if he did, it wasn't at my direction," Mikela said. She dropped her cigarette butt on the floor and mashed it out with the toe of her boot.

"He wouldn't let us take DNA from the body." I let her figure out what that implied.

"Look," Mikela said, "I didn't come up with the idea to pose as Rachael until after she died, so there was no motive to kill her."

"I'm sure the jury will take the word of two criminals for that," I agreed amicably.

Another item shot across my brain. "That's why you dug the bullets out of Orson, isn't it? So they couldn't be compared to the ones from that cop you shot."

"Orson?" Mikela balked. "Rachael's ex?"

She didn't need a yes so I didn't waste one. She read my face and leaned her head back, closing her eyes. "This can't be happening," she murmured.

"What about him?" I said, tilting my head toward Finn. He gave us another look over his shoulder.

Mikela shrugged. "Nalin and a couple of the other girls got him. I don't know where or why. Then after I told her about you, she decided to do the trade."

"Why? I'm not worth anything to the *Kokoi*."

"I couldn't have you running around loose not knowing what you knew about me," she said, "so I told Nalin that you were a collaborator. A couple of her women had gotten picked up by the cops a few weeks ago. I said that you'd turned them in."

I took a couple of breaths, thanking my lucky stars that I'd busted out when I did.

"Y'all buckle in," Finn advised over his shoulder. "We're fixing to hit some weather."

It was a rough ride the rest of the way back to Azula, so I didn't have a chance to do any more work on Mikela, but I was satisfied. I'd gotten her. Benny could do the rest.

CHAPTER 35

Finn had the air controllers call Benny before we landed, so that he could meet us and take custody of Mikela. The airport was a single-runway setup just south of Azula, and I could see Benny's cruiser parked in the nearly empty lot next to the hangar as we came in. He watched us land and then trotted out to meet the plane as it taxied over. I felt like I'd been gone for a million years.

The air that gusted in as I slid the side door open smelled of something burning off in the distance, and the temperature made the actual distance questionable. Ruben stood up and held his AK on Mikela while I grabbed her arm and guided her out onto the tarmac.

"Wow," Benny said as she stepped down. "She'd have got by me." He stepped around to her side, examining her like some kind of museum piece. "That's good work."

"Fuck off," Mikela told him.

"And an attitude, too," Benny tsked.

Finn had finished his flight check-in and turned in the pilot's seat to watch us. Ruben eyed Benny impassively from the side door. He didn't try to hide his AK.

"*Gracias,*" Benny said to him, shaking hands. "Don't take this personal, but don't hang around, OK?"

"We're going to head straight back," Finn said.

Benny gave him a salute, and Ruben slid the side door shut. Benny, Mikela, and I walked to the edge of the runway and watched them take off. Finn waved from the pilot's window.

"Maines is asking to see you," Benny told me as we headed for the parking lot.

"Right now? I haven't bathed, slept, or eaten anything remotely nutritious for the last three days."

"I'm sure tomorrow will be fine." He got Mikela into the back of the cruiser and then said, "Come on, I'll drop you home."

It was Wednesday, our closed night at the bar, and the square was deserted except for my truck, parked in front, and the ever-present assortment of cop cars on the other side of the courthouse. Benny pulled over to let me out at the curb. Mikela had been still and silent for the drive, and I glanced into the backseat as I opened the car door, to make sure she was still with us.

"I'll come over in the morning to fill you in before I go see Maines," I told Benny.

We hadn't said anything about the case on the drive, and he nodded. "I'm not going to try and get anything out of her tonight. I'm expecting the doc's full report on Orson Greenlaw tomorrow. That'll tell me where I need to start."

"You haven't done anything on him yet?" I said.

He shook his head. "Been waiting on Liz, and this one." He pointed his thumb at the backseat.

I got the feeling there was something he wasn't telling me, but I'd had it ever since I'd met him. He's a cop. It comes with the territory. I found my keys and got out.

As I walked through the dark bar, I got a ghostly whiff of Cuban cigar smoke again, and my blood went cold. Now what? I paused at the foot of the stairs, and the odor quickly dissipated.

There was food in Luigi's bowl when I got upstairs, probably courtesy of Mike, and the cat was lounging in his favorite spot in the exact center of the dining table. He opened his eyes a slit to watch me drop my duffel bag on the floor and come over to the table. When I sat down, he lifted his head and looked at me.

"Speak," I said. He'd done it before. If he did it again, I'd just go back downstairs and drive myself straight to the loony bin.

The cat gave me the feline version of a puzzled frown for a few seconds, then put his head back down on his paws. So I hadn't completely lost it. Not yet.

I took a shower and made some tea, then booted up the computer to look up Liz Harman's contact information. I knew she wouldn't be in the office at this hour, but I called to leave a message with her service, asking her to give me a referral to her head-shrinking colleague. It wouldn't be fun, but neither was not knowing if or when I could trust reality.

That night I dreamed about the devil smoking a Cuban cigar in the Mexican desert. I went out after him and discovered that he was me. I woke up tangled in sheets humid with sweat, and realized—because it was back—that the morning sensation of struggling up from under something heavy had been absent while I'd been out in the desert. I tried to remember if it had gone away before or after I'd seen my mother, but couldn't. All of it seemed so long ago.

Another shower was required to rinse off the night's

exertions, then I got dressed and walked across the square to the police station. The concrete on the sidewalk looked funny, the light poles foreign, the way those things do when you go someplace you've never been. I wasn't sure if it was because my brain was disintegrating, or because so much had happened while I'd been away.

Benny was in his office at the back of the low stone courthouse basement, the cast-iron pipes gurgling overhead as always. He had a folder open on the big oak desk in front of him and was looking at it like he'd just bet the farm on what it contained, and lost.

"Is that Liz's report?" I asked, pulling over the wood side chair. The noise it made sliding over the concrete floor caught my ear. Unfamiliar but remembered.

Benny nodded, pinching his lower lip. He did a little more reading, then closed the folder and creaked back in his chair. "Liz narrowed Orson's time of death down to roughly four months ago, so he croaked around February 15."

"OK," I said, waiting for him to tell me why that was making him look like he'd just seen a bad movie.

He closed the folder. "I was kind of hoping Rachael had killed him, just for simplicity's sake."

"You don't like Mikela Floyd for it?"

Benny pressed his fingertips into his eye sockets, then ran his hands down his cheeks, looking tired. "I just don't want to have to try and prove it."

He sat there for a minute, looking at the rough plaster ceiling, then sat up and went on. "If we buy her story, Mikela had no motive to kill Orson in February. The May Day protest hadn't happened yet, so the sisters were still ostensibly law-abiding citizens at that point. But this thing with Jennifer finding out something about the border-fence legislation—that happened before May. There could be a motive in there that's related to this job in D.C. that Orson took."

"What was the job?"

"Don't know yet, I've got a guy working on that now."

Benny looked at me for a minute longer, then said, "Maines wants you to run this case."

My chest contracted. A smart remark rose up into my mouth, but I swallowed it.

"I don't think it's a bad idea," Benny went on. "At this point, you and him know the salient details way better than me, and I don't have to pay either one of you."

I gave him the look that deserved. He got up and shut the door to his office. When he was back in his chair, he leaned forward and said earnestly, "Look, I know what I've got out there: high-school graduates who'd be working at Whataburger if they hadn't watched too many cop shows when they were younger. Nothing wrong with that, they're good kids, but none of them is a Merit scholar. Forget detective grade."

I continued to gaze at him with undisguised skepticism.

"You know how many murders we had on my beat before you arrived last fall?" he asked me, sitting back. He held up a zero sign. "We're not equipped to deal with stuff like this unless it's really simple—and I mean smoking-gun simple. Well, hell, you should know," he said. "We had our heads up our asses on your case last year, the whole time."

I liked him for admitting it, but I'd have liked him better if he'd done it nine months earlier.

"That ain't pretty," he went on, "but it's the truth. When

Maines got his PI license, I saw a light at the end of that tunnel. Well, now that light has gone out."

I caught his eye across the desk. There was some pain there, which surprised me. Benny and Maines had always seemed like two tomcats fighting over the same territory. I didn't figure there was much love lost between them.

"So, anyway—" He held a flattened hand out toward me.

"I'm glad you guys have my future all planned," I said, "but as soon as you get what you need from me to put Mikela Floyd behind bars, I'm out of here."

Benny looked at me for a while, then lifted his shoulders and got up. He went to the office door, opened it, and called out into the squad room, "Hey, Stella?"

The young Latina who usually occupied the dispatch desk appeared in his office doorway.

"Set up the interview room, will you?" he said. "I want to go ahead and get Julia's statement."

She nodded and disappeared.

"I'll talk to Mikela after I'm done with you," Benny said. "That way I'll have a better idea of how much bullshit she's trying to feed me."

I was still trying to process my unexpected promotion from bad guy to good guy. I wished I knew what it was that Maines and Benny saw in me. I certainly didn't see it.

"When do I get my gun back?" I said.

"After you get a legal-carry permit."

"You seem to forget that I was in WITSEC for a couple of minutes," I said, "which makes me worry about your memory. I'm not allowed to carry a gun."

"Sure you are," Benny said. "You're just a plain old American citizen now."

"Not according to my record," I said, remembering the Presidio cop looking me up in her database.

"Yeah, it'll show in the secure history, but there's no endorsements on it now. Your record was wiped clean by your deal with the feds, so you're free to do anything any other normal noncriminal person can do." He gave me a look. "That's not an invitation."

Stella poked her head into the doorway. "Ready for you, Chief."

We got up and went into the interview room, which was just outside Benny's office, tucked into the northeast corner of the basement. It was low-tech all the way: no windows, a couple of plastic chairs, and a folding table with a reel-to-reel tape recorder on it. Benny turned this on and gave the date, time, and our names. Then he hitched up his gun belt and sat down.

"Just go ahead and tell it from the beginning," he said. "I'll ask questions if I need to."

I got all the way up to Nalin's capture of Finn before he had one: "Why'd these *Kokoi* broads grab the monk? He doesn't seem like a valuable enough target to drag a hundred miles."

"Hector said the same thing," I replied. "I don't know the answer, either, and I'm kind of getting tired of the question. Why does it matter?"

"I dunno," Benny said, pulling at his lower lip. "But the fact that Hector picked up on it too makes me want to look at it a little more closely. Hold that thought."

He got up and turned off the recorder, stepped out, and came back in with a laptop computer.

"Finn what?" he asked me while it booted up.

"That's a nickname," I said. "I don't know his real one. Hector didn't, either."

Benny made a face. "Well, gimme what you got."

I relayed what Finn had told me about his record, his involvement in the death of the Mexican woman, and the approximate dates. Benny tapped as I talked, hit "enter," and grimaced. "Thirteen hundred hits and change."

"Wow, that's a lot of dead broads," I murmured.

Benny nodded, pressing his lips together.

"He must have a pilot's license," I suggested. "And if you can narrow by current residence location, he's been at the hot springs long enough to have formed some sort of working relationship with Hector."

Benny put that into the search filter, which reduced the field to sixteen. He turned the screen toward me, changed the list to include mug shots, and started scrolling.

Finn was the seventh one down. Real name: Travis Morse. He looked completely different with hair, but those wide owl eyes were unmistakable. Benny clicked on Finn's file and turned the laptop back toward himself, but I'd seen a disturbing factoid before he did so.

"Does that say the victim was nine years old?"

Benny was tapping and clicking, but he flicked an affirmative glance my way. My stomach turned over.

"Hmm, El Paso," Benny said, after a minute. "The Floyd girls' hometown. That's kind of interesting."

He finished reading, then took a deep breath and said, "This fucker is a pedophile, all the way down. A groomer for the trade—procures and traffics, but he's never been convicted of contact."

"He must have good lawyers," I said.

Benny shifted his mouth to one side and shrugged. "Meh,

some of these guys, they don't need to actually touch the kids. They get off on being providers for other 'philes. Some of 'em are voyeurs; some stick to the hands-off thing so they can tell themselves they're not really doing anything wrong."

I felt a little nauseous. Also slightly terrified. My radar had settled somewhere between "OK" and "slightly weird but not dangerous" regarding Finn. I've been wrong about people before, but never that wrong. I started to wonder if the dissociative episodes I'd been having were affecting my radar, which did nothing to settle my stomach. I couldn't imagine navigating reality without my secret weapon. I'd relied on it for so long that life without it would be like starting over from day one.

"She was working in a whorehouse down there," Benny was saying, shaking his head. His deep eyes under their heavy brows had lost their sleepy look.

The remark brought me back into the room. "As a prostitute? The nine-year-old?"

He nodded.

I swallowed my nausea and asked, "Was she one of Finn's— 'products'?"

"Hard to say. It ain't like these *pendejos* keep records. They're opportunists—they just grab the most easily accessible kid and work with whatever angle they can find. My experience, they have a genius for finding a child's weak spot, psychologically, and then exploiting it."

"When was his last run-in with the law?"

"That was it. He's been clean since he got out of prison." Benny gave me a look. "That don't mean he's gone straight. It just means he's gotten better at not getting caught."

I took his point, but couldn't decide whether Finn being vague about the victim's age qualified as a lie or not.

"Pedophiles don't reform," Benny continued. "It's a permanent personality trait. The only way I've seen any of 'em stay out of trouble is keeping themselves away from kids entirely."

"Shit," I said, remembering the couple I'd seen coming up the canyon with Hector. The woman had been carrying a baby.

I stood up, getting my phone out. Benny showed me the palm of one hand. "Hang on there, Trigger. We ain't done with your statement yet."

"Morse has access to a more-or-less steady supply of children with a built-in angle," I said. "Half an hour could mean the difference to one of them."

"What do you mean? Those Buddhist guys don't take kids. Said so on their website."

Benny and Hector had surely gotten reacquainted by phone when Hector had called him to try and track me out in the desert, but I doubted that Hector had told him what he was doing for a living. Benny and I were getting along fine, but he was still a cop, and *coyote* work was still illegal.

"Could you just take my word for it?" I said.

Benny put his head back, regarding me with a conflicted expression. "One of these days I'm gonna strap you in a chair and feed you some sodium pentothal. Then I'm gonna retire on all the dirt you have stored up in there." He pointed at my head.

"OK, but until then, I'm still free to make a goddamn private phone call, right?"

He made a reluctantly affirmative gesture, and I strode out of the interview room and onto the courthouse lawn, where no one could overhear me. I found a phone number for the hot springs and dialed. A young man's voice answered.

"I need to get hold of Hector Guerra," I told him. "It's kind of an emergency."

"Yes," he said, his voice rising at the end of the word, as if it were a question. Slightly disoriented by the inflection, I said, "Would you have him call me back at this number, as soon as humanly possible?"

"Yes," he said again. Same questioning tone.

"Also, who's in charge of the Buddhist group there?" I asked him.

"No one," the man said, a laugh in his voice, "but we are expecting a new abbot shortly. May I help in the meantime?"

I hesitated, then said, "There's a monk with you, a guy who goes by the name of Finn. He's not telling you the whole truth about his past."

"Ah!" he said. The exclamation managed to contain both curiosity and a sort of world-weary humor.

The man didn't say anything else, so I went ahead and relayed the facts as I knew them.

When I'd finished, there was a short silence at the other end of the line before he said, "I thank you for this information. I will contact Hector right now and ask him to call you."

He didn't sound shocked or even very interested. I told him he was welcome, but the line had gone dead. No good-bye or anything.

Back inside, I picked up where I'd left off with my statement.

When I was finished, Benny clicked the recorder off and sat back in the plastic chair with a sigh. I thought he was going to rag me about something, but he said, "I dunno how you did it without getting shot, but nice work."

CHAPTER 36

I made sure my ringer was set as loud as it could go before I headed out, so that I'd hear it when Hector called me back. Maines had been transferred to Memorial Hospital on Tuesday night, and the information desk told me he was in the gym, which occupied one large corner of the first floor. There were maybe a dozen people in it, most of them elderly except for one young amputee and a middle-aged guy who looked like he'd recently been run over by a truck.

It took me a while to spot Maines because he was practically unrecognizable. They'd cut off his springy strawberry curls, and the short brush of hair that was left was steel gray. He was at a large folding table, in a wheelchair, and he sat rigidly upright with his chin pulled in, his high-shouldered stoop a thing of the past.

A freckled youngster who looked like he'd been born too recently to have a job was helping Maines assemble some wood blocks on the table in front of them, and stood up when I came over. He introduced himself as Maines's physical therapist, then stepped over to help the amputee with some weights.

Maines couldn't raise his head, so I sat down next to his

wheelchair. He had a slight tremor, and when he saw me, he gave a grin that only moved the left side of his face. It wasn't the paralysis that made my heart ache, it was the grin. Maines wasn't a smiler.

"I got her," I told him.

It took some doing for him to get turned in my direction so he could look at me.

"Good," he said.

The look in his eye was still Maines, which tempered my sudden urge to put my head down on the arm of his wheelchair and sob. The man was still in there somewhere.

"What else can I do?" I asked him. "Do you need anything?"

"An op," he said, with some difficulty.

I paused to get hold of my temper. The man had been through enough. He didn't need me yelling at him.

"Yeah, Benny told me you wanted me running the case," I said. "I'll do what I can while I'm here, but after we get Mikela Floyd sorted out, I'm going back to Mexico."

A quizzical look came over him, and I realized he knew nothing of what had happened in the last forty-eight hours.

"That's the woman's name who took over Rachael's identity," I told him. "She did it so she could join a Native women's militia based in Sells. It's kind of a long story."

I didn't want to weigh him down with too many facts, but he kept looking at me with those water-clear eyes of his, so I gave him a short version.

"She and her sister killed a cop during a demonstration against the border fence in El Paso last year," I said. "The sister went missing, turned up dead, nobody went to prison for it. Mikela wanted to join the militia to try and avenge the sister, as well as hide out from the cops."

I stopped. Maines had pulled his chin farther in, letting his bushy eyebrows drop.

"What?" I said.

He half shook his head, turning it to one side quickly, and gestured at his physical therapist with a hand like a club. "Room, please."

The young man came back over to us, and wheeled Maines out into the beige-carpeted hall. I followed them to the cleanest-smelling elevator ever, which took us to the third floor. A gaggle of nurses greeted Maines as we passed their station, on our way to his excessively cheerful private room. There, he dismissed the therapist and pointed at the bedside table with his eyes. A business card was lying there. I went over and picked it up.

"My kid," he said. "Call her. Has all my notes."

I sighed. "For God's sake, Maines—"

He was making that jerky head-shake motion again, trying to communicate something. I stopped talking, and he said, "Notes. My notes. About Greenlaw. Political."

I took the Naugahyde chair next to the side table so that I could be at his level.

"Connection," Maines said. His eyes were alive, radiating the energy his body could no longer express. "That's it."

"What, politics?"

"Notes," he said again.

"I'll look at them," I promised reluctantly.

"More than look," he said.

My hackles were starting to get vertical. I tried to keep my voice calm, but I wanted to make sure he understood where I was coming from. "Maines. I hate cops. As a species. I always have. I don't want to be one."

He didn't say anything to that, but he wobbled one arm over

and tapped his fist on the card in my hand. A brief filmstrip of those freckled, broad-palmed hands before I'd destroyed them—passing me things, gripping the steering wheel of the Crown Vic, stroking Steve—played through my memory, making my chest flex painfully again.

"OK, look, I'll play 'op' for you as long as I'm here," I said. "But you know my methods, so no crying when you and Benny have to clean up the mess."

"New method," he said, lifting his arms and dropping them into his lap again slowly. "Settle. Think."

"If I had a year I might try that," I said, getting up. "But it's a lot faster to light a fire and jump whoever runs out of the burning building."

"Less effective."

"Maybe, but I'm good at it."

Since he couldn't move his neck properly, Maines had to tilt his torso back in the wheelchair to look up at me. "Not always."

My guts wrenched, but then I caught the glint in his eye.

"Really?" I said. "Emotional blackmail? That's low, Maines."

"Desperate times," he said.

CHAPTER 37

———— ◆ ————

I called Maines's daughter from the truck, and she gave me her address and told me I could come out immediately.

The house was outside town, in the ring of new suburbs. It was a starter model, freshly painted, the front yard littered with brightly colored plastic kids' toys. A young dark-skinned woman with liquid brown eyes and a baby on her hip answered the door. Her tightly curled black hair was up in a pouf, the bridge of her nose scattered with charcoal freckles.

I told her I was there to see Audra Maines, and, to my surprise, she said that's who she was. I sneaked a look at some family photos on the hallway wall as she led me into the house and spotted one with a much younger Maines and an elegant-looking black woman, both of them in full wedding drag. Now I understood why he seemed to have more liberal ideas than the average local white guy.

Audra led me into the kitchen, where another child of six or seven was enjoying a sandwich at a cluttered table. The little girl looked a lot like her mother except for her hair, which was braided into a collection of colorful barrettes that reminded me of the toys on the lawn. The house had that lived-in smell of warm bananas and laundry and human beings.

Audra put the baby down into a walker and said, "Have a seat. Do you want some coffee?"

"I'm fine," I said, joining the kid at the table.

The six-year-old watched me with suspicion. "What's your name?" she said.

"Julia. What's yours?"

"None of your business!" she replied.

"Ella, be nice," her mother said, then, to me, "Dad's stuff is upstairs. Can you hang down here for a minute?"

I said I could, and she disappeared through the kitchen door. Ella kept a jaundiced eye on me. I didn't try to make any more nice with her.

A clickety-scratch noise preceded her mother's returning footsteps, and Steve bounded into the room. He paused when he saw me, then tapped over and sniffed my knee, looking up into my face. Audra followed him in with a cardboard file box.

"I forgot y'all knew each other," she said, smiling at the dog.

Ella frowned at me. "You don't know Steve. He's Grandpa's dog."

"I took a little trip with your grandpa last week," I said, glancing at Audra. She met my look evenly. She was made of the same stuff as her dad.

The kid made a skeptical noise around her mouthful of sand-wich and looked away.

"He said to give you all of this," Audra said, sliding the box onto the kitchen table. "Are you really going to take over his detective practice?"

"Not permanently," I hedged. "I'm just helping out for a little while, until he gets back on his feet."

"He's never getting back on his feet," she said. Her voice didn't shake. Her eyes didn't water. She was sticking to the facts.

"Sorry," I said. "Figure of speech."

Steve had gone around the table and was eyeing Ella's sandwich. "Mom!" she said.

Audra exhaled a harried sigh and snapped her fingers at the dog. "I don't know what the hell I'm going to do with this animal after Dad moves in. He lets him get away with everything."

"Maines is moving in with you?" I said.

"Where else is he gonna go? My brother lives in a one-room apartment on the other side of the world, and I can't afford to put Dad in some rehab place."

I tried not to be obvious as I looked around the small kitchen with its boxes of cereal and crackers crammed into the corners, dishes in the sink, pots and pans stacked on the stove.

"It don't matter," Audra said. "It's always the girls. We end up taking care of everybody."

"What about your mother?"

She gave me an appraising look. "I guess Dad didn't talk to you about the divorce."

"Not so much," I admitted.

"Are your folks still around?"

The idea of my mother living with me got me out of my chair. "Yeah, but I don't see them very often."

"Sometimes that's a good thing."

"You said it, I didn't."

Audra gave me a sharp smile. I lifted the box and said, "If you need anything—"

"You've done plenty," she said.

It sliced me. I admit it. She saw the blade go in, and put a quick hand on my wrist. "I didn't mean it that way."

"Don't worry about it," I said. If she knew how many times I'd dodged my just deserts, she wouldn't have given it a second thought.

CHAPTER 38

When I got back to the bar, I went upstairs, fed the cat, changed into shorts and a tank top, then sat down on the bed and opened the box of Maines's stuff.

There was only one folder, the one for Rachael's case, lying on top of some miscellaneous office supplies, a holstered Smith & Wesson, a cell phone, and a half-full bottle of dry vermouth.

Maines's handwriting was as weird as he was, a gnarled cursive interrupted at intervals by big block capitals and random punctuation having nothing to do with the rules of grammar. It was all in pencil, but nothing had been erased—changes were made by crossing out old information and noting new stuff in the margin nearby. It made for some exhausting reading, despite containing precious little actual information.

He'd started with Rachael's coworkers, who had nothing interesting to say about her, except for one who'd waxed voluble about the state of her marriage and confirmed that Orson had left town "last summer" for a job in Washington, D.C. The coworker referred to Orson as a "piece of work," and Maines had made a note to follow up, but nothing anywhere else told me that he'd done so.

Behind this were his notes from several phone calls to the mysterious "H" in Mexico, establishing Rachael's appearance at the clinic. Maines seemed to have gotten access to Rachael's computer at that point, and apparently her private effects, as well, because there was a collection of photos in the back of the folder.

A couple of loose sheets from a small notebook rounded out the collection. One of them was the beginning of a timeline, which consisted of only two items:

Dec 5—(?—confirm) R. to clinic
Dec 10—death blood clot?

I went and got a notepad out of Hector's desk and made out my own timeline:

May 1—Demonstration El Paso, Floyd sisters kill cop
Jun 10—Jenny Floyd dead (find newspaper article)
Jun ?—Mikela starts job at clinic
Dec 5—Rachael to clinic
Dec 10—Rachael dead
date?—Mikela plastic surgery
ca. Feb 15—Orson dead

I left room between each item, thinking I'd go back and add stuff in as I found it. It seemed kind of stupid, but I was winging this being-a-detective business. I had no idea what I was doing.

The political thing that had tweaked Maines must have been Orson's job in D.C., though I didn't see anything in the notes to suggest why. Was Maines thinking about the demonstration the Floyd sisters had been involved in? I added a note to my timeline to find out where and when Orson was supposed to have gone to work.

The coworker's characterization of him, which tracked with the tidbits that I'd heard from others, was provocative, but if he was the asshole people said he was, talking to everyone who disliked him enough to kill him would be a lot of footwork and didn't really appeal to my inner arsonist.

While I thought about a more efficient way of getting the fire going, I went through the pictures, putting them in chronological order as best I could, based on Rachael's apparent age and other visual cues. There was a high-school graduation photo, a couple of wedding pictures, and half a dozen casual snapshots—outdoors in shorts and a T-shirt, at her desk at work, that sort of thing. When I got them all lined up, I looked through them again in order, noticing that while she had gained some weight over time, the most remarkable change was in her face. She'd had a look of basic contentment in the earlier pictures that gradually disappeared after the wedding. In the last couple of images, she looked definitively miserable.

Maybe she'd gone for the lap-band hoping that it would fix that. I knew plenty of women who invested their various appearance-altering efforts with magical antidepressant powers. She'd have had to go to Mexico to have it done because she certainly didn't qualify, medically speaking, for bariatric surgery by U.S. standards—in the later photos I guessed her weight at about 175 on a frame of slightly taller than average height. She was well-fleshed but nicely proportioned, and probably didn't even need to shop in the plus-size section.

I put the photos down and got the cell phone out of the box. Not surprisingly, the battery was dead, and there was no charger.

In any case, it probably wouldn't have anything pertinent on it, since I'd drowned Maines's previous phone while we were in Mexico.

That reminded me of Benny's phone call and his mention of Orson's job. I went and got my own phone and called Benny's number.

"Find out what the job was?" I said when he answered. "What was it?"

"Yeah, baby!" Benny laughed. "You're on it!"

"Don't make me come over there and beat you," I said.

"OK, wait, hang on." Papers shuffled. "Yeah, it was with the 'Baxter for President' campaign. Jesus."

"Baxter? You mean the wingnut who's been running these 'biblical democracy' ads?"

"That's the one. He runs for president every four years, like clockwork. Orson was gonna be his 'media contact manager,' whatever the hell that means."

"You got a number for them?"

Benny recited one and I wrote it down. I thanked him and hung up, going over to the computer. A quick search on Baxter yielded the basic neocon positions on just about everything. Not surprisingly, he was a big public supporter of the border fence. He was listed as being from San Antonio, but his hometown was El Paso.

I warned myself against drawing a connection with the Floyd sisters just because they were from the same city, and on opposite sides of the border-fence issue, but it didn't make many ripples sliding into the narrative I was making up in my head. If Baxter ran for president every four years, he had lots of spare change lying around. Could he be one of the hypocritical "powers behind the throne" that Jenny Floyd had uncovered?

I looked up his position on immigration reform, but he seemed to have avoided that specific issue entirely, which tweaked my radar. Opposition to illegal immigration and/or amnesty was a typical corollary to supporting the border fence, and most of the talking heads who occupied that ideological territory didn't make a big secret of it. Especially the ones from districts closer to Mexico, which naturally included San Antonio and El Paso.

Deciding that at this point it wouldn't hurt a thing to have all the facts I could find about Jennifer and Mikela, I went back to the Internet, put their names into the search box and hit "enter." That took me on a side trip to the news articles about the cop they'd killed. His name was Mike Reardon. He'd been on the El Paso force for twelve years, married, no kids. Half an hour of Internet searching turned up nothing about him that could conceivably make him worth killing, except by accident. He'd died on May 2, the day after the demonstration.

I couldn't find any newspaper article, Mexican or otherwise, about a dead white woman being found near Juarez on June 10. I tried all the Internet searching hacks I could think of: putting the Floyd girls' names in with Reardon's, singly and together; combining each name with the search term "border fence"; including "*feminicidio*," "Juarez," and "El Paso" in the search; and all combinations of the above. None of it produced anything but frustration. Casting the net wider, I tried including Baxter, Darling, Orson, and Rachael in my searches. Still nothing. I added "*Kokoi.*" Bubkes.

Giving up, I backed out of the search engine and did online background checks on the whole crew. Darling's record took almost ten minutes to read all the way through, but nothing in it set off my radar. Reardon was clean as glass, and Orson's only black marks were all misdemeanors, including several acts of vandalism against Rachael's property. Baxter's record had been sealed, not surprisingly. If you're going to run for president every four years you don't want people looking up your DUIs and parking tickets. There were plenty of pictures of him online, though, surrounded by his adoring wife and passel of kids. I guessed that they were Catholic by the sheer number, which was somewhere between four and ten, depending on which photos you used to count them. There was also the usual gossip that seems to follow any candidate for public office—that he'd been involved in any number of shady financial dealings, that he was gay, that he'd been the second gunman on the Grassy Knoll.

I got up and took a walk around the apartment to clear my head and had a thought that required another call to Benny.

"Did you guys ever figure out what kind of bullets killed Orson Greenlaw?"

"Not specifically," he said, "but the wounds were typical of standard pistol rounds, like a .38 or 9 millimeter, nonexpanding. Basic street ammo."

"Do you have access to crime reports for El Paso?"

"Sure." I heard him hit a key on his computer keyboard. "What am I looking for?"

"The cop the Floyd sisters killed, Mike Reardon. Just wondered if the rounds that took him down fit into the criteria for the ones that offed Orson."

"Yeah, I looked into that," Benny said. "His coffin nails were 9 millimeter Parabellums, which are, like, an incredibly common round. To match 'em up we'd need the actual bullets that went into both guys and, as you know, all we got in Orson is the holes."

"But it's possible the same gun killed both of them."

"Yeah. Possible."

"I don't suppose Jenny or Mikela had a license for a 9 milli-meter?"

"Way ahead of you on that one, too," Benny said. "Neither one. But ya know, most criminals don't register their firearms."

"What did she tell you about Reardon in your interview?"

Benny made a derisive noise. "Ah, she clammed on every-thing. Won't say a word until her lawyer gets here. She's due in a few hours."

"You want me over there for the festivities?"

"Nah," Benny said. "I doubt the lawyer will change much but the smell of the room. If Mikela gives up anything inter-esting, I'll let you know."

After we hung up, I moved toward the computer again but realized that I was just spinning my wheels. Searching the Internet probably wasn't any more efficient than going through the Azula phone book from A to Z. I picked up the slip of paper I'd written the Baxter campaign number down on, but I'd al-ready made as many phone calls that day as I could stand. It was four thirty, which meant it was past quitting time in D.C. anyway.

I wasn't ready to call it a day yet though, and after some thought, I decided to see what I could sieve out via the local gossip mill. Plus, I was hungry. I got dressed and headed over to the cafe.

CHAPTER 39

It was biscuits and gravy today, which, before I'd taken up residence in Azula, meant a couple of lumpy white Frisbees covered with some thick gray spackle. Lavon Roberts's biscuits and gravy were as far from that as Pluto is from the sun. His cooking was one of the few things that made me regret the fact I'd be moving soon.

His teenaged daughter, Neffa, brought me my silverware and a glass of tea a few minutes after I sat down. It was the tail end of the lunch rush and there were only a few other tables occupied, so she paused to chat, like she usually did when the restaurant wasn't running her ragged.

"Was it really Orson Greenlaw in your house?" she said.

"Yep."

"Man, that is harsh. But you know what? Someone was gonna do it. That man was a hot mess."

I'd never heard the term applied to a guy before and gave her a quizzical grin. She waited for her father to pass by, not letting him succeed at catching her eye, then said, "Orson used to come in here and pinch my ass black-and-blue."

"I don't see him getting away with that for long," I said, watching Lavon come back our way.

"Oh, I called him out," Neffa told me. "Every damn time. Daddy just about tore him up, too, but the fool would not stop."

A thought occurred to me. "You didn't happen to notice anyone coming onto my place around the middle of February, did you?"

Neffa started to shake her head, then brought a finger up quickly to her mouth.

"Oh, you know what? There was one night. I couldn't get to sleep, and some lights kept flashing over there. When was that?" She thought a minute. "Yeah, it would have been February 13. I remember because it was Daddy's birthday the day before and I had got up to have some of the cake that was left over."

"What kind of lights?"

"Car lights. Like somebody drove down your driveway."

The back of my neck thrilled. "You mean like just turning around? Or did they stay awhile?"

"They stayed awhile. Maybe a half hour. Their lights went on and off a couple of times while they were there."

"You didn't happen to get a look at the car, did you?"

Neffa shook her head. "I didn't pay it any mind, really. I thought it was you."

I hadn't been out to the Ranch after dark between November 8—the day Connie was arrested—and the beginning of March, when the weather had warmed up enough to make working at night comfortable. Between her trial and recovering from my near-fatal stabbing, I'd had way too much on my plate to even think about the house.

That car had to be the killer, transporting Orson's body out to my place. Without a description of the vehicle, though, knowing the date and general time wasn't that useful, unless I somehow miraculously stumbled across somebody who'd been MIA at the right moment. Still, it was gratifying to know that some of what had been put together about Orson's death was correct.

Neffa finally obeyed the hairy eyeball her dad had been directing her way, and I put the brain on hold. I don't like to think while I eat.

When I'd finished my sumptuous repast, I went back to the bar and updated my timeline:

May 1—Demonstration El Paso, Floyd sisters kill cop
Summer (date?)—Orson leaves for D.C. job
Jun 10—Jenny Floyd dead (find newspaper article)
Jun ?—Mikela starts job at clinic
Dec 5—Rachael to clinic
Dec 10—Rachael dead
date?—Mikela plastic surgery
ca. Feb 15—Orson dead
Feb 13—Car at Ranch

Thinking about the previous winter took me back to the events immediately following Connie's arrest and trial: the interminable wait while the lawyers played chicken with each other; moving out of my apartment and into Hector's place when it became apparent he wasn't coming home anytime soon; dealing with Tova and all the red tape that went with buying real estate from a convicted felon.

That made me remember that I'd taken the FOR SALE sign

down the day Connie had accepted my offer, November 4. It was possible that what Neffa had seen was just a couple of local kids pulling off the road to get stoned, but turning into a driveway at night and not backing right out again is likely to get you shot at, around here. The visitor must have known the house was vacant or they wouldn't have taken the risk. How did they know, if the sign was down? It must have been someone who knew the house had been for sale but wasn't occupied yet. That probably ruled out strangers to Azula.

Unfortunately, it didn't rule out much else. In a town this size, everybody knew everybody's business. All the locals had probably heard I'd bought the place, and would know that I hadn't moved in yet. That narrowed my field of suspects down to 5,412, give or take whoever had moved in or out since I'd checked the city population stats.

Stumped about where to go next, I got up and walked around the apartment, trying to think, but the brain wouldn't cooperate. I don't know what made Maines think I'd be able to solve his case by sitting down and meditating on it. If he wanted it solved that way, he should have hired someone else.

CHAPTER 40

———— ✦ ————

It was slightly cooler in Gatesville; some kind of weather system coming in off the gulf. Even inside, the air felt like moist slices of bread sticking to my skin.

They put me in a private visitor's room this time, and I had to wait five or ten minutes for them to fetch Connie. When she appeared, it looked like they'd woken her up from a nap. She wasn't wearing her glasses and her hair was wilder than usual.

"Sorry for the short notice," I said as she sat down.

She rubbed her eyes and frowned at me. I had my notepad with me and had sketched out a rough floor plan of the house, which I showed her now.

"This chase," I said, pointing. "Did it have a hole in the floor above it when you owned the house?"

"Yeah," Connie said. "The old furnace was in there. There was a—a thing, a thicker place in the floor, above the heater—"

"A plenum," I prompted.

"Yeah, where the heat would go up into it and then through a grille in the floor above. Dad took the grille out after the heater was removed."

"Did your dad put wood down to cover the hole afterwards?"

Connie nodded. "I was going to have it fixed to match the rest of the floor but I never got around to it."

"When did the linoleum go in?"

"Some renters installed it when Dad was still alive," she replied, her expression growing increasingly curious. "Is that where you found the body?"

I nodded. "I know that you just let people go out and look at the house on their own and that you left it unlocked so anyone could have gone in there and poked around, but who else besides me looked at it? Do you remember?"

She took a breath and gazed over my head. "Let's see. . . . Well, Lavon, and Charlie Eames, who used to run the salon . . . Mr. Hu from the corner store, Missy Black, she works for the county clerk. . . ." Connie went on to name about a dozen more people I'd never heard of, then stopped. "I think that's about it."

I was writing the names down. "Did any of them specifically notice the hole in the floor, that you know of?"

Connie shook her head. "Like you said, I just let people go out there on their own, whenever."

The high window in the glazed-tile wall behind her was open a crack, letting in the steamy weather. I gazed at the sky through it, thinking about what to ask next.

Finally, deciding that two noses were better than one, especially since I suspected that mine wasn't working so well at the moment, I leaned forward and folded my hands on the table.

"OK, you know that thing we talked about before? About how you and I are alike, the whole kicked-dog thing?"

Connie didn't reply, but her expression was affirmative.

"I'm going to ask you to rely on that thing to answer this question," I said. "Rely on that instinct."

"OK," she said.

"Were any of the people who looked at the house the type who would kill somebody?"

"Ohhh. . . ." she breathed, her head tilting back. She sat frozen like that for a few seconds, then said, "You know, this is probably going to strike you strangely, but I've always felt like there was a lot more going on with Neffa Roberts than most people think."

She was right; it did strike me strangely. "Neffa? Get real."

"No, I'm serious. She has a certain lack of affect that I see a lot in people with Axis two disorders."

"Axis?—"

"Axis two. Things like bipolar, borderline, schizophrenia. Which don't necessarily predispose people to homicide, you understand. Just . . . I remember noticing it one day and thinking she'd make an interesting study subject."

My curiosity got the better of me. "Are you on this Axis two?"

Connie smiled in her calm, sweet way. "No, I'm just a garden-variety psychopath, which isn't really a psychiatric diagnosis. It's more just sort of a handy catchall descriptor for a cluster of behavioral symptoms that don't fit anywhere else."

I pulled myself back to the subject at hand. "Why would Neffa want to kill Orson?"

"I'm not saying Neffa in particular. Just that of the people who've been in that house, she's the one I could see killing somebody."

"She did mention that he pinched her ass black-and-blue when he came into the cafe, but that doesn't seem like grounds for murder."

"Orson wasn't well liked around town," Connie said, tilting

her head to one side. "Figuratively speaking, he pinched every-one's ass black-and-blue. Perhaps that public behavior was the tip of a private iceberg."

I was thinking to myself that if Neffa was my killer, her report of the car at the house might be a deviously placed red herring. She didn't seem capable of that kind of subterfuge, but that's why I'd come out here.

As if reading my mind, Connie said, "You drove up just to ask me that?"

"You're the only other person I know with a radar like mine, and I'm not sure mine is trustworthy right now." Connie's face went quizzical, and I said, "I thought you might be able to give me some professional advice, as well."

"In my capacity as a former psychiatrist-in-training, impris-oned psycho killer, or something else?"

It always surprised me when Connie poked fun at herself like that; she'd been so pin-eyed scary after trying to kill me that I'd forgotten how much I'd originally liked her on sight, and part of that had been her self-effacing wit. There's a lesson somewhere in the fact that the person I thought the most sane of my social sphere in Azula had turned out to actually be the craziest.

"Maybe all of the above," I said. I gave a few seconds' thought to how much I wanted to tell her, then said, "That remark you made last time I was out here, about me not knowing myself. Someone else said almost exactly the same thing to me a couple of days ago. Do you think there's a relationship between that— whatever the hell you meant by it, and whatever the hell he did—and this dissociation thing that's been going on with me lately?"

Connie's face assumed the animated expression it always did

when dealing with her favorite subject. "Well, all 'insanity'"—
she made air quotes around the word—"is a bid by the unconscious to make itself known to the conscious mind. In that sense,
having less self-knowledge—that is, knowing less about where
your emotional and psychological weak spots are—could certainly make you more susceptible to things like dissociation."

"Weak spots," I snorted.

Connie smiled at me again. "That's what I meant about a lack
of self-knowledge."

"I'm not saying I don't have them, but if you'd lived my life,
you'd understand why they're not up here floating around on the
surface."

"That's how things like that cause trouble. When you get too
good at repressing things, you stop recognizing them as part of
you when they break through. That's what causes that feeling
of 'otherness' that's so typical of dissociation."

"It's not 'otherness,'" I said. "I go completely away."

Connie's interested expression intensified. "How so?"

"I'll be in one place in a room and then the next thing I know,
I'll be on the other side of it. Like, bam."

Connie's face went from interested to concerned. "As if no
time has passed?"

I nodded, and she crossed her arms, bringing one hand up
to her chin. She sat like that for a few minutes, thinking, then
said, "Have you seen a psychiatrist yet?"

"No. Liz Harman says she knows someone, but—" I lifted
my shoulders, looking away.

"Certainly see the colleague," Connie said quickly.

I looked back at her.

"Dr. Harman is a competent general practitioner," she explained, seeing my expression, "but I wouldn't see her for a

mental health issue. She has a pronounced ideological bias in that area."

"Ya think?" I laughed.

Connie smiled. "Just making sure you were aware."

It felt a little theatrical to me and I wondered if Liz had diagnosed her prior to the breakdown last year, producing this possible crop of sour grapes.

"So why are you asking these sleuthlike questions about Orson?" Connie asked, deftly changing the subject. "Has Maines finally prevailed upon you to come over to the dark side?"

"Sort of, temporarily," I allowed. "All things considered, I kind of feel like I owe him."

Connie quirked at me again, and I realized that she knew nothing of what had happened in the last few days. I gave her the *Reader's Digest*, watching her face grow solemn as I spoke.

When I'd finished, she slid her forearms across the table and put her small, cool hands on top of mine. She didn't say anything, but her eyes were full of feeling.

My phone rang on the drive back to Azula; her ears must have been burning, because it was Liz Harman, telling me she wanted to do a physical before she turned me over to her headshrinking friend. We made an appointment for the next day.

CHAPTER 41

Something was going on at the courthouse when I woke up the next morning. Two big black SUVs with tinted windows were parked at the curb in the rear, and a caricature of an FBI agent stood outside one of them. Dark suit, Ray-Bans, buzz cut, earpiece, the whole nine yards.

I turned off the water I'd put on to boil for tea, and walked over to see what was happening. As I came around the building on the narrow concrete sidewalk, the door to the police station swung open, and two more feebs came out, with Mikela between them. The guy on the left threw up an arm. "Step back, ma'am."

"If you're going to call me ma'am, you might want to put a 'please' in there somewhere," I replied, staying where I was.

One thing that's always puzzled me about G-men is their lack of humor. Like the world's going to come to an end if they crack a smile. This guy was no different; he gave me the blue steel and clenched up.

"I said, step back!"

Mikela's face, beyond his shoulder, was calm. She almost

looked happy. I got out of their way and watched them put her into one of the SUVs. Benny came out.

"What the hell?" I said to him. "I thought they blew you off."

"Couldn't be bothered when I really needed 'em, but they sure got the lead out when her arrest hit the database," he said, looking pissed off. "Bet you a hundred dollars none of us gets credit for picking her up."

"Did you ever get any kind of statement from her?"

"Yeah, after the lawyer showed," Benny said, shooting a disgusted look at the SUVs as they pulled away. "But they took the goddamn tape."

"You talk, I'll write," I said, moving toward the station door.

Benny had good recall, and the broad outlines of Mikela's statement didn't differ much from what she'd told me on the flight down. However, she'd filled in some details that made Benny a lot happier about what he had to prove.

She'd started work at the clinic on June 11, the day after reportedly seeing the newspaper article about Jennifer's death, and had gone under Darling's knife on December 13, the day after Rachael died. Darling had watched her like a hawk the entire time, right up until the day Maines and I had run into her on the street. Mikela said that Darling would vouch for the fact that she'd never been gone overnight, which would have been more or less necessary, given the time required to get to Azula, shoot Orson, dig out the bullets, drag his body to the Ranch, hide it in my floor, clean up the kill site, and then get back to Ojinaga. I wasn't sure how much Darling's word was worth, but Benny pointed out that giving someone an anonymous new face was an entirely different animal than felony identity theft. Darling was strictly a misdemeanor and malpractice man. He wasn't going to risk major prison time for some woman he didn't know from Adam.

"Mikela mentioned Rachael's restraining order against Orson when we found her in Ojinaga," I told Benny. "Did she go into any specifics?"

"No, but I was just fixing to look up the arresting officer's report," Benny said, dragging over his laptop, which had been sitting on the corner of the big desk.

"While you're at it, will you see if there's anything in your supercop database there about Jennifer Floyd? I can't find the newspaper article that Mikela says she saw."

Benny nodded without looking at me, tapping on the laptop keyboard. After a minute he gave a disgusted snort and turned the computer screen toward me so I could see the report. A crime-scene photo showed Rachael's newish little red Toyota with the words "fat cunt" scratched across the driver's-side door.

"Nice," I said.

"'Ridiculous' is more the word for it," Benny said, shaking his head. He went back to tapping.

"OK, Jennifer Floyd," he said, after what seemed like a long time. "There's a Mexican police report for June 8—the body they think might be Jennifer was found with seven others. It only made one paper, a local Socialist rag that follows the *feminicidio* thing, and they featured a picture because she didn't spec up with the other bodies."

"What was the difference? I mean, besides Jennifer being white."

Benny read his screen for a minute, then said, "The other seven were classic *feminicidio* victims: no hair dye, no makeup,

petite and slim with long dark hair. Jenny was blonde, taller, and
kind of . . ."

His eyes wandered in my direction. I raised an eyebrow. He
cleared his throat and went on. "None of the rest of the usual-
victim profile fits Jennifer, either—she was thirty-six, educated,
divorced. The *feminicidios* all tend to be country girls—single
working mothers between sixteen and twenty-five."

"That's a pretty specific demographic," I remarked.

Benny nodded solemnly. "And they are all, every single one
of them, *maquiladora* workers."

"Did they work in the same one? Or factories owned by
the same company? Anything like that?"

"No. Which drives me—and every other cop who sees this
stuff—nuts." Benny adjusted his belt, annoyed. "I mean, with a
victim profile that specific, anybody with half a brain should be
able to find a connection."

It was making my brain itch, too, but probably for different
reasons. "How'd Jennifer die?"

"Lead poisoning. Same garden-variety rounds as the cop
they killed: Parabellum .38s."

I put my pen down and sat back, thinking.

After a while, Benny made a "come on" gesture at me, and
I said, "Baxter's from El Paso and supports the border fence.
He's got to be the guy that Jennifer found the dirt on."

"Why?" Benny said.

"Because he's connected to this whole thing, through
Orson."

Benny snorted a short laugh. "You're doing that backwards.
You don't decide who did what and then massage the evidence
into place. You follow the evidence to the answer."

"It's a connection," I insisted.

"No, it's not. It's a desperate investigator throwing shit at the wall to see what sticks."

"I'm not an investigator," I shot back, my temper finally going nuclear, "and if you and Maines don't like the way I do your jobs for you, you can fuck right the hell off."

All this did to Benny was make him lean back and cross his legs, lacing his fingers behind his hedgehog head.

"You went after Mikela Floyd like a bulldog," he said. "You'd have done it even if I'd said no."

"So what?"

"So you *are* an investigator. Whether you like it or not, you've got the instinct," he said.

"I've got the instinct to make people pay when they cross my personal lines in the sand. That's not exactly what cops are supposed to do."

"No, it's not what we're supposed to do," Benny agreed. "But nobody becomes a cop solely because they want to enforce the law, out of the goodness of their virtuous hearts. That shit's just glurge for public consumption."

I felt my face turn into one big question mark.

" 'Every cop is a criminal, and all the sinners saints,' " he quoted, grinning.

"Oh, for Christ's sake," I groaned.

"If you developed some kind of professional relationship with law enforcement, you might not have to worry so much about your own security."

"Yeah," I snorted, "because the Brotherhood would find me a hell of a lot faster."

"But you'd be a much more difficult target. You wouldn't be some random woman on the street. You'd be one of ours."

"If you think that would stop them from killing me, you don't know much about their organization," I said.

Benny sighed and got up. "Fine. But think about it, OK?"

I didn't say so, but I had a feeling that I was going to think about it whether I wanted to or not.

CHAPTER 42

———— ◆ ————

Liz Harman's office was in her house, a big ramshackle place at the very edge of the old part of town, to the north. She'd taken advantage of the house's two front doors—typical for its age, which I guessed to be about seventy-five—by using one as the entrance to her medical practice, which occupied two front rooms of the house. She didn't have any staff, you just walked in and there she was. Her office was nicely decorated with vintage furniture and an eclectic collection of artwork, including a large framed print that looked like it might be an original Picasso.

She got up and shook hands with me across her desk, and indicated I should have a seat while she pulled over a tablet computer that was lying nearby.

"Nice setup," I said.

She retrieved her glasses from the top of her head and put them on, glancing over at me with a grin. "I'm old-school, baby."

"That's good, because I don't have any insurance."

She tapped on the tablet, pursing her lips. "Hm. Not a problem for me, but I'm not sure how Jean works all of that."

I made a face, and she said, "Let's burn that bridge when we get to it. First, tell me what-all's been going on with you."

"You know," I said.

"I only know generally. Give me the specifics."

I sighed and told her about the high, cool feeling, the olfactory hallucinations, the feeling of morning suffocation. She already knew about my dissociative episodes, but I described them in more detail including the stuff I'd told Connie and mentioned that I'd experienced an associated decline in radar. Balking at that last, she asked what I meant.

"I've just always been good at picking up on what other people are feeling and thinking," I explained, "but since I've been having these episodes, not so much."

"Everybody thinks they're good at that," she chuckled, raising an eyebrow in my direction. "Most of it is wishful thinking. You're just getting old enough to stop believing your own crap."

It felt like a slap in the face, and I had to take a breath to keep from losing my temper. I wondered if she were that dismissive with all her patients.

She continued to tap on her computer keyboard for a few minutes, then got up with a grunt and said, "OK, let's have a look at you."

She gestured toward the door behind me, which led into a small exam room. I got undressed and put on a worn cotton gown. She had me lie back on the exam table so she could poke and prod, asking me the usual doctor questions: any shortness of breath, dizziness, weird bleeding, new appendages, etc. I copped to some dizziness but told her I was pretty sure that it wasn't physical. She had me sit up, listened to my heart and breathing, took my blood pressure and temperature, and then went over to a small chest in the corner of the room and pulled open the top drawer.

"I'd like to get a full blood profile on you," she said, taking out a pad of lab orders. She scribbled on the top one, hesitated, then tore it off, crumpled it, threw it in the trash, and started another.

"The address is on the back," she said, handing me the form. "You don't need to make an appointment."

She seemed suddenly disturbed and jerked the drawer open again to replace the pad. Instruments clinked as she shoved it closed, harder than was necessary.

"Give it to me straight, Doc," I said. "How long have I got?"

She snorted a short laugh and didn't answer right away. I got the feeling she was looking for something to use as an excuse for whatever was really bothering her. "Those lab tests are expensive. I just get pissed off every time I think about it. People are going without basic health care because they can't afford to pay doctors anymore. Meanwhile, most of my colleagues are driving from the golf course to the country club in thousand-dollar suits behind the wheel of this year's Mercedes."

"How come you're not doing the same thing?" I asked her.

"Because I have ethics," she snapped. "I became a doctor because I wanted to help people, not bleed 'em dry. Somebody like you, if you get cancer, you get the very basics, if you're lucky. But Joe Millionaire, he can afford a Cadillac insurance plan that pays for nutritional support, exercise program, spa treatments, and private rooms for his chemo. How is that morally defensible?"

"Don't ask me," I said. "I was raised by wolves."

That made her laugh. "OK, get out of here. If anything weird comes up on your blood test, I'll call you."

CHAPTER 43

I was on my way to the lab when it hit me. I pulled into the nearest driveway and did a 180 to head back to town.

Benny was still in his office, on the phone behind his big desk. When he saw my face he told whoever he was talking to that he'd call them back, and hung up.

"What?" he said.

"The kids," I said. "What happens to their kids?"

"You're gonna have to be more specific."

"The *feminicidios*. You said they were mostly working mothers. What happens to their kids after they die?"

Benny looked puzzled. "I don't know, I guess they go back to the family or something. That would be the typical thing where most of these gals are from."

"Underpaid factory workers, country girls, you said," I reminded him. "They're poor, barely making ends meet, away from their families. If their kids had someone else to go to, wouldn't they be there already?"

Benny just frowned at me, keeping his mouth shut.

"You said it yourself, when we were looking at Finn's record," I said. "Pedophiles, they grab the most susceptible children. Along the border, that'd be illegals with no guardians, wouldn't it?"

"OK, just wait a minute." Benny held up both hands. "You're way out in left field here."

"If you build a fence and stop whoever's killing these women, the supply of vulnerable kids—undocumented kids—across the border stops. That's the connection. You said yourself, anybody with half a brain could figure it out if they tried."

"Jesus, Julia," Benny said, with feeling.

"Mikela said that Jenny discovered there were people on record as supporting the border fence who didn't really support it," I said. "Why would someone kill her just for that, unless it was connecting to something bigger?"

Benny sighed, looking away, and I stepped closer to his desk. "No-fault red-light districts along the border. Nine-year-old Mexican girls working in whorehouses. International sex tourism. That's an American industry just as valuable as steel production or building cars or coal mining, and it's surely got a lobby just as powerful."

Benny shoved his chair back, leaving one arm on the blotter, and said, "Even if Jenny Floyd discovered that Baxter was somehow helping, or looking the other way, or even messing with their kids himself, you can't take that all the way to personally killing all these women. At worst, he's taking advantage of an awful situation."

"What if his lobby money is helping the Mexican government look the other way? Don't you think that makes him at least partially culpable?"

Benny continued frowning up at me, his expression black.

"Look," I said, leaning toward him, "we've got a woman who fucking *changed her identity* to join a group that avenges this kind of thing. The identity she stole just happened to belong to a woman whose husband was going to work for someone who—maybe—funds it? That can't be a coincidence."

"It's a wild hair, Julia. Leave it."

My frustration had reached terminal mass. "Why? Why should I leave it?"

"Because there's nothing we can do about it, even if it's true," Benny said.

Our eyes met across the desk.

"It's how the American sausage gets made," he said. "Supply and demand. You take down one fucker, and people think, oh, OK, we've fixed that problem. You haven't. He's just one fucker among thousands of others. As long as there's a demand for kids, or dope, or snuff porn, or shark fins, or rare rain forest wood—*anything*"—Benny's hand shot out, and he paused to look at it as if it weren't part of his body, then let it drop—"anything there's a market for, someone, somewhere is gonna supply it. It don't matter how many people you put in prison. *The suppliers are not the problem.*"

Benny stopped talking. He was breathing hard and looking right through me. I leaned back off the desk, a little out of breath myself, and gave it a couple of minutes to see if he'd say anything else, but he didn't. He just closed his eyes and sat back in the chair. I turned and left.

CHAPTER 44

The brain was still processing what Benny had said when I got to the lab and handed my paperwork to the receptionist. She gave me a quick professional smile and told me to take a seat in the waiting room.

I did, but I couldn't get comfortable. My head was going about a hundred miles an hour, arguing with Benny after the fact. OK, yeah, maybe taking out one fucker wouldn't do any good, but did that mean you should just let him run wild? You don't dig a tunnel out of prison all at once. You do it grain of sand by grain of sand.

I had my little notebook with me and I got it out to update my timeline, but the only new thing I had was Jennifer Floyd's cause of death. I ripped out the page and tore it into small pieces. I still didn't know who'd killed Orson Greenlaw. I knew something much bigger instead, something I couldn't change. So much for my detective days. If this was how it worked, I wanted no part of it.

A young black girl called my name from the doorway next to the reception desk, and I got up to follow her into a tiny white cubicle with a padded chair in it that looked disturbingly like a medieval torture device.

"Which arm, do you care?" she asked me, snapping on some rubber gloves.

I shook my head, my bad mood still clattering around my head like loose change. The girl took my left arm in her cool gloved hand, and ran her finger lightly over the inside of my elbow.

"Hm," she said. "Let's see the other one."

I gave it to her and she made an approving noise, then went over to the small counter where she'd left my paperwork. She chuckled. "Looks like you tried to do it yourself, huh?"

I glanced at her, reluctant to tear myself away from the cacophony inside my skull, annoying as it was. "What?"

She held up the form that Liz Harman had given me, indicating a small brown splotch along the edge. "Paper cut?"

"Must have been the doc," I said. "Wasn't me."

"Lucky," she replied, coming over to my right side with a couple of syringes. "I hate those things."

She slid one of the needles through my skin and into a vein, and as I watched my blood jump into the glass cylinder, I felt another dissociative episode coming on. For once, I thought ruefully to myself, it was happening at a convenient moment.

However, when the mental tornado suddenly shut off this time, it left a single, blazing thought standing: Orson Greenlaw hadn't died from a paper cut. He'd been full of holes, and not only that, someone had dug the bullets out of those holes. That meant there had been a great deal of blood, way more than most people—people who've never seen anyone get shot—know. Wherever he'd been killed had to have looked like a slaughterhouse when the thing was done. Unless he'd been killed in a bathtub or some other conveniently cleanable location, he'd left a nice big spot.

Of course, that spot would be long gone by now, but with that much blood involved, if anyone had seen the scene of the crime, it would have made an impression.

The lab tech pressed a cotton ball against the end of the needle and withdrew it, and my brain kept going. Since the killer had gone to some pains to hide Orson's body, they'd almost certainly also cleaned up after themselves, which meant bloodstained rags, towels, and/or clothing—a lot of it. Yeah, you could throw it all in the washing machine, but blood isn't that easy to get out, and if I was right about the quantity involved, it would require more than one load of laundry. Myself, I wouldn't feel that comfortable leaving a basketload of bloody clothes lounging around the utility room waiting for its turn in the washer. I'd want to get rid of it pronto.

On my way out of the lab, I called Benny to ask him where the city garbage collection was and, who would talk to me if I wanted to ask some weird questions. He wasn't there, but Stella told me where it was, and said she'd call ahead to let them know I was coming.

Azula Solid Waste was housed in yet another corrugated-steel agricultural building, near the river east of town. A chain-link fence surrounded the concrete parking lot where two garbage trucks were parked. It was midafternoon, and the place was deserted except for a couple of middle-aged black guys sitting on upended plastic buckets next to the open overhead door on the loading dock. I walked over and asked them where I could find the boss.

"He's gone home already," the one who looked like the older

of the two said. "Night shift coming on right now . . . we help you with something?"

He was wearing a faded plaid snap-front shirt with the sleeves cut off, and a red-and-white gimme cap perched on top of his natural. He had an open, friendly face, a ready smile, and a badly chipped front tooth. His companion was younger, maybe in his mid-forties, with shoulder-length cornrows hanging out from under a paisley do-rag. Both of them wore stained tan khakis and steel-toed boots.

"Are y'all collectors?" I asked them.

"Yes, ma'am, official," Chipped Tooth acknowledged with a grin. "We do the night commercial run."

"Were either of you working here this last winter?"

"Shee-it," Cornrows said, shifting on his bucket. "Been at this damn job since I graduated high school."

Chipped Tooth nodded agreement, and I asked them, "Did you happen to hear about any of your coworkers picking up some bloody stuff in early February?"

"Bloody stuff?" Cornrows said, glancing at Chipped Tooth. "What you mean? Like field dress? City don't let nobody put that stuff in the trash. It's gotta go to biohazard now."

"No, I mean towels or clothes, things like that."

Chipped Tooth pursed his lips and shook his head, but Cornrows said, "Not February, but there was a pickup on the west side last summer, hoo-wee. You remember that, man?" He poked his companion's bare biceps.

"You talking about that Dumpster over on Porter?" Chipped Tooth said.

Cornrows nodded. "Yeah, yeah, man. You remember." He looked back at me. "I thought it was paint at first 'cause it looked brown, you know? But then that smell." He shook his head. "Damn. Like spoiled meat, you know what I'm saying?"

"When was this?" I asked him.

"August sometime. Man! That stuff stunk so bad. Big bag of clothes and stuff, sitting up in that Dumpster all day in the heat."

"Where'd you pick it up?"

"Porter Street," he repeated. "Just west of downtown."

"Can you remember which block?"

Chipped Tooth was rubbing his stomach up under his shirt, listening to us talk. Cornrows looked out past my head, squinting and thinking. "Man, you testing me now."

He made a motion at me to follow him and got up. I stepped up onto the loading dock and we went through the overhead door into the warehouse, where a stained city map with the garbage routes marked on it in different colors was tacked up on one wall. There was an old punch clock next to this, and time cards in one of those steel slot holders.

The odor of garbage and bleach wafted around us as Cornrows stepped up to the map and traced the route with a finger thick as a tree branch, stopping at a spot two blocks west of downtown. "Yeah. Two hundred block. Dumpster. The stuff was in a bag, but they ain't put a tie on it, so it just sorta fell out when we did the pull. I hadda get in after it." He shook his head. "Nasty."

I looked at the map again, trying to remember what was there. It was the next street over from the one that ran behind the bar, home to a row of nondescript office buildings whose occupants I'd never paid any attention to.

"Did you notice whether it was men's or women's clothes?" I asked Cornrows.

"Now, how am I gonna tell the difference?" he chided me, clicking his tongue. "I mean, I didn't see no evening gowns or nothing, it was shirts and pants, some towels and sheets, too, all of 'em soaked through. Looked like somebody had tried to mop up after the Alamo or some shit."

"Did you report it to anybody?"

"The boss," he said. "Dunno what he did about it, though. Ain't my job to ride him, goes the other way up in here."

I ripped a sheet out of my little notebook and wrote down my phone number. "Would you ask him to call me when he gets in?"

Cornrows took my ad hoc business card, looking apologetic. "He ain't gonna be back 'til tomorrow."

"Don't worry," I said with a sigh. "I doubt I'll get to the bottom of this before then."

He laughed at that and followed me back out to the loading dock, where Chipped Tooth was still sitting on his bucket, smoking a cigarette.

CHAPTER 45

———— ◆ ————

The buildings on the block the garbage collector had pointed out looked like they'd all been built at the same time—around 1945—by the same guy. They were one-story brick with flat roofs and concrete floors. Some of the brick had been painted and none of the storefronts looked original, but the buildings were all the same size and shape, five in a row along a wide sidewalk that ran all the way to the curb. The other side of the street was the start of the residential area—small, run-down rent houses that formed a barrier between downtown and the nicer homes farther in.

There was a Dumpster in the alley behind the commercial buildings, near the south end of the block. The other side of the alley was the back of the bank, with its parking lot alongside.

The Dumpster was one of the single green ones, with those plastic lids that make an annoying banging noise in the middle of the night when the trucks come by to empty them. In other words, anybody who wanted to could have walked by and dropped in a bag of bloody laundry at any time. It wouldn't be my quarry, since it had been six months before Orson died, but that didn't shut down my interest. Hunting season in these parts was a winter affair, as I remembered from hearing echoing rifle shots daily between September and February, and nothing but a large mammal bleeding out produces the quantity of blood described.

I stood there thinking about it for a couple of minutes, then walked down to the end of the alley and turned toward the square. Benny was walking into the cop shop as I came around the courthouse, and paused to let me catch up. He held the door for me, not saying anything, and came in behind.

"What was last August like on your beat?" I asked him as we went into his office.

He strode around his desk, putting his hand on his trusty laptop. "Lemme look."

I watched him do his thing until he made a face and shook his head. "Pretty quiet. A couple of B-and-Es, the usual speeding tickets and DUIs, domestics, that kind of stuff. Only thing out of the ordinary was somebody hitting a cow out on 281 around the end of July. Sent a couple of locals to the hospital."

"Bad injuries?"

"Not life threatening, if that's what you're asking."

"Did anyone bleed a lot?"

"Yeah, the cow," Benny said, looking amused.

My heart sank. "Who did the cleanup?"

"We did," Benny said. "It wasn't bad, just some glass and shit from the car."

"No, I mean the blood."

He gave me a surprised look. "Nobody. The driver and his passenger were banged up, but they weren't bleeding. We sent 'em to the ER because of possible closed head injury—the driver had face-planted pretty hard on his steering wheel, but it didn't break the skin. The cow was in the ditch. We just left her there."

I made a face and Benny explained, "If somebody complains, we'll have Hazardous Waste go out and get roadkill, but this was outside town. No reason to waste tax money on it when the buzzards will take care of it for nothing."

"Well, damn it," I muttered.

"What's the problem?"

I told him about the bag of bloody clothing, and he went back to tapping and scrolling on his laptop. "Nothing that summer to explain it."

"Well, where the hell did it come from, then?"

"I dunno, but I can see why it would get your panties in a wad," Benny said, pulling at his lower lip, like he often did when thinking.

"The collector said he reported it to his boss."

"Never made it over here."

"I wonder why."

"Sheer ornery laziness, most likely," Benny said. "Far be it for me to bad-mouth my fellow city employees, but those guys want to go home at the end of their shift. They don't want to have to fuck around with anything extra, even if they get paid overtime."

"I guess it wouldn't make any sense to try and test that Dumpster for blood now, would it?" I asked him hopefully.

"We could test it," he allowed, "but I wouldn't trust the result at this late date."

"What about DNA? If it could be matched to Orson?"

"Orson wasn't dead until February," Benny reminded me.

"Maybe Liz fucked up somewhere. Forgot to carry the one or something."

"She's never been wrong before, but I guess it's possible. I'll ask her to check her math."

"And test that Dumpster for DNA?"

He sighed. "Sure. What the hell."

CHAPTER 46

My phone rang as I walked over to the bar. It was Liz Harman.

"Speak of the devil," I said.

"What'd I do now?"

I relayed the salient details, and she said, "If we were talking the difference between January and February, maybe, but no, I wouldn't be off by six months."

"Could there have been some kind of environmental thing that made the body look newer?" I asked her.

"Several things," she said, "but they'd only change the date by maybe a week, at most, and I don't see how I could be off on any of that. I checked the almanac and averaged the local daily temperature and humidity percentage for the time period. Since that house is so old and didn't have any environmental systems running, I feel pretty confident that the indoor and outdoor conditions would have been equivalent."

"The hole where I found him was the top of an old heating chase," I said. "Those are typically built a lot tighter than the rest of a house."

"OK, fine, but in old wood-framed houses, especially those

with no heat or A/C or weather stripping, everything tends to normalize to environmental conditions, tight or not. Especially with nobody living in it. I've never measured a statistical difference in indoor versus outdoor climate in a place like that. Plus, like I said, it's not going to make a January time of death into a June one."

I trusted what she was saying but I was reluctant to let the issue go. "Just for laughs, could you do a DNA test on a Dumpster for me?"

There was a brief silence, then Liz sighed, and I heard her shuffling papers. "I'll need an order from Benny."

"It should be in your fax machine right now."

I heard her grunt and the squeak of her desk chair. "You want me right now?"

"If you can."

She sighed an assent, and I gave her the address. She said she'd be over in a few minutes, then added, "Oh, the reason I called was, Jean Conroy, my psychiatrist colleague, can see you this evening, if you're open."

"This evening?" I said. "A doctor?"

"She's leaving for Maui in the morning."

There was spite in the doctor's voice, and I chuckled. "In her Mercedes?"

She chuckled back. "Don't get me started."

"What time?"

"Here, give her a call." Liz relayed the number, and I dialed it after we hung up. A light feminine voice with an Alabama twang in it answered, and I asked for Dr. Conroy. To my surprise, the voice replied, "This is she." She sounded like she was barely out of high school.

I told her who I was and we made arrangements to meet at

her home office, which was just a couple of blocks from Liz Harman's, at six.

It was hotter than hell in the apartment, as usual, and I gave myself some shit for not thinking to schedule meeting Liz in the morning instead. That alley was going to be an odiferous swamp at this hour—close to four—and I kind of wanted to lie down for a little while before meeting with the shrink.

Instead I splashed my face with cold water, and turned on the fan to ventilate the place while I was gone, then headed down through the bar and out the back. I crossed the vacant lot behind the bar and turned south, walked the block to Porter, and went around behind the row of commercial buildings. Liz was parked at the other end of the alley, getting out of her car.

"I'm too old for this shit," she puffed as she trundled up to me with her field case in hand. She wiped her face and neck with a white cotton handkerchief and nodded past me at the Dumpster. "This our victim?"

"Yeah," I said, not happy to see that it had been a while since the trash guys had been by.

Liz put her field case down and got out some latex gloves, which she handed to me. I took them, giving her a puzzled look.

"I ain't climbing up in that thing," she said.

"I've never taken a DNA sample," I told her. "I don't know how to do it."

"Nothing hard about it. I'll give you a couple of sterile wipes and you just run them over whatever areas you think might have what you're looking for on them. Then we throw the wipes in a plastic bag and send 'em off."

I gave the Dumpster a sidelong look. "There's going to be all kinds of stuff on there."

"That's right, there is," Liz said, getting out the wipes. "In-

cluding, probably, human DNA from the trash collectors, from
people's home trash, from any bums or Dumpster divers who
might have been in there—you name it."

"But they can run all of them against a profile from a specific person and get a match, right?"

"Sure, but it's gonna take a while, and depending on how
long the sample's been in there, it will have degraded over time.
Matching DNA doesn't work like you see it on TV."

I hesitated, wondering if it was worth it. Neffa's sighting of
the car at my house in February suggested that the doctor's timeline was correct, but a bag full of bloody clothes and rags, even
at the wrong time, was too provocative to ignore. I put my foot
up on the Dumpster bracket and held out a hand toward Liz.
She stepped forward and steadied me while I climbed up. Her
hand was dry and slightly rough on my arm, like a dog's paw.

I didn't look down to see what I sank ankle deep into as I
dropped from the Dumpster's edge. The smell was bad enough,
I didn't need a visual. Breathing through my mouth, I opened
one of the packages of wipes and shook one out, then ran it
around the rim of the Dumpster and handed it to Liz. I used six
in all, covering everything except the stuff I was standing in,
then climbed out.

Liz made a face at my shoes as I jumped down. "Shoulda
brought some hip waders."

"Do you smell something burning?" I asked her. I'd just
caught a faint whiff of smoke.

Liz looked at me, her eyebrows up, and shook her head. The
smell grew stronger, overpowering the scent of garbage. It was
Hector's Cuban cigar again.

"God damn it," I muttered.

Liz gave me a quizzical look, sealing up the last bag of wipes.

"I'm having a moment," I told her.

Her tools clinked as she dropped the bag of wipes into her leather bag, and the smell of the cigar grew stronger. I started to cough, my eyes watering.

She gave me a severe look. "You make an appointment with Jean?"

"Yeah, for six," I said.

"Let's go sit for a minute," she suggested, gesturing toward her car.

I followed her and eased into the plush passenger seat. She set her case on the hood and got out a stethoscope and blood-pressure cuff. I waved them off, but she barked, "I humored you, now you humor me."

The cigar smell persisted while she took my blood pressure and pressed the frigid stethoscope against my chest, her eyes intently averted. She listened for what seemed like a long time, then wrapped up her instruments and put them back in her case. The cigar odor grew, impossibly, even stronger. I felt as if I were almost choking. I got out of the car, alternately taking deep breaths and coughing.

"You take drugs?" she asked, putting one hand on her hip.

I laughed between coughs, and her scowl deepened. I held up one hand. "OK, it's a fair question, but the answer is no. The inside of my head is weird enough already, thanks."

"It's something, all right," she agreed.

She came around to put her case in the trunk, and as she slammed it shut, the cigar odor disappeared. I took another couple of deep breaths, feeling like I'd just stepped out of a burning building. "It's gone now."

Liz shook her head, getting out her keys. "Keep that appointment, will you?"

CHAPTER 47

———————◆———————

Jean Conroy was a tallish redhead in her early forties who looked and sounded a lot younger. Part of her youthful air was her hair, which she wore in loose waves down around her shoulders, and part of it was her vernal wardrobe: linen shirt over a tank top, skinny jeans, and flip-flops. She looked about as much like a psychiatrist as I did.

"All right," she sighed, dropping down into the comfortable-looking armchair in her neat office and opening a folder. "Let's see what we've got here."

She pursed her small mouth, peering at the notes in front of her. She read over them for a few minutes, then took off her tortoiseshell horn-rims and tucked her legs up under her in the big chair. She looked like a college coed at a slumber party. "So what's going on?"

I told her and watched her face take on the same look of concern that Connie's had when I described my little mental vacations.

"No memory of anything that happens in the time going by?" she said, returning her glasses to the bridge of her freckled nose. "At all?"

I shook my head, and she made a note in the folder.

"You guys are starting to worry me," I told her. "Have I got something terminal?"

"Most mental illnesses won't kill you, in and of themselves," she said. "But some are easier to manage than others. That's where the mortality risk is with these things—when a psychiatric condition becomes so difficult to live with that the patient decides death is easier."

The comment made me remember the thing that had hit me out in the desert, taking the sun away from Mikela. "Is that always a conscious decision?"

"That depends on what you mean," she said, giving me a guarded look over her glasses.

I didn't want to recite my entire life story, so I just said, "Sometimes I do dangerous things."

"Hmm," she said, putting a slim white finger to her lips. "Do your episodes seem to coincide with those times?"

I thought about it. "It's hard to say."

"Why don't you describe what you were doing the last couple of times you've had a spell. Maybe I'll notice a theme you're not seeing."

The word "spell" made me smile, especially the way she said it, but I hesitated, and she looked up from her notes.

"How ironclad is your doctor-patient confidentiality thing?" I asked.

"I'm legally required to report child abuse, domestic violence, or criminal activity, but I'm allowed professional discretion on all those things," she said. Her fine-featured face had grown curious.

Salt-and-Pepper's death was the only thing that might technically fall into any of those categories. I wasn't the one who'd shot her, but I didn't know enough about Conroy yet to depend on her personal discretion, so I left it out.

"The most recent was hearing that a coworker had undergone a disabling stroke. Previous to that, it happened after a dead body had been found in my house. I checked out when the cops were moving it."

"Hmm," the doctor said, listening intently. I could tell she wanted to ask questions, but was holding back.

"Oh, and I sometimes hear and smell things that aren't there," I added, thinking about the cigar, and Luigi's verbal skills from last winter.

"Do those hallucinations occur along with the dissociative episodes?" the doctor asked.

"Yeah, near them, usually, but I get them on their own at other times, too. Like, I just hallucinated the cigar smell a couple of hours ago, but I didn't dissociate. Well, that I'm aware of."

The doctor was scribbling in her folder. She had her feet on the floor now.

"The other thing is, a lot of times, as I'm waking up, I have this feeling like I'm drowning or suffocating." I hesitated, then decided to come clean. "I had occasion to talk to my mother recently, and she told me that she tried to drown me when I was little."

"How old?" the doctor asked.

"Less than a year, she said."

"So you've had this waking-up thing all your life?"

"No, it only started recently, along with this dissociation stuff."

"Hmm," Conroy said again. "And how long ago was that? That this all started?"

"About three years, give or take."

"And what happened to you three years ago?"

I widened my eyes at her, and she made a rueful face. "People always react like it's rocket science, but it's just simple math. You've got all the symptoms of PTSD, starting at a particular point in time. So the T part must have happened at that point."

This again. Irritated, I said, "I wish you people would make up your minds."

The doctor gave me a quizzical look.

"I've heard the PTSD suggestion before," I told her, "but I don't buy it. Another shrink told me she didn't think I had it." I didn't tell her that the other shrink was in prison for trying to kill me.

"Give me the history," she urged gently, "and I'll give you my opinion. That doesn't mean you have to accept it."

"My husband was shot and killed in front of me," I said.

She took this in without batting an eyelash. "Yep, that'll do it."

"I've seen people killed before," I said.

Her curious expression returned. "In what context?" I hesitated again, and she said, "OK, I can tell there are things there you don't want to talk about, and that's fine. Let's just concentrate on physical symptoms, shall we?"

"I thought you guys wanted to hear all about my unhappy childhood," I said, perplexed.

"No, psychotherapists do that," the doctor explained. "I'm a brain mechanic. I look at physical symptoms and figure out how to fix those, if I determine that they have an organic cause. There's some overlap, but I try to stay out of counseling. I'm no good at it."

She gave me a quick smile, and I started wondering what

side of that divide my WITSEC head-examiners had been on. There had been two of them, and I saw one or the other weekly, but had never paid much attention to their official credentials. As far as I'd been concerned, they were just part of the machinery keeping the Brotherhood out of my hair, so I answered their questions and did what they told me.

"Unfortunately," the doctor was saying, "there aren't a lot of treatment options for PTSD. Medication is typically aimed at symptom relief, but we don't have a pill that will stop dissociation."

"So you're going to stick with PTSD as my diagnosis?"

"It fits your symptoms," she said. "The next closest things are dissociative identity disorder or schizophrenia, but those typically present much earlier in life, and have much more severe effects."

I gave an annoyed sigh.

"The highest success rate for PTSD is with cognitive behavioral therapy," the doctor said, reaching for a small pad on the desk behind her. "I'll give you some names of therapists in the area who work in that modality."

"What's cognitive behavioral therapy?"

"Basically, you figure out what triggers your symptoms, and then learn techniques to keep you grounded when you know you're going to encounter your triggers. Over time, as you use the techniques, you become desensitized to your triggers."

"So what you're saying is that I just have to learn to live with it."

Her blue eyes sharpened, but she smiled. "I guess you could put it that way."

"Great," I said.

"If you've seen people killed before and didn't develop the

disorder, I'd suggest you look at the difference in the situations. That might tell you where your major trigger is."

"I can tell you the difference right now," I said. "I was married to Joe. I loved him. I wasn't close to the others."

Conroy sat back. "Well, there you go."

But I hadn't been close to Orson Greenlaw or Salt-and-Pepper. Nor, really, to Maines.

"I can prescribe you a sedative if you have trouble sleeping," the doctor said. "I don't think you need a mood stabilizer, but that's an option, too, if you find yourself really getting your head twisted around." She closed the folder and put it on the desk. "I'll have a look at your blood when it comes back, to rule out any organic causes, but I'd say at this point your best bet is to start some kind of therapy. You might also consider meditation, which is something you can start on your own."

"Meditation?" I frowned.

"Yeah. There's research that shows it helps, and it has no side effects." The doctor smiled again. "Well, except for good ones."

She was making end-of-session motions, so I got up and took the slip of paper she held out. "What do I owe you?"

"No charge for the initial consultation," she said.

"Kind of like a drug dealer, huh? First one is free."

Her expression told me she didn't much care for my sense of humor, but I wasn't here to make friends. I stuck the slip of paper in my wallet and left.

CHAPTER 48

My brain spent the short drive back to the square trying to figure out the contradiction between my reaction to Joe's death and my "spells." If my "trigger" was seeing something horrible happen to someone I cared about, how come it happened with people I barely knew?

I thought back to before I'd found Orson, calling up past situations where I'd floated off. It had happened upon receiving the first payroll check from Hector; one afternoon when I'd overheard some local gossip in the cafe; arguing with Tova about an item on the Ranch title; and talking to some guy at the gym just after New Year's. I replayed each event in my head, trying to determine what these things had in common, but for the life of me I couldn't figure it out. Especially when I added in the most recent examples.

Luigi was giving himself a bath on the table when I came into the apartment. I gave him some kibble and set about making dinner, still working on the trigger problem in the back of my head. It was too hot to cook, so I made a sandwich and some iced tea, scarfed them, and lay down to watch a little TV.

The phone woke me after dark. I got up and went to the kitchen to get it. It was Audra Maines.

"I hope you don't mind me calling," she said. "And, even more, I hope you don't mind me asking what I'm about to ask you."

"I won't know until you do it," I said.

"Would you consider taking this dog?"

It took a second to penetrate my only recently awakened consciousness. "You mean Steve?"

Audra sighed. "I just don't see how I'm going to manage him, with the kids and Dad, and I don't want to take him to the shelter. They'll just gas him."

"Are you sure? He's pretty well-behaved."

"You ever been down there?" she asked. "It's like Dachau."

I looked over at Luigi, his white patches glowing under the dining-table light. Over the phone, I could hear Steve's tags jingling and the voice of Audra's daughter. My feet began to tingle. I tightened my grip on the phone, feeling something coming up from underneath something, inside my head.

"Are you there?" Audra said.

"Shhh!" I hissed.

"I beg your pardon?"

I wanted to click the phone off, but something made me hold on to it, listening to the background noise. That sound, that jingling. A cool thrill of expectation was rising up my legs. I shut my eyes.

"Lady, I don't know what you're shushing me for. If you can't take the dog, then just—"

Audra's voice faded away. The only thing I could hear was those tags jingling. I waited, gripping the phone, my hand going sweaty.

Walking the canyon from the hot springs to Ruidoso. Something there, a jingling sound—what had it been?

The cartridges in the box, when I'd loaded the little Glock. That unique hollow rattle they made against the stiff pasteboard. I'd heard it again later. Where?

"I'm sorry," I said to Audra. "I'll have to call you back."

She'd been in the middle of a sentence. She made an affronted noise and hung up. I stood there with the phone still to my ear, afraid to move lest I disturb the process taking place between my ears.

Shapes and sensations finally began to solidify in my head. I opened my eyes. I remembered.

CHAPTER 49

It was just after nine, but most of the houses on the block were dark and quiet, including the one I was interested in. There was no car parked in front, and I sat in my truck for a few minutes after turning off the motor, making sure that I was willing to commit breaking and entering to confirm what the brain had just told me. I knew it wouldn't be difficult. I'd had a look at the locks when I'd been here earlier.

Reason said I should just call Benny and tell him what I suspected, but all I had to give him was a remembered sound. I doubted he could get a search warrant on that. My plan hardly qualified as a crime anyway, I told myself. I wasn't going to take anything, and getting in was almost certainly a simple matter of using the skeleton key I had for my own house. Little-known fact: Old mortise locks will almost always open with any skeleton key.

I shut the truck door as quietly as I could, then nipped across the street and up onto the porch. My luck was good; the key worked. I stepped quickly through Liz Harman's office and into the exam room where she'd looked me over the previous day. I didn't dare turn on a light, lest the neighbors be awake, so

I paused to let my eyes adjust for a minute before going over to the chest in the corner where she kept her lab forms.

I pulled the drawer open and heard that telltale rattle, but I couldn't see inside it, in the dark. I didn't want to just feel around and get my DNA on possible evidence, so I held my breath and switched on the exam light. I pulled the drawer out as far as it would go, and there they were, at the very back: five spent cartridges and their bullets, rolling around in a shallow cardboard box. There were brown stains on the box, and one side had soaked through, transferring to the edge of the lab pad. The blood on my form hadn't been from a paper cut, and it hadn't been Liz Harman's.

I quickly pushed the drawer closed and turned off the exam light, pausing again to let my eyes readjust to the city-lit darkness. While I was doing this, headlights turned into the driveway.

My immediate instinct was to leg it or hide, but then I thought: What's the point? She'd probably seen the light, driving up, and my pale yellow truck, parked at the curb directly across the street, was as unique as a fingerprint. I went out to the office, turned on the desk lamp, and sat down in the leather desk chair.

"Julia?" I heard, as the house door swung open. Footsteps to the connecting door, and then Liz stepped into the office, her eyes wide. "What's wrong? You OK?"

It's funny how people change when you know they've killed someone. I don't mean that they actually change, but you suddenly notice that their mouth is cruel, or that the set of their shoulders is arrogant. Liz's round, pink face didn't look friendly to me anymore.

She dropped her bag into the patient chair, and made as if to come around the desk. I got up and kept it between us. She stopped moving.

I took out my phone, keeping my eyes on Liz, and dialed Benny. When he answered, I asked him to come over to the house. He must have heard something in my voice because he didn't argue.

Liz's face had relaxed. She glanced at the exam room door with a sigh. "I knew I shoulda put those somewhere else."

"Why didn't you?"

"I dunno. I guess I just didn't want to touch them again. They feel like they have bad voodoo on them or something. Or maybe I've been punishing myself. Or wanting to get caught." She sat down in the desk chair, saying again, "I dunno."

"Just please tell me you have some hard evidence somewhere of what Baxter is up to."

Liz looked up at me like I was from outer space.

"Jim Baxter," I said. "The pedophile running for president. The guy Orson was going to work for."

She frowned at me. "Are you having one of your episodes?"

"Why don't you just tell me why you killed Orson?" I suggested.

"It was him or Rachael," she said with a shrug.

Puzzled, I sat down in the patient chair, which seemed to relax her. She folded her hands on the blotter and leaned forward.

"I see a lot of people at their worst, but that guy deserved a category all his own. The things he did and said to Rachael—" The doctor shook her head, looking away from me. "I could almost excuse it if he was sick or something, had some kind of mental problem. But Jean didn't think he did. He was just mean. He was purposely trying to break Rachael down."

"Why?"

Liz lifted her plump shoulders. "Why does anyone do a thing

like that? Entertainment? Don't ask me. All I know is I watched that girl turn from a nice, normal human being into a suicidal wreck because of him. Her blood pressure went up. She developed tachycardia and a skin rash. Had stomach ulcers, was losing her hair, and couldn't sleep more than a couple of hours a night." Liz looked at me across the desk. "It was just a matter of time before she developed a life-threatening health condition. That's murder, in my book."

"You might get some argument on that," I said.

Liz sat back and slammed her palms down on the armrests of the leather chair. "I don't care! People come in here, fighting for their lives, every damned day. Good people who shouldn't have to be doing that. And nine times out of ten, there's some son of a bitch in the background, grinding them down, making it worse. It's just cruelty, plain and simple."

"I find it hard to believe that Orson is the only person in Azula who drove his wife nuts."

"Way to trivialize Rachael Pestozo's experience," Liz snorted.

I held up one hand. "I'm not trying to trivialize it, I'm trying to figure out why you decided that he was the one who deserved to die when there are surely other people around who were as bad as him, or worse."

Liz shifted in the chair, looking away. "I didn't really decide it. He did."

I raised my eyebrows. "He asked you to shoot him?"

There was a short pause, then Liz said in a low voice, "He got personal."

My eyebrows stayed where they were.

"Came in here, started telling me I had no business being anybody's doctor with my 'fat ass.' That I was disgusting, an embarrassment to my profession."

I've had people make fun of my weight often enough to understand how she must have felt. I've even sincerely wished that one or two of them would drop dead. But I'd never seriously considered becoming directly involved in the process.

"Then he started in about Rachael," Liz went on. "How *I* was killing her, not letting her get a bypass, not giving her enough shit about her weight, not putting her on some diet. The woman was perfectly healthy before he got hold of her. Nice, normal blood chemistry, strong heart, clear lungs—everything."

She stopped talking and bowed her head. I thought she might be crying, but I didn't move toward her. After a minute she reached forward and pulled the middle drawer of the desk open, and took out an old .38 revolver.

Seeing the look of alarm on my face, she said quickly, "It's not loaded." She set it down on the desk and closed the drawer.

"You shot him in here?" I said, glancing at the papered walls and pine floor with its patterned wool rug.

"No, we were in the exam room," she said, nodding toward the gun. "I kept that in there. I had a thing a few years ago where I was working on a rancher and he came at me."

A car door slammed, and I got up and took hold of the .38, watching Liz carefully while I did it. She didn't move. Benny's step sounded on the porch; I walked over to the connecting door and greeted him as he came into the office, holding the gun toward him by the muzzle. He took it with a quizzical look.

"That's the gun that killed Orson Greenlaw," I told him, leaning my head toward the exam-room door. "The bullets are in there."

Benny's dark eyes jumped toward Liz. "I'll be damned."

She didn't say anything, and he did his belt-hitching thing, muttering. "It never occurred to me that the bullets being dug out of him pointed at someone with medical training."

"Me, neither," I admitted.

He looked back at Liz. "And finding blood traces in a doctor's exam room would not be weird."

She shrugged, giving him a rueful smile. "All of that was just luck, really. It's not like I've done this before."

Benny was looking at me with an I-told-you-so expression.

"Fine," I said. "You were right. There's no connection to all that other stuff. Happy?"

"Not really," he said, motioning to Liz and reaching for his cuffs.

CHAPTER 50

—————◆—————

"The feds are going to want your testimony in Mikela's case," Benny said. We were sitting in his office after getting Liz booked, and I'd just told him I was going to pack up and head back to Mexico.

"I'll come back when they want me," I said. "It's going to be months before they get to that point. Federal cases take forever."

"I'll need you for this one, too."

"Damn it, Benny."

"Look, I'm sorry," he said, raising his open hands. "That's how this shit works."

"The last time you told me not to leave town, that didn't stop anything from going to hell. If it's going to go to hell either way, I'd just as soon be in Mexico while it does."

"This is a nice little town," Benny said. "Why you in such a hurry to get out of it?"

I gave him a look. "Seriously. Your memory. Have it checked."

"All right," he said, setting his jaw. "Go ahead and leave, but think about this: If you blow me off, one or both of these cases will go to hell, and all the shit you've been through will have been for nothing."

He was hitting me where it hurt, but that rarely slows me down. "You don't need my testimony for Liz. She's pleading guilty."

"What if her lawyers change her mind?"

"Then you call me," I said. "It's not like I'll be on Mars."

"Fine," Benny said, putting his hands up. "I can't stop you. But God help me, I'll probably keep trying."

"Every man needs a hobby," I told him as I left.

I went back to the apartment and packed up my clothes and other necessities. It was getting on toward ten, but I was full of nervous energy, and I'd gotten several extra hours of sleep the night before. If I got tired on the road, I could stop. I wasn't trying to beat the clock anywhere.

I filled up Luigi's food and water bowls and wrote a note for Mike to find when he opened up the next afternoon, explaining that I'd be out of the apartment for a while but that I'd be back when the trials got started, and that I'd be in touch after I got settled. I felt bad not telling him I'd be with Hector but decided it was better he not have any information that could be gotten out of him.

Shouldering my duffel, I took a quick look around. I'd spent a lot of time in this place over the last year, some of it enjoyable. It felt like I was closing a chapter, even though I'd be back for the trials and to take care of business with the Ranch. It wasn't going to be the happy homestead I'd share with Hector 'til death did us part. That was a fantasy I hadn't even been aware I had until that moment. It made me kind of misty.

Crossing through the dark bar, I spotted something bigger than a bread box lying in the recess of the storefront, against the door. We didn't usually get street people, right across from the

courthouse and police station, but there's a first time for everything.

I pulled the door open gingerly so as not to wake him, but
when I saw who it was, I couldn't suppress a whispered, "God
damn it."

Steve's ears pricked and he lifted his head to look at me.
Audra had tied his lead to the door handle, and there was a
note under his collar. I pulled it out and read:

*Sorry to do it like this, but I just can't bear to be the one to
take him to the shelter, after all this stuff with Dad. If you
really can't keep him, I won't hold it against you. Thanks—AM*

"God damn it," I said again.

Steve cocked his head as if wondering why I kept swearing
at him. I stood there trying to figure out what to do for a few
minutes, then untied him and headed for the truck. He'd rid-
den with me and Maines to Presidio once, he could do it again,
and he'd be just as happy living with me and Hector in Mexico
as he probably was living in Azula with Maines. It just meant
I'd have to make more stops on the way. The dog jumped into
my truck like he was as ready for a vacation as I was, and we hit
the road.

Just west of Sonora, right around midnight, I stopped to let
Steve take a leak, and as we were getting back into the car, my
brain sent up a flare. I turned off the radio, which I'd had tuned
to a vintage country-western station just to see if I liked it,
and paid attention to my gray matter. It laid out the deduction it
had apparently been working on behind the scenes since my
visit with Jean Conroy: My "spells" occurred in situations where
the radar sensed something big and dangerous hidden but didn't

feel safe enough to keep me conscious while it worked. It put me to sleep unless there was something in the situation that made me feel safe—the presence of Hector, for instance, when we'd found Maines, or having Steve with me when I'd gone into Darling's clinic.

The logic seemed to hold as I ran through my memory of situations where I'd checked out. Maybe not a hundred percent, but often enough that it could be considered a viable theory. I looked over at Steve, wondering if I could claim him as a service dog for something like that. He looked back, giving me that doggy smile of his, and I couldn't help letting out a laugh.

CHAPTER 51

The sun was just coming up when I turned onto the rough dirt road that led to the hot springs. Steve sat up as the truck began to rattle, looking slightly alarmed. He took it in stride, though, going philosophical and playful by turns as we bumped down into the canyon. When we finally stopped, I took a minute to sit and let my bones settle before getting out to go into the office. The young monk who'd checked me and Maines in on our visit was there behind the counter.

"I need to get in touch with Hector Guerra," I told him.

"Ah, Mrs. Smith," he said, doing that same thing with his eyes, as if they were more interested in my face than anything else in the world.

"Um, no," I admitted with what I hoped was a disarming smile. "Kalas. Julia Kalas."

"One moment," he said, stepping to the end of the counter.

He picked up a phone and dialed, but there appeared to be no answer. He left a short message, then returned to where I was standing.

"Do you happen to have a vacancy?" I asked him. I was dead

tired after driving all night, and there was no telling how long it would be before Hector called back. I could use a nap.

The monk gave me the same cabin Maines and I had stayed in before. After throwing my stuff on the bed, I put Steve's lead on to take him out for a bathroom break, and almost walked right into Finn.

He'd been passing the cabin, heading down the gravel path toward the office, and sidestepped the door as it swung open. He looked up to see who'd almost KO'd him and his wide eyes went still and angry.

He was dressed in jeans, boots, and a light tan jacket, and was carrying a suitcase. "Thanks for ruining my life," he said.

I remembered Benny's comments about pedophilia and felt a weird sympathy for the man in front of me. I stepped out of the doorway and shut the door, giving Steve's lead some slack so he could do what he needed to do at a respectable distance.

"You ruined your own life," I told Finn. "All I did was turn on the lights."

He took a deep breath and seemed to gather himself. "I'm sorry. It's not your fault." He looked at me again. "You know, I didn't just sit in prison doing the crossword puzzle. I worked on myself and my issues. I'm not the same person I was when I went in."

In his street clothes, still covered with bruises and cuts, he lacked the gravitas of his robes. I wondered if they would have made me more receptive to what he was saying.

"People don't change," I said. "That's something I know. Behaviors, maybe, but you are who you are. Trying to pretend otherwise is just going to land you in trouble again one of these days."

He was looking at me again now, his bright eyes frank. "Let me ask you something. Where do you think you come from? I mean, whatever it is that makes you *you*. What is that? Where is it located?"

I didn't answer. It sounded like another one of his dead-end philosophical questions.

He kept his clear, disconcerting gaze fixed on my face. "Imagine if that thing, that thing that made you *you*, that indelible part of your personality, caused an almost irresistible urge to do something you found reprehensible. Physically sickening. How would you live with that?"

The sun was already bleaching the sky out to that blazing white, and the temperature felt like it was getting close to eighty despite the early hour.

"If you're looking for sympathy, you won't get it from me," I said, even though I felt some. "Everybody's got something in life they have to deal with."

"No, no," he said, shaking his head emphatically. "I'm not trying to justify anything, I'm trying to *explain* it. The Sangha, this place, they taught me that this thing I call *who I am* is actually the least durable part of me. I learned that thoughts cause feelings, and that feelings cause craving, and that craving causes suffering, and that gave me the ability to separate myself from my urges, to understand that they are not *who I am*."

Despite my aversion to what I suspected he'd done, what he was saying drew my attention. "What is, then?"

"Nothing," he said, his wide-open hazel eyes fixed on mine. "Everything we think we are is transitory. It can't be pinned down or pointed to because it's always moving toward dissolution. We literally do not exist."

Steve was pulling on the lead, distracting me, which was probably a good thing. I've met a lot of spiritual weirdos in my day, but this guy was in a class all by himself. I could easily see him hypnotizing himself into thinking that nothing he did was wrong, because it was all meaningless.

"Not that you'd admit it, but I'm curious," I said, wanting to slap him back into this nonexistent reality, "how many of Hector's clients' kids have gone astray at your hands?"

"None of them!" Finn burst out. "Not at my hands!"

The force of his response surprised me. Not that I'd spent enough time around him to know, but he didn't seem like the passionate type. Also, something about the way he said it struck my ear oddly.

"Just because you didn't touch them doesn't mean you aren't responsible for what happened to them," I said.

He gave me one more look with those wide eyes. "My conscience is clear."

He stepped over Steve's lead and disappeared around the corner of the office. The dog, who'd lain down about halfway through the conversation, pushed himself up off the ground, and we went back into the cabin.

Not at my hands kept ringing through my head while I brushed my teeth and got dressed. I hadn't sliced Maines's throat open, but I'd been responsible for it happening. If Finn had committed a crime, so had I. OK, I hadn't been looking to cause harm, but in Finn's mind, neither had he.

It occurred to me that maybe he'd meant it more literally—as in, not *his* hands, but someone else's. Then I remembered Benny's rant about supply and demand. Even if I could find out who Finn catered to, it wouldn't solve the problem. There'd be another Finn a few miles down the border somewhere, plying the same nasty trade. That didn't stop me from wanting to chip a couple more grains of sand out of the escape tunnel.

CHAPTER 52

It got past noon without Hector calling me back, and I started to get impatient. I put Steve's lead on and walked down to the office.

"Listen, could you just give me his address?" I asked the young monk.

He lifted his shoulders. "We don't have it. Only his telephone."

I sighed, annoyed, and went back to the cabin. I didn't feel like moldering around the place all day waiting for the phone to ring, so I got my purse, put Steve in the truck, and headed for Ojinaga. There, I asked directions to city hall, and was directed to a nicely kept two-story brick building with an arcade going all the way around the first floor. It was painted a pale orange, and the wrought-iron balconies on the second floor were shaded with bright blue awnings. Like almost all of the public buildings I'd been to in town, it fronted on a treeless plaza, this one paved with tan brick.

The public records office was on the second floor, down a hallway lined with colorful majolica tile. The woman at the reception desk in the motor vehicles section spoke fairly good

English, and it was just a matter of a few minutes to find the address of Juan Obregon, owner of a 1965 Norton motorcycle. No American privacy concerns to deal with, no red tape to cut through.

Hector's place was a tiny little house on the very southernmost edge of town. A few siblings stood between it and the desert, but not much else. The Norton was parked in the front yard, assuring me I had the right place. I stepped up onto the porch and knocked, leaving Steve in the truck.

It took a few minutes before Hector opened the door, and when he did, his face went shocked, then wary. "I told you to give me some warning."

"I tried," I said. "Did you change phone numbers again?"

Steve emitted a short greeting bark, and Hector pushed the screen door open, coming out onto the porch and closing the house door behind him. "I see you brought the whole family."

He trotted down the wood steps and walked over to the truck to pet the dog. I followed, and he said to me in a low voice, "It's not a good time." His face hadn't relaxed.

I wanted to ask him why, but something wouldn't let me. Looking back on it now, maybe I didn't want to know.

"I'm not here permanently yet," I told him. "I'll have to go back for the trials."

He raised his eyebrows at the plural, and I relayed the details of what had happened since the last time I'd seen him. When I got to the truth about Finn, his face went murderous, and he started toward his bike. I grabbed him and held on, knowing that if I could just stay in his way for thirty seconds I might save a man's life.

"He says nothing happened to any of your kids," I said, keeping my eyes fixed on his face to make sure he heard me.

"I'm gonna make him prove that," Hector said through gritted teeth.

"Good," I said. "I'd like to know for sure if he's telling the truth. But later. When you won't kill him."

Hector's eyes had simmered down to mere coals now. He was back under control.

I let go of his arms and he wiped one hand across his mouth. "I never gave much thought to the kids alone. I figured they were safe as long as they were with their parents."

"They very well may be," I said. "Finn claims nothing happened to them on his account."

Hector gave me a quizzical look, and I explained the odd wording of Finn's denial.

"That doesn't make me feel much better," he said.

"Me, neither," I admitted, "but don't worry. I intend to get to the bottom of it, one way or another."

He opened his mouth to reply but was interrupted by a woman's voice calling, "Hector?" from inside the house.

My eyes jumped to his face. "I assume that's the old ball and chain," I grinned.

He tried to laugh, but I could see that something was very wrong. When she opened the door, I realized what it was. This was no *coyote*. She was somewhere in the vicinity of twenty-five, with shiny long curls, stylishly dressed in a crochet wrap over a tank top and wide-leg silk pants. She was tall and slim everywhere but in the middle, where her pregnant belly peeped over the top of her waistband.

I returned my eyes to Hector's face. "Anything you want to say here?"

He didn't reply, but his expression told me everything I needed to know.

"Wow," I said softly. "Not even going to try to lie, huh?"

The woman came out onto the porch and Hector stepped up to join her. She put a proprietary hand on his shoulder, eyeing me with shy curiosity.

I didn't hesitate. I turned and left.

CHAPTER 53

The lights were still on in the hot springs office when I got back. It was late, past ten, but I didn't feel like staying.

The young monk behind the desk had been joined by a tiny brown woman with no hair and teardrop-shaped golden eyes shimmering between plump, straight eyelids. She wore the same yellow and red robes, and as I came in, they both smiled at me. Her teeth were small and pointed. She looked kind of like a Tibetan jack-o'-lantern.

"I need to check out," I said.

"Of course," the woman answered. "Which number?"

Her voice was American and accentless, which surprised me, given her appearance. The young male monk hovered behind her as she drew the ledger over, and he watched her with rapt attention as she began to leaf slowly through the pages. After a minute, she said something to him in what I assume was Tibetan, and he bowed low, raising his hands on either side of his head, palms up. I'd never seen any of them do this before, and I gave him a puzzled look.

"We are so happy to have our new teacher," the young monk explained, seeing my expression.

I raised my eyebrows at the tiny brown woman. "You're the abbot?"

She nodded, keeping her eyes on the ledger, but another radiant smiled bloomed on her face. "It is my honor."

The young monk nodded to me, and exited via the side door behind the desk. The abbot continued to leaf leisurely through the ledger, as if she were studying a bistro menu. I fidgeted with the desk pen, hoping to speed her up by showing my impatience.

She finally got to the end of the big green-bound book and laughed, looking up. "Wrong one!"

Moving a stack of newspapers, she pulled another ledger down the countertop. As if mocking me, an ad for Baxter's campaign stared up from the top page of the stack. I began to draw a goatee and devil horns on him, and the abbot laughed.

"Ah, Mr. Baxter," she said. "I did look forward to meeting him."

I started filling in the whites of his eyes. "Hmm?"

She opened the second ledger in her sedate, methodical manner. "He was a frequent visitor, I am told. He and his many children, and their young companions. Unfortunately, his friend is leaving us."

It took a second for what she was saying to sink in. When it did, I moved over and got right in front of her, pulling the ledger away. "Are you talking about Finn?"

"You are a friend of his, as well?" she said. Her golden eyes widened with curiosity, and something else.

"No," I said. "No, I am not his friend."

I watched the something else in her eyes turn to guarded relief. "I'm glad to hear that."

"Why?" I said, staying right up in her grill. "Tell me why."

"He misused the dharma," she said. "Used our spiritual teachings for immoral and selfish purposes. There is some very bad karma coming his way, and for Mr. Baxter, too, I'm afraid."

"These immoral and selfish purposes, they involved children, didn't they?"

The abbot's eyes told me I was correct.

"Did any of your group witness Finn's and Baxter's activities?" I asked, my breath getting short. "Witness them first-hand?"

Her short, thin eyebrows rose. "Of course. We wouldn't expel a member on mere hearsay, especially in a case like this."

I couldn't help myself. I leaned across the counter and pinched her rounded cheeks. "If you were any closer, I'd kiss you."

She looked surprised for a moment, then laughed.

CHAPTER 54

The baby came on Halloween, which I found darkly humorous, not least because it horrified Hector's wife, who was superstitious in the extreme. Hector called me that evening, as was his weekly habit since I'd taken up residence at the hot springs, despite the fact that I never called him back. It was a girl, and Carmen wanted to name her after her mother, who'd been called Guadalupe. Hector was emphatic that no kid of his was going to go through life at the risk of being called Lupe, and he clogged my voice mailbox to the brim that night with lengthy arguments to that effect. I listened to all the messages, laughing at some parts and wincing at others, but thinking about Hector didn't hurt anymore.

Geshe Jampa, as I'd come to know the abbot, was teaching me how to meditate, and it had been a long time since I'd dissociated. In fact, the last time had been after Mikela Floyd's trial, when the indictment against Jim Baxter had come down. Finn had been named, which wasn't a surprise, and so had Miles Darling, which was. It was reading the paragraph outlining his pediatric surgical duties for Baxter that sent me out of my body. There are some things that are better left to the imagination.

Mikela went to federal prison for life, and seemed happy about it, given that she'd been up for the death penalty. Liz also got life, which she'd serve at Gatesville, alongside Connie. She admitted to falsifying Orson Greenlaw's autopsy report. She'd actually killed him in August and stashed his body in the morgue as an unidentified cadaver until she couldn't get away with it any longer, and had to find another place to put him. The car Neffa had seen at my place on February 13 had indeed been her, transporting Orson's now practically mummified corpse into the heating chase at the Ranch.

Mike looked after the house for me, and every now and then made me an offer on it, but I always turned him down. I don't know why. There was something about it that made me want to hang on to it, even if I never lived there. I think, in the back of my head, it had become a fantasy future love nest for me and Hector, a place to put all of those thoughts and feelings until I could stand to look at them again.

I heard from Benny regularly, and every month or so, Steve and I made the drive up to Azula to visit Maines, who did move in with Audra, much sooner than his physical therapists predicted would be possible. It was a crowded house for a man in a wheelchair, but they made do, and every time I visited, Maines and I spent an obligatory hour bickering about my future. He'd gotten some speech back, including a new propensity toward swearing, but not enough to win an argument against me. It didn't stop him from trying. He told me I was wasting my talent with all this spiritual crap, and that eventually I'd stumble across another body, and have to use my goddamn brain again.

While I waited to see if he was right, I found myself enjoying things that were downright prosaic: not having to wash my hair because I'd shaved it all off; wearing the same thing every day; changing sheets and filling up gallon water bottles for tired and thirsty Mexican families on their way to El Norte. It wasn't an exciting life, but it felt kind of good to be bored for a change. I doubted that I'd want to do it forever, but I didn't have to decide that now. Forever would get here soon enough.